Wreckers
JULIE HEARN

Other books by Julie Hearn

●

Follow Me Down
The Merrybegot
Ivy
Hazel
Rowan the Strange

JULIE HEARN

Wreckers

OXFORD
UNIVERSITY PRESS

Quotation from 'The Napoli' used by kind permission of West Country
singer-songwriter Steve Knightley (*www.showofhands.co.uk*)

OXFORD
UNIVERSITY PRESS

Great Clarendon Street, Oxford OX2 6DP
Oxford University Press is a department of the University of Oxford.
It furthers the University's objective of excellence in research, scholarship,
and education by publishing worldwide in

Oxford New York

Auckland Cape Town Dar es Salaam Hong Kong Karachi
Kuala Lumpur Madrid Melbourne Mexico City Nairobi
New Delhi Shanghai Taipei Toronto

With offices in

Argentina Austria Brazil Chile Czech Republic France Greece
Guatemala Hungary Italy Japan Poland Portugal Singapore
South Korea Switzerland Thailand Turkey Ukraine Vietnam

Oxford is a registered trade mark of Oxford University Press
in the UK and in certain other countries

British Library Cataloguing in Publication Data

Data available

ISBN: 978-0-19-272929-3

1 3 5 7 9 10 8 6 4 2

Printed in Great Britain
Paper used in the production of this book is a natural,
recyclable product made from wood grown in sustainable forests.
The manufacturing process conforms to the environmental
regulations of the country of origin.

'Everyone's a wrecker 'neath the skin'

from 'The Napoli' by Steve Knightley

'If all of life on land were to vanish tomorrow, creatures in
the ocean would flourish. But if the opposite happened and the
ocean life perished, then the creatures on land would die too.
Life, if it went on, would have to start over.'

Alanna Mitchell, *Seasick, The Hidden Ecological
Crisis of the Global Ocean* (2008)

For my brothers, Andy, Paul, and Danny

Cornwall, England, 1732

The box was nothing special. No carvings. No swirlings of gold. And so light compared to, say, a barrel of rum or a sea-sodden roll of tapestry, that the wrecker who claimed it would have left it for driftwood had a half-drowned sailor man not risen from the waves and fought for it with surprising strength and fury.

'No you don't,' the wrecker had scolded, raising high a chunk of rock already slimed with sailor-gore.

'Please . . . ' The sailor man had fallen, his torn shirt dripping and flailing, his fingers still clutching for the box. His face, upturned, had been as dark as the storm and unmistakably foreign—the easiest kind to smash in. 'I beg you . . . '

The howling wind had taken his words just as surely as the next wave to crash would take his body, but the wrecker had heard them clearly enough as he brought the rock hard down.

'DON'T OPEN IT!'

When it was over . . . when the wreckers were certain that no one from the broken ship had lived to tattle tales . . . that only their God could see them now . . . they hurled away their murderous rocks and bent their heads in prayer.

'Have mercy' . . . 'Forgive me' . . . 'You know how hard these winters are for those who fish the sea' . . . 'You have seen our empty nets . . . heard our children squabble and cry over scraps fit only for gulls.'

1

The storm had eased. Soon dawn would break and others would come hurrying down to the cove: men with sacks, wheel-barrows, empty pots and scuttles—anything in which to carry away whatever might remain for the taking. Women with hunger and greed etched deep in their faces as they raced one another into the boiling surf. Children hoping for treasure this time; for Spanish doubloons littering the tideline like golden crabs; for oranges and lemons bobbing towards them on the waves.

The ship was groaning, like something mortally hurt. She had never stood a chance, that ship, so fierce had been the gale that blew her too close to the Cornish coast and smack onto rocks that rimmed the cliffs in a perilous, toothy curve.

She was a wounded thing, a ripped up thing, spilling cargo from her guts into waves no longer mountainous but rough, still, and relentless in the way they crashed through rigging no man would ever climb again, and slathered the tilting deck in foam.

Prayers over, the wreckers set to work, roping and reeling, rolling and hauling. And they cheered, hoarsely, as two barrels from the ship's shattered hold arrived at their feet like gifts hurled there by Neptune.

'His lordship'll be wanting his cut this night. Joe? Joe Tonkin? Ride out to the manor. They two barrels'll be enough to keep him sweet, I reckon.'

'It's late, Perran. Too late, I'd say, to be bothering his lordship.'

'No mouthing back at me, Joe. Do you not see the lights, up there in the windows? 'Tis her ladyship's twenty-first birthday. They'll be making merry fools of theyselves for a good while yet, and expecting their share of the spoils whatever the hour. Go now. Take the cart. Michael Killick? Lend a hand up the beach with the barrels. No—wait—what's in that box?'

2

Joe Tonkin did not look down, only kept one foot on the plain wooden box that a man's last breath had begged him not to open.

'French lavender,' he lied. 'All waterlogged.'

Perran Carthew owned most of the port's fishing boats. He was leader, of sorts, on nights such as this, and had yet to encounter trickery from a man wanting more than his due.

Had Joe Tonkin been a stranger, and the box just a shade more ornate, Perran might have insisted on looking for himself. But the box was plain. And Joe was a neighbour. And it was share and share alike when it came to the spoils of wrecking, always had been, always would be, and young Joe knew that just as surely as he knew the timing of the tides and the colour of his baby daughter's eyes.

'French lavender eh?' Perran's voice was pleasant. 'Then take that as well, up to the manor. A birthday gift for her lady-ship. Dried out, she can use it to sweeten her drawers—and I'm thinking linen, not mahogany, eh, lads?'

The wreckers laughed, muckily. Laughter was good—necessary—at the close of such a sorry night's work. Sniggering like schoolboys at the mention of women's underthings would help them feel normal again. Normal and almost innocent.

The road to the manor wound giddily upwards, curving away from the cliff edge and then back again. Twice Joe Tonkin hauled on the reins, bringing horse and cart to a halt in the drizzly pre-dawn light.

The first time he stopped he gave the box a tentative shake (aware, as he did so, that a pounding from the sea might have smashed the contents already, to unmendable smithereens).

Nothing.

Holding his breath, and pressing one ear flat against the

sodden wood, Joe shook again, a bit harder this time.

Still nothing.

No clatter of coins. No rattle of gems. No chinking of china, broken or otherwise. Whatever was inside, Joe realized, was clearly fantastically light. Certain butterflies, so he'd heard, fetched high sums for their colour and rarity, but wouldn't air holes have been made for things that were—or had been—alive? There were no holes in this box that Joe could see, not even a big one for a key. And butterflies, even dead ones, would have rustled, he was sure, like petticoats or leaves.

What about gold dust? That had to be almost weightless. He imagined it so, as light as air shot through by sunbeams; although, on second thoughts, a box crammed full of the stuff would more likely be as heavy as a cube of wet sand . . . wouldn't it?

The second time Joe Tonkin stopped he tried to raise the lid, but it was sealed so tight that after a few minutes' struggle he gave up.

That sailor man was raving, he decided, crossly. Or lying through the stumps of his rum-rotten teeth. For anything worth having, either to keep or sell on, would definitely rattle or roll around—show some sign, however slight, of its existence.

Face it, Joe, he told himself. This box is empty. My guess is it held rations once, enough for a week, and now the most it contains is stale air and the husk of a weevil. Her ladyship is welcome to it. I will say I smelt lavender, down in the cove, but must have been mistaken. A trick of the storm . . . the whiff of a sailor man's soul flying by on the wind. No one will doubt me, for a wrecker's mind will play what tricks it must to ease the torment of all he does, and all he bears witness to, on nights when a tall ship is broken.

4

And so Joe Tonkin made his delivery to the manor house above Port Zannon—two barrels of rum and a box he no longer wanted—and returned to the cove with a clear conscience. And a footman in a powdered wig carried the box through to the drawing room where her ladyship clapped her little hands and demanded it be placed dead centre of the room and opened straightaway.

'The person who brought it, my lady, was in two minds as to its contents,' the footman said, as he set the box down. 'He asked me to tell you that, on hauling it from the ocean, he caught the unmistakable scent of . . . '

'Stop, Rogerson—not another word!' Her ladyship leaned forward, her face flushed in the candlelight, her wig a towering shadow on the wall. 'A box with a smell from a faraway land? My dears, what can be in it? No, no, Henry dear. Don't open it yet. Let's try and guess.'

'A monkey!' whooped a middle-aged man with a claret-coloured nose. 'A stinky little beastie from some jungle or other.'

'Dear George, pray not. The very idea . . . '

'Honeycomb,' guessed a woman with white roses clotting her wig, like big spoonfuls of cream.

'Tea,' guessed her neighbour after a few hearty sniffs. 'Enough to last a year.'

'A dead monkey,' George guffawed. 'Dead this past fortnight and smelling to high Heaven.'

'George—please!' Her ladyship wrinkled her pretty nose. 'I, personally, cannot smell a thing—apart from candle wax and camellias, and those scents have been with us all evening. Henry? Pray open the box before I die of curiosity.'

His lordship tried, but fared no better than Joe Tonkin had done, out in the rain and the mire. 'Lid's stuck,' he grunted.

5

'Rogerson—fetch a crowbar.'

A crowbar was dutifully fetched. Her ladyship leaned even further forward and her guests leaned with her. They had heard, every one of them, the tall ship running aground; had thrilled to the crack of timbers against rock; the sound as loud as cannon fire booming up from the cove.

Each guest had known, at once, the significance of that noise. And each had thought it the most marvellous entertainment; almost as good as fireworks, only not quite, as it had been too dark to see the stricken ship or any goings-on in the cove.

Through all eight courses of a truly excellent dinner they had wondered aloud what goodies might be tossed to the sea this time and swept ashore by the obliging waves. And if his lordship and Sir George had licked their lips while laying odds on how many of the crew would drown, and how many make it to dry land, it was surely in anticipation of the lemon sorbet, and not the murder of innocents.

His lordship positioned the crowbar. The young footman hovered, preparing to hold the box steady, but his lordship waved him away.

'Be careful, Henry,' her ladyship warned. 'Pray mind your fingers.'

'Nearly . . . got it.' His lordship adjusted his grip on the bar and hunkered lower on his heels. He was already panting and sweating from the strain. 'Not easy . . . feels as if it's been . . . shut fast . . . for a thousand . . . years.'

The lid gave, eventually, with surprisingly little noise. Nothing splintered. Nothing broke. No hinges flew, or even creaked, and for a second or two nothing happened at all.

His lordship turned aside, to mop his brow on his sleeve. 'Nothing in there, I'm afraid,' he said, raising the lid a little higher and then turning back to check. 'Although . . . what in the name of all . . . '

Her ladyship was the first to scream. It blew out a candle, that scream, and brought servants running from all over the house.

'Shut the lid!' she cried out, above the babble and shriek of her guests . . . the clatter of dainty chairs, knocked flying in a panic . . . the shattering of glasses as the butler dropped a tray.

'For the love of God, Henry . . . SHUT THE LID!'

DILLY

It was Danzel's idea. The best ones always are. At baby school, which is where we all met, it was his idea to liven up toilet training by sticking a potty on his head and peeing into his hat.

That was clever. For a fifteen-month-old boy-child that was pure genius. I mean, potty on head: vaguely amusing and kind of cute, right? Something any smart baby might do, to get attention. But to use your sunhat to pee in; to go one step further than anyone else would have done, at that age, in that situation. Well, that's Danzel for you.

He got a smack. I remember that. A whole handprint on his bottom, like a strawberry birthmark. *Bad boy!* If you ask me, it was his cleverness that rattled the baby instructors. More than his disobedience, or the puddle on the floor (it was a very small hat and Dan's aim, back then, was poor) it was the sheer maturity of the joke that earned him that wallop.

Most adults, in my experience, are at best wary and at worst driven crazy around too much smartness in the very young. And even as a toddler, Danzel Killick was as clever as a trick and as sharp as a crab claw. He dumbs it down now, which is a cleverness learned with age.

We are all fifteen. That's me, Dilly Tonkin, Danzel, Jenna, Gurnet, and Maude. We are The Gang, which sounds sing-song but actually isn't, because we know one another inside out and back to front. We know one another so well that we can finish each other's sentences off, like psychics or quintuplets.

Being so jam-sandwich-close ought to have all kinds of good points, but in our case it doesn't. It's dull. It's boring. It's an endless yawn knowing that nothing any of your friends will ever say or do is going to surprise you in the slightest.

Having said that, I didn't see Danzel's brilliant idea coming. None of us did. We were sitting in The Crazy Mermaid (that's my mum's café), moaning into our milk-shots over having nothing exciting to do on Hallowe'en when he came right out with it:

'Let's spend the night at the old manor house.'

Nobody replied straightaway, although I could guess, easily enough, what the others were thinking:

Jenna: *Danzel, you are soooo amazing. I adore you. I want to marry you and have lots of clever babies.*

Maude: *Ooh no. Let's not. We'd get into terrible trouble.*

Gurnet: *Bags I first to smash a window.*

And I, for what it's worth, thought: *Whoah! I had a dream about this. Last week—or was it the week before?— I dreamt I was in the old manor house, exploring it room by room. There was sunlight and dust and things from a very long time ago. A doll in a blue coat—velvet, I think. A wheezy old clock. A high bed with a slippery eiderdown. And it was like I belonged in that house, and never wanted to leave. Waking up felt like being kicked out of Heaven. I nearly cried.*

'Just an option,' Danzel said, grinning round the table. 'Just something a bit more daring than hanging around here all night, eating pie.'

Maude's face had gone as white as her milk-shot.

'Although if Maudie's going to have a sissy-fit over it, or Gurn's planning to trash the place . . . '

No, no, insisted Maude and Gurnet, both together, while Jenna placed one hand on Danzel's shoulder and said, 'Let's do it.'

'Dils?'

I was looking at Jenna's hand, which still rested on Danzel's shirt, like it had been stitched on. And I was thinking how only Jenna could make those words 'Let's do it' sound smutty, even out of context.

'Hey, Dilso? Dilly Daydream? Are you with me, or not?'

'What? Yeah . . . yes. I'm with you. Only . . . don't they have cameras up there? Or a live-in guard, or something?'

Maude gave a little shriek, then clapped her fingers over her mouth and looked, apologetically, all around, even though the café was empty apart from us and about two hundred flipping mermaids.

'I'm *sure* there's a guard up there,' I insisted. 'An armed one. Day and night. I thought it was common knowledge.'

Danzel leaned back in his chair. An antique mermaid, with a tail made out of the silver tops that used to go on milk bottles about a hundred years ago got caught in his hair, and we all watched as he untangled her and set her free.

'It's time your mum opened a museum, Dils,' he said, laughing. 'You can't move in here any more. And the ones dangling from the ceiling are *weird*, my friends. Like a load of hanged women.'

Gurnet snorted. He's into all of that. Hangings and so on. Whenever there's a beheading on the inter-telly, he'll watch it, and if the king ever goes in for public executions, instead of private ones in the gaols, Gurn will be right there, at the foot of the block, hoping to get splattered.

'There's no guard at the house,' Danzel told us. 'Hasn't been for ages. Not since the Council had all the precious stuff put into lock-ups. And the cameras got so snarled over by twigs and things that they switched them all off. No one will pay, any more, to keep the garden from going wild. It's a jungle up there.'

My mum came in just then, saying everyone should shunt along home for their teas because the café was about to close. We close early from October through to April, partly to save on electricity, but mostly because the locals aren't big eaters-out and no one else comes to Port Zannon out of season. The fishermen call in for breakfast, and we—The Gang—always have our milk-shots after school, but that's about it.

It was all very different, according to Mum, before The Attack. Just about everyone over the age of seventeen drove a car then and could go anywhere, at any time: to remote seaside resorts like ours, on a whim; to enormous shops that sold everything; even away from England, if they felt like it, on boats that took cars, as well as people, to all kinds of foreign lands.

I don't know anyone with a car. None of us do. Not a car that goes anywhere, anyway. Grandpa Tonkin has one which, for some obscure reason, he calls a four by four. He says he never got round to getting rid of it after The Attack even though he could have used his garage as a stable, or rented the space out, easily enough, as a shelter for displaced and traumatized Londoners.

It's falling apart, that car, and no good to man nor beast. But the little kids like it, for playing in (pretend driving being the only kind they'll ever get to do, unless they end up in Emergency Services, or working for the National Summer Bus Corporation, like Danzel's cousin John).

'Scoot, young people,' Mum chivvied. 'I'm closing.'

It was already dark when we got outside, with clouds scudding over the moon.

'Yeeeooooooow!' howled Gurnet, throwing back his head. 'Yeow, yeow, yeoooooooow!' It's his werewolf act. He's been doing it since he was three, on cloud-scuddy moonlit nights. He's been doing it for so long that the rest of us no longer jump out of our skins when he starts, or tell him to put a brick in it.

The tide was high and all the boats were in. *The Dolphin. The Daydream. The Merry Maid. The Sunray* . . . I noted each one silently to myself: her name and her place at the ropes. There's not much to be had out at sea right now. *Fish are fickle,* Mum says. *Like spinsters and cats. They'll come back when they're good and ready.*

Gurnet's dad, though, says it's odd, this scarcity; that it shouldn't be happening any more. For three nights in a row, apparently, he's been ranting in the tavern that other countries must still be messing up the eco system, only we don't know about it, because nobody tells us anything in this part of the world and the inter-telly's one big fix.

Gurnet's dad drinks too much. The mackerel probably smell his breath, from half a mile off and four fathoms down, and scarper.

We sat in a row on the harbour wall: girl (me), boy (Danzel), girl (Jenna), boy (Gurnet), girl (Maude), just like at school and even—yes, you've guessed it—at potty training. Even though it was dark, with no instructors around to chivvy us into line, we slotted into place naturally and easily, like the boats below our dangling feet.

'So,' said Danzel, 'shall we vote?'

But we didn't need to do that. We didn't even need to bat the idea around, or ask important questions like: How does anyone without a scythe and a spare couple of months actually get to the manor house through the nettles and briars and whatever else is tangled all around it? Or how, exactly, are we going to go in without raising an alarm somewhere?

Because for all that Maude is scared out of her boots, and I am still dubious about the practicalities, and Jenna hasn't thought it through at all, and Gurnet hasn't promised, yet, not to trash the place, we all know we are going to do it.

We—The Gang—are spending Hallowe'en night in the old manor house. We'll get in somehow. There'll be a way. Because Danzel is our smart one, our razzle-dazzle boy, and what he says goes. It always has.

Dust. Not as much as you might expect after all this time but enough to fur the mantelpiece and discolour the upholstery. In the drawing room, to the left of the fireplace, is an ageing chair. Its brocade seat was once a delicate shade of green—sage, her last ladyship called it—but it's dark now. Unpleasantly so. And you wouldn't want to get too comfy on it, because of the mouse nibbling up through the stuffing in a leisurely yet determined way.

Mice and dust. Dust and ghosts. The occasional fly.

Fifteen years have passed since his last lordship, and his lady wife, went off on a jolly to the capital and got blown to oblivion. It is not they, however, who haunt this place. They went too fast, and too far away from home. Like hundreds of thousands of others, they are more likely to be haunting the memorial wastelands of London. Perplexed. Invisible. Jostling for space.

Fifteen years . . .

It is a long time, even under current circumstances, for a house to remain empty. But the West Country Council has never known quite what to do about this one. Applying to the king for a deed of ownership would have been a straightforward enough procedure, given that his last lordship died childless, and no one has ever claimed inheritance, or so much as squatters' rights, since the terrorists did their worst.

But whenever the matter arises (as it does, at Council

sessions, at least once a year) someone always gets cold feet. Port Zannon's manor, you see, is high maintenance. Always has been, right from the long ago day its foundation stones were laid and her first ladyship dreamed of watching the sea shift and change colour through a kaleidoscope of diamond-paned windows.

And right now, with the National Trust a thing of the past, and no money in the Treasury for tarting up old piles, who's going to pay for the roof to be patched up? Or for pipes and wires to be kept in good repair? Who's going to prod gulls' nests from the chimney pots, or stem the tide of rhododendrons creeping over the drive?

Not the West Country Council. Not any more.

The authorities have given up on the place, which just leaves the ghosts. Not apparitions, as such—no ladyships running down corridors in their nighties; no lordships appearing, blurrily, in their favourite chairs; no children's faces, moth-pale in the mirrors. Nothing so obvious as that.

Only sometimes (and there is no rhyme or reason for this, no set time of day or night, and no clue to be had from the weather) the house will tense. Something about the air . . . the atmosphere . . . will alter, minutely, as if the building is holding its breath.

It's been happening for years. For centuries. And while the house was full of people, clattering about their daily lives, or trooping, as visitors, through rooms full of gorgeous things, no one noticed.

Dogs sensed something, though. Generations of guard dogs, lap dogs, hunters and mutts have, from time to time, whimpered . . . shivered . . . gone skulking under beds or sideboards; getting a chocolate or a kick for it depending on their owner's temperament.

They say that a dog's hearing is four times more acute than a human being's; that their ears work like hairy radars, detecting threats. They say that a dog can pick out a sound that bodes ill though it be as faint as a sigh in a rookery.

Perhaps what all those animals detected, here in this rich man's house above the sea, were sounds trapped in time. Sounds destined to repeat themselves, randomly, down the ages, at levels undetectable to the human ear. Sounds so awful, or important, or both, that they will echo for ever more.

> *The sound of a tall ship running aground.*
> *The clapping of a young woman's hands.*
> *The shattering of crystal as a butler drops a tray.*
> *A scream that blows out a candle.*

Or maybe something far more immediate, and a thousand times more ominous, sent those dogs all of a quiver. A noise a thing might make if it had been trapped for a very long time, in a very small space, and is desperate to get out.

A curse? A hiss? A slither?

Or simply the sound of a lid being raised, one tiny bit at a time.

GURNET

I get the stuffing teased out of me; at home, at school, in the café, everywhere. I've got used to it. It doesn't bother me any more. Much.

My real name is Gary, but nobody calls me that. My dad, so the story goes, took one look at me after I was born and said, right into my face: 'Flaming heck, what a weird-looking kid!' If I'd been a fish, he would have thrown me back.

'Hey there, Gurnet!' was the second thing he said to me (a gurnet being the ugliest catch on the planet; all goggle-eyes, pinkish spines and a massive lumpy head).

Mum laughed at that, apparently. She laughed so hard that she bust all the stitches she'd had to have put in a certain place, due to my head being the size and shape of a pumpkin while she was pushing me out. There are things I think of sometimes that make me feel peculiar; and knowing that the very first thing I ever did in this life was rip up a woman's certain place is one of them.

I don't do well at school. I have a go. There are things I like, and try to do good in, but it never works out and those instructors . . . those instructors should be pushed out to sea on a raft. They don't get me. Nobody gets me nowadays except my Dilly, and my Maude, and maybe my Danzel Killick, although sometimes I wish that boy didn't get me at all, or even know me from Adam-of-the-Bible because then I wouldn't have to pretend not to care when he makes smart remarks about my head, or my nature, like he has the perfect right.

'Good old Gurn,' he says. And (when he senses I'm feeling peculiar): 'Hey, Gurn, let's do some hurling.' Then we go up on the cliffs, my Danzel and me, and we scream, and shout swear words, and throw big stones, hard, at whichever rock I decide looks most like my social skills instructor, or my mad uncle Tom, or some kid at the school who's upset me.

The last time we hurled it was Jenna Rosdew who'd done the upsetting but I knew, if I said so, that Danzel wouldn't throw so hard, or would make sure he kept missing the Jenna-rock, because he is too much of a gentleman to ever hit a girl, even in pretend. So I lied—said my dad had cuffed me for watching heavy sleaze on the inter-telly—but Danzel didn't believe that, not for half a second, so neither of us hurled for long that day, or with much whack.

I go out on the boats, with my dad and my uncles. I'm a deckie, which means I do as I'm told. Gutting is what I do best. Some deckies botch that job, getting bored and cack-handed while there's half a haul still to go, and another one swinging in. Me, I never get bored, and my slicing's always clean. I get everything out, including the kidney line, in four seconds flat. And I can do the bones too, ripping them clear in one whole piece, like doing up the zip on my trousers.

My Maude says I'll be all right. Never mind, she says,

about inter-communications, or preserving the arts, or any of the other bilge they teach us at the school. For as long as there are fish in the sea, Maude says (which will be for ever, now that everyone has stopped fouling up the water) there will always be a job for me on my dad's boat.

Maude wants to be a doctor one day. I cannot see it happening. She is too squeamish, that girl. I, on the other hand, could be a top doctor—a surgeon—if only the tests for becoming one were based on gutting and filleting and not on writing things down.

My Danzel wants to be an entrepreneur. This country will need more of those, he says, should the king ever decide to relax his laws a bit and allow some foreign trading to take place, like in the old days. My Dilly doesn't know, yet, what she wants to do, and is getting all restless about it. Jenna would like to go to the United States of America, to star in films. She has more chance of growing a dorsal fin and making a new life for herself under water.

I have lived in Port Zannon from day one of my life and wouldn't mind not leaving. It is a good place to be, especially in the winter when there are no visitors and it gets dark by four o'clock. I like the dark. I like cupboards and caves and cellars. I like colouring things in with black charcoal sticks and wearing my highwayman coat.

The other night they showed a concert on the inter-telly. It was from the archives and the band was called The Rolling Stones. The lead singer was jumping around like a puppet-man, even though he was well into senior-hood, but there was something about him that I liked. He sang this song, about painting things black; about seeing a red door, and girls in summer clothes, and having to turn away because of the darkness right there in himself.

Then he sang another song, about having sympathy for the Devil, and the crowd began to chant and sway, and I got the peculiar feeling I sometimes get that is blissful as well as bad, like being swung way up out of my skin.

The day after tomorrow is Hallowe'en, a seriously dark time. Me and my Danzel and the three girls, we always do stuff on Hallowe'en. When we were little our families took turns having parties for us, with pies and apple-bobbing, and tales told out loud about dead smugglers and Port Zannon's very own ghostly rider.

It was fun back then; I enjoyed that stuff. But we're too old for it now. The girls all have their periods. Me and Danzel are as tall as our own fathers. It's a long time since we dressed up as kitty-cats and wizards, and those stories haven't scared me for at least six years.

Last Hallowe'en we took a tent up on the cliffs. My Maude got frightened, thinking she could hear the ghostly rider coming, and because the sides of the tent kept blowing in and out, like a lung. But the rest of us just got bored. The little kids in the port would have sneered, though, if we'd packed up our things and gone home. They would have said we were milksops and scaredy-pants, which is just kiddie talk, but all the same . . .

This year was looking like being another big waste of time. I'd decided to stay home, watching the goriest thing I could find on the inter-telly, but my Danzel has other ideas. He says we should bust into the old manor house, up on the cliffs, and spend the whole night there.

'Although *tech*nically,' he told us all today, on our way home from the school, 'we won't really be breaking in, or even breaking the law. *Tech*nically, so long as we don't smash a window, or force a lock, or steal anything once we're in there, we'll only be exploring.'

I couldn't see how that might work. But then Danzel made us all stop walking and sit down on the turf, so that he could talk to us better and claim our full attention. And he said that his brother Ned's girlfriend (who works for the Council) let on the other week that there's been a path cut through the manor grounds. A path no one's supposed to know about but which is there so that surveyor-men, or councillors, or nutters thinking about buying the place, can get to the house if they want to without spraining their ankles or getting smacked in the teeth by branches.

According to Danzel's brother's girlfriend, a contractor goes up there on the fifteenth of every month, to make sure the path is clear. He puts weed killer down, kicks things out of the way and cuts stuff back. And that's all he does. He doesn't hang around, and he never goes into the house even though the servants' door into the kitchen doesn't lock properly, and anyone could go in if they wanted to.

That's word for word, apparently, what the contractor told Danzel's brother's girlfriend, over a milk-shot in the Council's canteen. And there's no reason, my Danzel says, for anyone to think he was big-mouthing. Nor would the authorities have a leg to stand on if someone who happened to notice that kitchen door swinging open went into the house, like a good citizen, to make sure all was well.

'If we get caught,' he said, 'which we won't, we'll get a sharp telling off for snooping, but that's all.'

'We could get whipped, I'd've thought,' said Jenna. 'Not yet, but once we're eighteen. They could defer it.'

'Horse dung!' my Danzel said. 'We won't have broken any *laws*, Jen. I've just told you. Not a single one. According to the contractor, there aren't even any signs up nowadays, telling people to keep out.'

Some inland kids came into sight just then. We knew they'd ride as close to where we were sitting as possible— not close enough for their horses to kick our heads in but close enough to be a big irritation—so we all got up and carried on walking, down onto the cliff path and out of their way.

Jenna, who does not want to walk the cliffs on Hallowe'en, said, after a while, that Danzel's brother's girlfriend, or the contractor, or someone, is bound to have told the authorities by now about how easy it has become for any old vagrant to get inside the manor.

She reckons that the servants' door will have had a bolt the size of a murderer's shackle fitted, so we'll end up coming home, or camping out like we did last year, and having a miserable time. What's more, she said, it will probably rain, and that is not good for her hair.

My Danzel just tossed his school bag up in the sky, caught it again and said that it's worth us going anyway, rain or no rain, just to find out.

'Wear your oilskins, Jen-Jen,' he told her. 'And stop being a smother-all. I'm telling you—that door will be open; the path is clear; there are no cameras or alarms up there . . . no guards with whips or guns . . . how much easier could it be? Like I said, there aren't even any "trespassers will be jailed" signs, because no one flicking well cares any more, or wants the bother of having to deal with people caught picking bluebells, or whatever.'

I must have sniggered just then, at the thought of someone getting whipped or slammed away just for picking flowers, because Jenna spun round on the path and gave me one of her looks.

'Did you hear what Dan said, Gurnet?' she asked, in the lady-instructor voice she started using with me about eight years ago, only it's even hoitier now and is really needling my works. 'Before. About not stealing anything when we get to the manor, or smashing anything up? Did you make a mental note of that?'

I said I had. I said it pleasantly. Once upon a time, I would have bitten that girl or taken one of her toys and thrown it into the sea. I would have made her cry for being a she-witch to me.

I deal with torment better now. On the outside, anyway.

Secret chambers and passageways have exciting reputations, along these rocky shores. Priests have hidden in them. Smugglers have used them. Families have stashed diamonds and bank notes away in them rather than trust the banks.

The way in is often a thrill in itself: a trapdoor beneath a rug . . . the mouth of a cave . . . a library shelf that swings open when a particular word on the spine of a book is pressed a certain way.

But the secret chamber in the manor house above Port Zannon has no more glamour than a drain. His first lordship added it for fun. It wasn't even a secret, then, for he showed it to everyone—dinner guests, servants, carol singers, chimney sweeps—just as he showed off the oranges swelling in his conservatory, and his panoramic views of the sea.

Little bigger than a boot cupboard, it was put in behind one of the drawing room's panelled walls, and his lordship had a mural painted to disguise the presence of a door. The mural was of Roman influence (appropriately as it turns out, but more of that later . . .) but so poorly done that its vineyards and marble columns looked all out of kilter, as if knocked that way by a small earthquake, and the cherubs resembled nothing so much as a score of flying pigs.

A Botticelli it was not. His first lordship, however, had about as much artistic appreciation as a bird dropping and thought it quite superb.

'Come and see our mural,' he would say, ushering unsuspecting visitors into the drawing room. 'Enchanting, don't you think? Look at the sheen on those grapes . . . and the sublime expression on Cupid's face.'

And he would run his hands over the panelling as if enjoying the touch, as well as the sight, of all that art work, but secretly feeling for the mechanism that would throw open a door and reveal his 'secret chamber'—along with the human skeleton he kept in there, for a wheeze.

'Gadzooks!' he would exclaim, leaping backwards, with one hand on his heart. 'So that's what became of poor old Uncle Richard!'

And his visitors would roar with laughter, or burst into tears, or stand very still thinking 'you ridiculous little man' depending on their age, impressionability and station in life.

The next lordship threw the skeleton into the sea and used the secret chamber as a drinks cabinet. The one after that shut his children in there, whenever they misbehaved. The next, having endured more than his fair share of cramp and terror, shut away for the most trivial of boyhood misdemeanours, hung a vast tapestry over the mural and pretended that the secret chamber wasn't there at all.

His young bride was never told of it and nor, as time passed, were his own two sons. And, since the tapestry was never moved, or even properly cleaned, servants soon forgot about the space behind the wall. All except one, a footman called Rogerson who, you might recall, took delivery of the box that Joe Tonkin brought up through mizzling rain in the year of seventeen hundred and thirty-two.

Rogerson was a lad with ideas above his station. He reckoned himself as fine as any gentleman and, as a consequence, was not very good at his job. Everything, it seemed, was beneath that boy's dignity, from scraping dung from his lordship's riding boots to answering the door. And he doted on her ladyship so openly and brazenly that it was only a matter of time before his lordship noticed.

The butler had done his best to turn Rogerson from a swaggering upstart into a humble servant, if only because the boy's father, grandfather, and great-grandfather before him had dedicated their lives to the smooth-running of the manor house, and been respected for their loyalty. But by the morning of her ladyship's twenty-first birthday it was clear to just about everyone that Rogerson's days as a footman were numbered.

'Don't take it personally,' the butler told him, after luncheon. 'But you are to leave at the end of the month. You are young, healthy, and strong. There will be other opportunities for you, beyond the manor gates.'

But Rogerson did take it personally. Very much so. He didn't let on (he had his pride) but it bothered him, immensely, that no one had pleaded his case, or appeared to care two figs about his dismissal.

'What does her ladyship have to say about this?' he grumbled, only just managing to sound as if he didn't really care.

'She says she hopes your replacement will have better manners,' the butler told him. 'And that, unlike you, he will be capable of serving a meal so that the food is still warm when it reaches her mouth.'

At that, Rogerson flinched. In his arrogance, while serving at table, he had allowed himself to believe that the blush that always rose in her ladyship's cheeks as he ladled out the soup, meant that she hankered after him every bit as much as he lusted after her.

But, no. It must, he realized now, have been annoyance that had reddened her. Embarrassment too, by the sound of it, over the proximity of his person as he leaned in over her cleavage and ladled out that soup as slowly, and suggestively, as possible.

He grew angry then; so angry that he made up his mind to go that very night, and to hell with any wages owing. It was a pitiful wage they paid him anyway, and he would make it up, three times over, before the year was out. A life on the ocean wave, that's what Rogerson was planning for himself. A sailor's life with no woman to distract him until he was back on dry land and could pick one up, and cast her off, as the fancy took him.

He would leave before dawn, he decided, and walk to his sister's cottage on the moors. His sister, he knew, would lend him the money to get to Bristol, and to lodge there, cheaply, until he found a merchant vessel to sail away on.

He had it all mapped out, did Rogerson.

Then the storm blew up, and the tall ship ran aground. And her ladyship's birthday party continued on into the small hours, fuelled by fine wines, silly parlour games, and much speculation about what his lordship's cut would be this time of the goods spilling out of the wreck and tumbling ashore on the waves.

When the box that was said to contain lavender was opened in the drawing room, only to be hastily slammed shut again amidst all manner of hubbub and mayhem, it was Rogerson who was called for and sent running to the nearest outhouse, for something—anything—to weigh down the lid. And as the guests fled, and her ladyship was taken, trembling and crying, to her room, it was Rogerson who was instructed to take the box fifty miles along the coast and hurl it into the sea.

'I'm going to lock this door behind me,' his lordship told him, once they were alone in the drawing room. 'Just to be on the safe side, and because I promised my wife that I would. Then I must go and sit with her ladyship until she is fully recovered. Perkins will let you out once a horse has been saddled and brought round. Will you . . . will you be all right?'

'Of course.'

Rogerson was sitting astride the mooring chain that he had dumped, like a pile of snakes, on top of the box. He wasn't scared. For one thing, he had neither seen nor heard whatever it was that had frightened the wits out of her ladyship and sent her guests a-fleeing. For another, he was too busy marvelling at the sudden twist of fate that would enable him to make his getaway after all—and on horseback too!

Out of all the servants, the butler had been the only one to catch a glimpse of the thing in the box. 'Ghastly . . . ghastly . . . ' were the only words he'd seemed capable of uttering as Rogerson sprinted past him, en route to the outhouse. And he had been muttering them still as Rogerson ran back to the drawing room, clanking like a convict under the weight of the mooring chain.

'Ghastly . . . ghastly . . . '

'Some kind of animal is it, sir?' Rogerson asked his lordship, now.

The older man shuddered, then glanced, fretfully, at the box as if whatever was inside had two good ears and an intelligent brain and might act, with menace, on any information received.

'Just deal with it,' he replied.

Rogerson adjusted his position on the chain as if making himself more comfortable on a cushion.

'I will,' he agreed, amiably. 'Despite the risks to my own self should this animal—if indeed that's what it is—get out and attack me before I'm far enough away from here to dispose of it, in accordance with your wishes.'

With an impatient 'tssk' his lordship pulled a soft leather pouch from the lining of his waistcoat, shook out a coin and tossed it.

'Much obliged.' Rogerson caught the coin neatly, thinking: *A horse, and a guinea . . . this truly is my lucky day!* And as soon as his lordship had left the drawing room, locking the door behind him, just as he'd said he would, Rogerson moved, fast.

The tapestry covering the far wall was huge, its threads heavy with years of dust and grime. Rogerson grabbed the hem, and began rolling it up. And as he rolled, stretching both arms as high as he could manage, he uncovered vines and columns and cupids as vibrant, and revolting, as when they were first painted.

Where is it . . . where?

Rogerson's grandfather had spoken, often, about the hidey-hole behind the drawing room wall. Indeed, he had made quite a tale of it to dazzle and frighten the young. There was a latch, or a lever, or something, that opened a secret door . . . but where?

Using just his right hand, now, to keep a large section of tap-estry out of the way, Rogerson ran his left palm over the panel-ling, searching . . . searching . . . He neither knew, nor cared, what was in the wretched box, but whatever it was it could *stay right here and rot. He meant to gallop away in completely the opposite direction to the one he'd been told to take, and he wanted no passengers, human or animal, dead or alive, boxed or breathing the air.*

More than that, he was determined to get one over on this high and mighty household. To have the last laugh. He wanted the pleasure of knowing that the final order given to him here had not been carried out, and that one day—next week, next month, next year, when it was too late, anyway, for anyone to come after him—someone would discover the box and realize they had all been taken for fools.

From outside in the courtyard came the slow clip-clopping of hooves.

Holding the tapestry was slowing Rogerson down so he ducked behind it, and let it drop, leaving both hands free to sweep this way and that. He thought of using a chair to stand on; was about to back out to fetch one when yes! He felt the nub of something, a tiptoe's stretch away, pressed it . . . twisted it . . . tugged it . . . and—

Whoomph!

So abruptly did the door to the secret chamber fly open that it blew the tapestry outwards, in a peppery cloud of dust, and sent Rogerson scuttling, crab-like, part-way across the room. Luckily the tapestry was too firmly attached to the top of the wall to come crashing down, and too billowy, despite the weight of its grime, to have been ripped by the force of the door.

No one would rumble him, Rogerson told himself. Not straightaway. Not if he was quick, and the door had been designed to shut as easily as it had opened.

Catching hold of the box, he dragged it, chain and all, across the floor. And if he noticed a teeny shred of something, trapped by the lid, it neither bothered him unduly or slowed him down. One shove and the box slid behind the tapestry. One more and it was in the secret chamber.

'Cheerio,' Rogerson crowed. 'Whatever the merry-hell you are.' And he pushed the lever, finding it immediately this time among a cluster of badly-painted grapes, and held his breath as the door sealed itself shut and the tapestry fell back into place.

Right then . . .

Quickly, with only seconds to spare, he snatched up the first box-shaped thing he set eyes on and flung his own coat over it. If Perkins checked, the game would be up, but Perkins wasn't about to check. On the contrary, having unlocked and opened wide the drawing room door, Perkins took three giant steps backwards as Rogerson came loping towards him.

All kinds of rumours were flying, by then, about what was in the wreckers' box. Cook had sworn blind it was a disease-ridden monkey that would rip out your throat as soon as look at you. Her ladyship's maid said a naked imp, with eyes like burning coals. The butler said a dark insubstantial thing that had seemed to both flutter and pulse and which had made him feel quite . . . hopeless.

A strange response, Perkins thought, for the butler to have made. Not frightened half to death, or so revolted that he had puked like a herring all over the carpet, but that one word . . . 'hopeless'.

'Good luck,' he called, tentatively, as Rogerson ran past him, the box clutched close to his chest. 'Take it steady.'

'I will,' Rogerson called back, pretending to stagger a little from the weight in his arms.

'See you later then.'

'Yep.'

But Rogerson was never seen in Port Zannon again. It was feared—indeed it was rumoured for miles around, becoming legend by and by—that both he and the horse had come to a sticky end. Mauled to death, the cook said. And then eaten. By a rabid monkey. Bewitched, her ladyship's maid said. Sent screaming and whinnying over a cliff by an imp with burning eyes.

'Let's hope, for all our sakes, that whatever happened did so a long ways off from here,' the maid declared to anyone who would listen, 'and that the creature that did it don't go beating a path back to us. Let's hope that the Cornish winter proves too much for it and that it perishes, wherever it be . . . God rest poor Rogerson's soul.'

Only the butler wondered, and continued to wonder for the rest of his life, whether Rogerson had pulled a fast one.

No one in that household ever found the wreckers' box behind the drawing room wall. And no one missed the one that Rogerson had taken in its place (although the person who left it behind, as a birthday present for her ladyship, would be most put out at never receiving a single word of thanks).

As for Rogerson, he made it to Bristol, sold the horse, and had a high old time for a while, drinking himself dizzy and showing off to the ladies. He still intended to go to sea one day, but not until his money ran out.

One night, he invited a good-looking girl back to his lodgings and gave her, on a whim, the box containing her ladyship's birthday present.

'Oooh!' the girl exclaimed, setting aside the lid. 'I ain't never seen such a luverly hat. Can't take it, mind. Can't see you again, neither. My man, Jake, he'd be hopping mad . . . '

Even as she spoke, though, she was lifting the hat from its

33

wrappings, her eyes shining as she touched the red velvet roses that rambled all over its brim.

'Keep it, darling,' said Rogerson, with a lordly wave of his hand. 'Keep it . . . hic . . . and wear it tomorrow. I'll meet you . . . hic . . . down at the docks . . . Same place . . . hic . . . as earlier.'

The girl reminded Rogerson of her ladyship. Same height. Same honey-coloured hair. Not an ounce of good breeding, of course, but in poor light, and with that hat on . . .

It was the hat Rogerson was thinking of as he stood in the shadow of a warehouse, late the following night, waiting for the girl. Staring out across the Bristol channel—as black as a lick of pitch in the dark—he imagined himself back at the manor house above Port Zannon, watching her ladyship open her present.

It was a fantasy he had taken to re-playing over and over again, and, in it, the hat was a gift from him. Smiling, he allowed his imagination to linger on her ladyship's slender fingers, untying ribbons . . . lifting the lid . . . and then on her face, tip-tilted for a moment, and flushed with adoration as she gazed into his eyes.

'Keep going,' he imagined saying to her. 'Look at your present. Go on.'

He didn't hear the man—Jake—sidle up behind him. And as his lungs were punctured—once, twice—by the in and out of a blade, he felt himself confused, more than anything, by the sudden interruption to his thoughts.

His legs were kicked from under him, yet his mind, in its shock, still clung to visions of ribbons falling prettily away, and to her ladyship's smile.

Wheeling . . . falling . . . wondering how and why . . . he heard a woman scream . . . thought he saw a face . . . beautiful . . . appalled . . .

Then everything blurred, as he toppled from the quay and all he had left was a rush of cold air and a dreadful tightening in his gut.

Hitting the water was like going head-first into a box, and having the lid slammed down.

DILLY

We thought it would rain and were glad when it didn't. We wore our oilskins anyway, and made sure our torches were fully-wound.

It was 3.30 in the afternoon when we set off for the manor, not dark yet but getting there. On the sills of one or two houses you could see turnip lanterns, already lit and grinning. I saw Danzel's little niece looking out of her parlour window, pulling a face. She was trying to be like her turnip, all teeth and menace, and hadn't noticed us.

'Look at Sheila,' I said. 'Just look at her.'

Everyone laughed, including me, and when Sheila saw us all staring and laughing, she straightened her face, mortified, and backed away out of sight. I felt cruel then, like I'd stamped on a fledgling or something.

'We'd better get going,' said Danzel. 'Thanks for the pie, Mrs Tonkin.'

'Bring the dish back,' Mum said, as she waved us off. 'And be sure to peg that tent down properly. The wind's getting up.'

We said we would, meaning we'd remember about the dish. Danzel had the tent in a roll on his shoulders, but planned to shove it under a gorse bush as soon as we got up on the cliff. We had sleeping bags and water bottles and spare socks and vests. And, because it was a Saturday, we had permission to stay out until next day's dinner, if we wanted. We looked like turtles, the five of us, with our rucksacks on our backs, or like kids going away on 'foreign exchanges' the way kids used to do all the time, before The Attack.

'Watch out for the ghostly rider,' Jenna's mum called after us, and she began to recite, in a quavery voice: *'That footman he rode like a bat out of hell, lickety-lickety-split, but the imp bit his throat and down he fell, lickety-lickety-split . . . '*

'Moth*er*,' groaned Jenna. 'Behave!'

My mum and Jenna's mum were standing arm in arm on the cobbles, both dressed in black, with their hair slicked back and their good shoes on. They would be meeting the others later—Maude's mum, Danzel's mum and Gurnet's mum—in The Crazy Mermaid, to drink cider, remember our dead, and prepare to go into the dark part of the year.

When Jenna and Maude and I are twenty-one we'll be allowed to join them, if we want. No offence to the mothers, but the very thought of still being in Port Zannon in six years' time makes me more than a little depressed.

We set off in single file—me, Danzel, Jenna, Gurnet, and Maude.

'Do you want to swap?' Danzel asked me, once we were past all of our homes and climbing away from the harbour. 'Just this once?'

'If you like,' I replied.

But Jenna, Gurnet, and Maude didn't want to

swap—Jenna because she would no longer be close to Danzel, and Gurnet and Maude because they simply don't like change.

Three against two.

We stayed as we were.

'That path through the grounds better *had* be clear,' I said, as I reached the clifftop and forked left. 'That contractor, whoever he is, better *had* be doing his job properly. I don't want thorns blinding me, or roots tripping me up. It's all right for you lot.'

'You fall, we all fall,' Gurnet said. 'Like bowling pins.' He was wearing his highwayman's coat over his oilskins. I could hear him strutting and swishing.

'I told you I'd swap,' Danzel reminded me.

'Nah,' I replied, aware of Jenna bristling and Maude tensing up. 'I'll be all right.'

And I was too, to start with. I felt like an explorer; an old-fashioned adventuress leading her followers into undiscovered territory. And I found myself thinking, as the track curved towards the cliff edge, that I really ought to be braver than I am, more confident than Danzel even, given that I've always been first in the line.

Perhaps, I thought, tonight will be a turning point for me. Perhaps I can make it one, by being more assertive. A proper leader, for once.

We walked in silence for a long time—our own, not nature's, for we could hear the wind getting up, just as Mum had said; scraping through the gorse and making all the rigging sing, way down in the harbour. I thought of the ghostly rider (the footman who gallops, so legend has it, away from the manor on stormy nights, *lickety-lickety-split*) and found I was straining my ears for the sound of hoof beats.

'Torches on,' Danzel ordered while I was still wondering whether it was dark enough, yet, for those.

The wind grew stronger, the closer we got to the cliff edge. It blew my hair loose and whipped it all over my face. I slowed the pace, for safety's sake, shoved my hair back behind my ears and gripped my torch harder. I thought of my mum and Jenna's mum setting cider cups out in The Crazy Mermaid, and of little Sheila getting ready to bob for apples in her parlour.

We—The Gang—are too old for apple bobbing and too young for cider. We had our pie, our spare socks, and Danzel's crazy plan, and that was it, pretty much. We were, I realized, between two worlds—child and adulthood—with no rituals of our own and no idea, really, about what kind of fun we actually wanted on this Hallowe'en night.

Having such a profound thing dawn on me, up there on the cliff with the wind buffeting me around, and darkness closing in, made me feel wistful and clever, brave and uncertain all at the same time. I would have liked to sit down, to think about it some more. I would have liked to record it in my 'Dilly's Daily Doings' book (don't probe . . .) while it was still fresh in my head. But the track curved inland again, just then, marking the halfway point to the manor, so I re-focused my torch and forced myself to concentrate on the way ahead.

Adventuress, I reminded myself. *Intrepid explorer.*

'When we get to the house,' Danzel announced,

breaking our silence and making me jump, 'Gurn and I'll go in first to make sure it's safe—no ceilings about to come crashing down; no rats waiting to rip out our throats.'

Jenna gave one of her shrieks. 'You're not leaving us girls outside by ourselves,' she protested. 'Absolutely no way are you.'

'In that case,' Danzel answered her, *I'll* go into the house, and Gurnet will stay with you three knicker-wetters until I give the all clear. All right?'

'All right,' we girls said, none of us caring, at that moment in time, that we'd just been sneered at, badly.

The way ahead seemed even darker, to me, after that, and being first in line no longer an honour, or a challenge, or worth carrying on with for a single second longer than I absolutely had to. I was just a girl after all. A potential knicker-wetter; terrified of rats and the great unknown.

Then Maude's small voice came from the back, saying that if I wanted to swap with Danzel, now that it was really coming dark, she honestly wouldn't mind.

'Me neither,' Jenna added, in a tone that said, in no uncertain terms: *Swap with Dan, Dilso. Do it now or I'll twist your arm.*

'OK,' I agreed, moving sideways straightaway so that Danzel could squeeze past. It was too dark to see if he winked, but I noticed the swagger as he took the lead and *Dan*, I thought, with a shake of my head. *Even in the dark, I can read you like a text. You frightened me on purpose, scoundrel-boy.*

Then Maude spoke up again, wanting to swap with

Gurnet so she wouldn't be at the end, with who knows what snapping at her heels.

Oh, go on then, we all said.

And that—the swapping around—was our first big mistake. It changed our pattern . . . disturbed the norm. These things shouldn't matter, but they do.

GURNET

I had cider in one of my water bottles and so did my Danzel. I drink cider at home, even though I'm under-age. Mum would throw a cat-fit if she knew, but Dad lets me, after Mum's gone to her bed. Dad says if I'm old enough to do a man's job on the boats then I'm old enough to enjoy a proper drink in the privacy of my own parlour.

When Dad gets lashed he talks horse dung, or picks a quarrel, or both. I don't. Cider doesn't fog me up, it makes me a sharper person. I've been known to tell a good joke after my third cup, and it was just a shame there was only my dad there to hear it.

My Danzel and I weren't going to tell the girls we had cider on us. We were going to drink it very late, once they had all gone to sleep. We had it in our minds, then, that they would all sleep by and by; that nothing would stop them nodding off—Maude first, then Dilly, then Jenna—because nothing ever had before; not even on Hallowe'en.

It was one mighty walk, to the manor. We're used to walking, we walk most days, but not in that direc-tion because there's never been any point. It had never crossed our minds to go as far as the old manor until my

42

Danzel gave us the urge.

The gates were closed. Padlocked.

'Oh, brilliant,' Jenna said. 'Absolutely sing-song. Back home for some apple-bobbing is it then, Dan?'

It was the closest I've ever heard Jenna Rosdew come to calling our Danzel a splat-brain. Usually you would think he had a halo above his head; a great big one, like a flying saucer, that means he can do no wrong.

'Sorry,' she said, almost straightaway. 'But that was a long walk, all for nothing. My legs hurt and—'

'But we can't go back,' Dilly interrupted. 'Not now. Danzel, this is your fault.You said there'd be a path.'

'Stay the axe, you two,' Danzel told them. He sounded perfectly cheerful. Nothing gets to that boy. Nothing bothers him. 'No one said this was the only way in. I'll walk round a bit . . . see what I can find. Wait here.'

'I'm coming with you,' said Jenna, straightaway. 'Come on, Maude. Stay by me.'

I thought my Dilly would want to go as well, but she'd stepped right up to the gate and was shining her torch through the bars.

That gate was sing-song. Think horror movies from the archives. Think old Count Drac. Think lost travellers bumping up against iron bars—great tall bars with spikes on the top—and one of them saying: 'Thank you, Lord. We will not freeze, now, or be eaten by wolves, for whoever lives beyond this gate will give us dinner and a bed for the night.'

Yeah, right.

I went to stand beside my Dilly and I, too, shone my torch through the Dracula-gate. There was no driveway any more; the plants and trees had covered it. No driveway, and no path, either, just a mass of garden, gone wild over the years. I swung my torch to try and spot a house through all the overgrown stuff. It might have been magicked away, though, or knocked flat by a demolisher. You couldn't see a thing through all the wildness.

'It's like that story,' my Dilly said, dreamily. 'Remember? In baby school? The one about the Sleeping Beauty? She'd been asleep for a hundred years and a prince had to slash his way through acres and acres of briars, just to get to where she lived.'

I'd forgotten that story. It sounded like slop to me. Dilly remembering it made me smile though. It made me feel all soft and warm standing next to her while she thought her pretty, dreamy thoughts. It made my darkness go.

Then: 'Hey!' yelled Danzel, from somewhere off to our left. 'Hey, Gurnet! Dilly! Get yourselves round here. We've found a path. We've found a way in!'

Coincidences are all around; invisible threads joining events, places and people in a web of cause and effect. It is a very small coincidence—tiny—that the wreckers' box has been hidden, for all this time, behind a Roman mural, but it remains significant, nonetheless, and pleasing, in its way.

The box, you see, has Roman connections. Strong ones.

The Romans themselves never bothered, much, with this straggly stretch of the kingdom after they occupied Britain way back when. Their aqueducts, fountains, and sewers; their straight roads, pretty floors, bear fights, and baths were imposed on other more convenient locations, leaving the people of Cornwall to go their own ways, pretty much.

As for the Roman gods, they never got a look in down here. True, a few Romans did, eventually, come sniffing around after supplies of silver and tin, but if they brought their deities with them you'd never know it now.

Shrines and stories. Temples and tales . . .

The Romans controlled Britain for the best part of four centuries but the beliefs they arrived with never gained more than a toe-hold and eventually fell right out of favour.

Imagine though, if you will, how things might have turned out had the Romans stayed on in Britian and Emperor Constantine not found it politically expedient to convert to Christianity.

Consider what it would have meant—not only for Britain but for large chunks of the world—if Christianity had been suppressed, or allowed to fizzle out, and belief in the Roman gods had grown instead . . . grown like wildfire, or a snowball gathering speed . . . grown so big, and so powerful, that given a few more centuries and enough vested interest, nothing could challenge or topple it.

Imagine temples dedicated to Apollo, the god of truth, music, and healing. Picture marble statues of fun-loving Bacchus, gobbling grapes in market squares. See yourself tipping a nod, at sunrise, to Aurora, goddess of the dawn, and, at night, greeting Luna, goddess of the moon.

There would be no Christmas, of course, and no promise of Heaven. Sorry.

But what might have been made, instead, of the Fates? . . . the Muses? . . . the Graces? And of Ceres, the corn goddess, who so loved her only daughter, that she followed her beyond death and bartered with the King of the Underworld for her safe and immediate return?

Shrines and stories. Temples and tales . . .

The beliefs of ancient Rome have gone the way of the toga: laughably out of fashion now; a poor fit for modern man. Here in Port Zannon, folk would no more conceive of Jupiter hurling thunderbolts from Mount Olympus than they would of a fresh-caught lobster telling them the time. But, then, most of them don't know what to believe in nowadays; not since a swarm of aircraft crash-landed, with terrible precision, on London, in the name of religion, or revenge, or whatever it was.

London.

Londinium, the Romans called it.

Boudicca, queen of the Iceni Tribe, flattened the place to teach

46

Roman invaders a lesson, but it got rebuilt. That hasn't proved so easy, second time around. The land remains raw. An unlicked wound. Few people want to live there despite new incentives to do with housing and trade. And trees in the memorial parks are taking a long time to grow as if their roots can't help recoiling from what lies, reduced to atoms, beneath the surface of the soil.

The kingdom—the world—is still reeling from The Attack. People cling to whatever they can: to faith; to happy memories; to each other . . . to a belief, if they can muster it, in the ultimate goodness of mankind.

They say it cannot—will not—happen again.

They say that man did his worst on 20/3.

They cling, above all else, to hope.

Hope: i) to trust and believe; ii) to have faith in a favourable outcome.

Ancient Romans had a story about hope coming into the world. It used to be taught in schools, but not any more.

The young people of Port Zannon have probably never even heard of Pandora's box. And if they have, you can bet they know of only one ending to the tale: that after hope was released, to flutter in the face of cruelty, greed, and all the other nasties in the world, that was it. The box was empty.

Wrong.

DILLY

The path to the manor house begins where part of the wall surrounding the property has either crumbled or been knocked down. Unless you were looking, you wouldn't know it was there. After a bit of a rough start (there are brambles over the first bit, which Danzel reckons have been trained there deliberately, for camouflage) it goes in a long, straight line right up to the house.

And although the garden is totally out of control, with rhododendrons grown as tall as ten men, the path itself has been so well-tended that we found ourselves hurrying—running, almost—confident that we wouldn't trip, or find the way ahead blocked by fallen branches.

Even Maude, who might so easily have pigeon-stepped her way along, fearing everything from cobwebs to a mad axeman, seemed lulled by the smoothness under her feet and kept up.

We moved silently, like Red Indians in ancient films. And the closer we got to the house, the more eagerly I stepped, almost treading on the heels of Danzel's boots and doing my best to see ahead of him.

And when we reached the house, when the beams of our torches crept up its steps, hit the main door and went skittering over the great swags of ivy draped like a shawl all over the walls, I got a sensation in my stomach like butterflies fluttering, and an ache, to go with it, that I can only describe as a yearning. It's a feeling I only usually get when I think about my mother—my real mother, who dumped me on my dad while I was still so new that I fitted, easily, and with room to spare, into the daffodil crate she left me in, on Grandpa Tonkin's doorstep.

I've always thought I'd get a similar feeling, part flutter, part ache, when I finally fall in love, particularly if it ends up being a one-way thing—a sweet but hopeless craving. I never thought to get it over a building.

'This way,' said Danzel. 'I think.'

The contractor who's keeping the path clear must also be stopping the garden from coming right up to the house. You can walk all the way round. It's like the manor covers most of an island, the track around it is the shore, and the grounds are a deep green ocean, spreading away on all sides and cutting off the rest of the world.

We found the kitchen door easily enough, in the light of our torches and, as Danzel had predicted, it opened.

'Don't. Don't go in there.'

Danzel had one foot over the threshold. I was trying to see round him and, at first, I assumed it was Maudie having one of her sissy-fits behind us. It wasn't, though, it was Jenna.

'Don't do it, Dan. There's something . . . I don't know . . . something really bad about this place. I don't like it. I want to go home.'

This wasn't like Jenna. This wasn't like her at all. She wasn't being dramatic just to get attention; she'd sounded genuinely scared. I shone my torch at her—shone it right into her eyes, I was so surprised.

'Oi!' she snapped, more like her usual self.

'Sorry,' I mumbled and swung the beam away.

Danzel looked back and frowned at Jenna as if he really didn't need her, of all people, going skittery on him just then. 'You're in charge, Gurn,' he said. Then he stepped into the house, the first one of us to go.

GURNET

I liked being in charge. I would have protected those girls against any kind of evil—man or beast—if I'd had to. I had my gutting knife on me, and would have used it, too.

My Danzel was gone a long time. He was gone so long that Jenna began to fret and pace around.

'Stop walking away,' I told her. 'Come back here, where I can see you.' I was very firm about it, because I was in charge.

We had put our torches down on the ground with their lights slanting up. And although I could hear Jenna's feet, scrunching the gravel, she had gone right away from our safe patch of yellow and it was making me uneasy in my head.

'Come here, you,' I called out, really angry this time because she hadn't replied, or done as I'd asked straight off. 'Come and be with us, in the light.'

'Flick off, Gurnet,' she yelled back. 'Don't talk to me like you're my dad, or my instructor, or someone with more than half a brain cell.'

There were clams, once, on the Great Barrier Reef, that took two hours to shut their mouths. I've seen them on the inter-telly and they reminded me, a lot, of Jenna Rosdew. Those clams are extinct now, unlike the big-mouthed Rosdews.

My Maude took hold of my arm, and my Dilly patted my shoulder, to reassure me that it was Jenna in the wrong, not me, telling me to flick off the way she had, and insulting my mind. Both of their faces, in the torchlight, were as pale and as pretty as flowers. Jenna, I decided, could go where the merry hell she liked. She could wander off and get her leg mulched in a badger trap for all I cared.

'Are you frightened, Maude?' I asked.

She said she wasn't. Not as much as she'd thought she'd be, and not while I was there.

I nodded, proud. I didn't need to ask my Dilly the same question. She wasn't scared. She was so excited I could feel it, like the buzz from a cattle fence, going from her right through to me. It puzzled me then but I understand it better now. My Dilly loves that house.

I fixed my eyes on the kitchen door, wishing that Danzel would hurry up. I wondered if there was stuff in there—old carving knives or silver dishes that I might be able to filch. Then my stomach growled, reminding me that we'd had a long walk and I was as hungry as a wolf.

'Who's got the pie?' I asked. 'And cake. Did we bring a cake with us?'

I heard Jenna curse me under her breath. She was still pacing on her own in the dark, and that curse was nasty. There was no need for it.

I opened my mouth to reply to her. To give her what for. Those were scalding words I was about to address Jenna Rosdew with. I could feel them coming up in my throat, like cider-sick.

Then we heard our Danzel scream.

So here it is, the story of Pandora's Box: a tale embellished and hacked about, down all the years, but still worth paying attention to. Heard it before? Tempted to skip ahead? Let's remind ourselves, shall we, that this box is still with us, and that its continuing presence in the world does not bode well—for anyone.

Once upon a time the only mortals on earth were male. They were a dull lot, compared to Jupiter and his cronies, but that was how the gods wanted it, particularly Jupiter, ruler of all, who would have seen off any man who'd turned out smarter or more charming than him, with a well-aimed white-hot thunderbolt.

Each mortal had been fashioned out of clay by the Titan, Prometheus, and had the life force breathed into him by a goddess. Each mortal knew his place, pretty much, but Prometheus did not. He was a joker. A kidder. The kind of man you wouldn't want at parties in case he over-stepped the mark, embarrassing everyone but himself.

At a sacrificial meal, Prometheus tricked Jupiter into choosing bull bones wrapped in fat, instead of a helping of good meat. Nobody laughed. Nobody so much as sniggered. And Jupiter, instead of smiting Prometheus stone-dead on the spot, took his temper out on the whole human race by taking fire away.

53

How they shivered, then, those mortal men. How they missed being able to cook their food, and longed for the means to banish darkness from their thresholds on nights when the goddess Luna turned her face away from Earth.

Prometheus, knowing this was all his fault, considered his options:

1. Go grovelling to Jupiter, to ask for fire back;
2. Do nothing;
3. Steal a bit of the sun, and take it down to Earth.

Being Prometheus, he went with the third option. It was like sticking two fingers up at Jupiter. It was the craziest, bravest, riskiest thing anyone could have done under the circumstances. And when Jupiter, peering down from Mount Olympus, saw the glow of re-kindled torches; heard the crackle and snap of enormous bonfires, and noticed mortals leaping around like happy frogs, his fury knew no bounds.

The punishment of Prometheus went beyond awful. Jupiter had him tied to a rock and sent an eagle to rip out, and eat, his liver. Death, you might suppose, came as a welcome relief to that young man but no . . . death was considered too good for Prometheus. His liver grew back, to be eaten all over again the following day . . . and the next day . . . and the next . . . in an infinite cycle of agony.

As for the mortals: they assumed they'd got away with it. They thought, as time passed, and fire stayed, and nothing made a swoop for their own vital organs, that Jupiter had let the matter drop. They really were as thick, still, as the clay used to mould them. Happy though; as happy as larks, for there were no evils in the world, then, to trouble their days or haunt their nights. No crime. No jealousy. No famine or disease. No fear of anything or anyone (except Jupiter, swiper of fire, torturer of Prometheus, but they were used to that).

Then Jupiter created the first woman: Pandora. He was pleased with her; the men were going to love her to distraction. But Jupiter was crafty, and Pandora part of a plan.

The goddess Minerva breathed life into Pandora and clothed her in a silvery gown. Venus gave her beauty. Apollo taught her to sing and play the lyre. Ceres, the corn goddess, showed her how to tend a garden. Neptune's gift was a pearl necklace and the promise that she would never drown. Then Mercury, the messenger-god, instilled in her the power to charm and to deceive, particularly around mortal males, the poor clods.

Pandora was sent to Earth as a bride for Epimetheus, brother of Prometheus. And she was given a box to take with her. Nothing special. No carvings or swirlings of gold. But a box that would intrigue and bother Pandora because the very last thing Jupiter said to her, before sending her on her way, was: 'Don't open it.'

Imagine the temptation. Imagine having that box under your own bed, or stashed away in a cupboard. It would haunt your dreams, wouldn't it? It certainly haunted Pandora's. And after a while the longing to know what was inside grew desperate. An obsession. She could think of nothing else.

'Come with me,' she said to her husband one day, when the longing to know had become unbearable. 'Let's open it together.'

Epimetheus must, surely, have hesitated. His brother, after all, was having his liver pecked out for around the eight hundred and forty-seventh time. Epimetheus, of all people, should *have been more than a little wary of disobeying Jupiter.*

Perhaps he tried a few excuses. Drinks with the boys. Exhaustion. An urgent appointment with a soothsayer. Pandora cajoled him into following her, to the place where the box had been stored, and before he knew it, he was kneeling down beside his wife as she placed her two hands on the box, palms flat against the grain of the wood.

'Are you sure this is a good idea?' he might have said, at the very last minute, keeping his own hands behind his back, or clenched in his lap. 'Shouldn't we—you—give this a bit more thought?'

But Pandora, by then, would not have been listening.

Her fingers, on the box: did they tingle? All power was hers, just then, and she could—yes, she could—(surely?)—have changed her mind.

Curiosity though . . . it's a terrible thing.

The lid would have lifted easily. The box was still new, after all, and no one had thought to seal it tight, with magic or glue or anything else. No mortal, back then, would have considered it necessary.

The rush of all evil was both foul and immediate. Like bats they flew, or midges; some big, some small, but all of them healthy and moving fast. Pandora, expecting—what? Jewels? Stars? Frankincense and myrrh?—gasped in horror, almost swallowing a speck of something deviant that would have killed her on the spot.

She couldn't move. She was numb to her bones; incapable of closing either her mouth or the lid of the box. And the smell . . . the smell all evil left behind would have turned the stomach of a whale.

'Ow!' Epimetheus slapped at his arm, as something nipped

him in passing. Opening his mouth to yelp made him retch. That appalling smell . . . he could taste it. But: 'Shut the lid . . . ' he managed, between great, dry, heaves. 'You stupid . . . bitch. You stupid . . . thoughtless . . . crazy . . . '

Pandora burst into tears. Epimetheus had never spoken to her like that before. And she, herself, had never been so frightened or so washed through with despair. She would grow old, she realized. She would get sick and know pain. She felt the need to be cruel—to kick an animal, whip a servant, or tell a child it would always be ugly. She wanted to die.

Epimetheus pushed her—a shove so unexpected; such a shock to Pandora's whole being, that her fingers loosened their grip, and down crashed the lid. It was too late though, Pandora could tell. Ghastly things were no longer streaming past her head or whirling like cinders in the room. They had gone—through the open window and out into the world.

'You stupid . . . '

'Wait . . . '

Pandora raised her right hand. Pleading. Halting.

'Listen,' she said. 'Please.'

Epimetheus listened. He heard nothing, at first, and then . . .

'Let me out.'

The voice was gentle, drifting from the box like three perfect notes of music. After the wordless, graceless, rush of the other things it seemed trustworthy—lovable, even.

Epimetheus shook his head. There were tears in his eyes, come out of nowhere; confusing him. 'It's a trick,' he said, thickly. 'Ignore it.'

Pandora, blinking back tears of her own, wondered what to do. She was falling deeper into despair with every passing second and asking herself what kind of punishment Jupiter might have

*in store for her. She was willing it to be a thunderbolt and try-
ing hard not to think about Prometheus.*

'Let me out.'

*Pandora found she didn't much care if this was some kind of a
trick. In disobeying Jupiter she had let loose some terrible things.
One more of them, she felt, would make very little difference, to
herself or to the world.*

And so, once again, she lifted the lid of the box.

*Hope rose in a corolla of light, hovered a while above the
tearstained oval of Pandora's face and then flew. Straight for
the window she darted, in the wake of all evil. She was a filmy,
flimsy thing and neither Pandora or Epimetheus would have
been at all surprised to see her fall, like a snowflake, and melt
away to nothing. They did not realize, then, how tenacious hope
can be.*

*As hope disappeared—through the window and away—
Pandora shut the box, pressing the lid down, hard. She felt
better. Not enough to go on as before, for she knew that was
going to be impossible, but enough to want to live. Neither
she or Epimetheus had spotted the slow-moving thing—the
worst of all evils—making a last-ditch attempt to enter the
world before the lid of the box slammed down again and
stunned it.*

*'I trust you're satisfied,' Epimetheus yelled. 'You just couldn't
leave it alone, could you?'*

Pandora bowed her head.

*'We must make offerings to the gods,' Epimetheus contin-
ued, in the loveless tone that would be the norm from then
on, whenever he spoke to his wife. 'We—you—must beg for
Jupiter's mercy. And if he allows us to live we will set this box
on a pedestal where we—you—will always be able to see it.*

Not a day, not even an hour, must pass in which you aren't reminded of the terrible things that are out there now, all because of you.'

Endless torment, Pandora realized, did not have to be physical. For one split second, she almost envied Prometheus.

JENNA

I swear, I could have killed Danzel Killick for screaming like a flicking whistle and frightening me half to death. I thought a rat must have gone for him, or that he'd fallen through floorboards into some mouldy old cellar. I thought we'd find him paralysed, or with half his face chewed off, and that's the only reason I set foot in the manor house—to get to Dan before any of the others did, so that I'd be the one holding his hand while he bled, or whimpered, or whatever.

Nothing, apart from Dan's scream, would have got me into that place. I'm not a superstitious girl, and it takes a lot to frighten me (although I fake being scared, sometimes, so that boys in general, and Danzel in particular, won't think I'm turning into one of those brass-hard women who think men are only good for chopping wood, or donating their sperm), but that house put the shivers into me the second I saw it.

When Danzel went in, ahead of the rest of us, to check the place over, I didn't know where to put myself. I felt poorly, to tell you the truth, and was seriously considering heading back to the port, even though it was a grungy walk and I knew no one would want to go with me.

The others—Gurnet, Dilly, and Maude—seemed fine.

Even Maude, the biggest scaredy-boots in the kingdom, was looking up at the house like it was just another place, not somewhere to run a mile or ten from, which is how I was seeing it. I couldn't bear to be near her, or to Gurnet and Dilly either; I was too jumpy. So I took myself off a little way and took deep, slow breaths to try and calm down. It didn't work.

When Danzel screamed it was like I'd been expecting it. It confirmed the frightened-sick feeling growing in my stomach that there is something about the manor that visitors (oh all right, intruders) need to beware of. Something truly nasty. I almost made a run for it, in the general direction of away, but this was my heart's desire in there, shrieking, so, of course, I was up the steps and in through the kitchen door while the others were still reeling and looking gormless.

Turns out, a toad was to blame. A big fat toad, plonked like a poo on the third stair down from the first floor and puffing its throat in and out, like they do. He'd almost skidded on it, Danzel said, when I finally reached him, through a maze of little passages, by calling 'Where? Where?' to his 'Here! Here!' He'd almost squished that toad with his boot, which had been enough, he said, to make him holler, and to almost go head over heels down the rest of the stairs, or straight over the banister and splat!

The others came tumbling in behind me and we all stood in a huddle, at the foot of the staircase, not daring to move in case one of us skidded on Danzel's disgusting amphibian. There was a ripe smell in the air, like you get in old sheds; sort of mushroomy with tinges of soot and fox. The boys shone their torches up and all around but toady had hopped it—that's if he ever existed in the first place.

The hall we were standing in was enormous. The walls were of dark wood, divided into rectangles, and from somewhere way above our heads hung a great long chain which I'm guessing had a light fitting on the end of it, once upon time—one of those ugly antique things, made of dangly glass. A chandelier.

The chain, by itself, looked sinister. The entire situation was as scary as scary ever gets, and way too much for me.

'If I thought for one minute,' I yelled at Dan, 'that there wasn't any toad, and that you only hollered just then to frighten me—us, I mean . . . I'll . . . I'll . . . ' I sounded more furious than I actually was, which was partly my way of covering up how relieved I was to have found Dan in one piece but mostly to disguise the fact that being inside the house was scaring me a thousand times more than standing outside it had, which the night sky knows was bad enough.

Danzel shrugged and then he grinned at me, in that teasing way of his that makes me believe he can read my thoughts. I flicking well melt, nowadays, when he looks at me like that and I reckon he can tell. His face, in the torchlight, had shadows in interesting places, making him look older than he is—eighteen, at least.

I smiled back, and for a moment I didn't care that I was standing in a derelict old ruin that may, or may not, have been infested with toads as big as teacups or haunted by ghosts in powdered wigs and tatty coats. I just wished that Dilly, Maude, and Gurnet had decided to stay home, the wastrels.

'I'm starving,' said Gurnet. 'Let's eat the pie.'

'Can't we explore first?' Dilly wanted to know. And Danzel looked from me to her, his expression changing; becoming nicer, somehow, and definitely keener because he and Dilly-flicking-Daydream were on exactly the same wavelength in their excitement over the house. It bonded them, this eagerness to go poking around, and I didn't like it. I didn't like it one little bit.

'Pie,' said Gurnet, firmly.

'Oh, all right . . . '

Danzel swung his torch, so that it shone down one of the passageways. 'There's a room along there with a picture all over one of the walls,' he said. 'A mural-thing. You'll like it. Dils—come and look. We can eat in there and go exploring afterwards.'

I hung back, with Maude, while Dan led the way to the room with the stupid wall-picture. Maude whispered to me that she was all right. She thought I was sticking with her to be kind; looking out for her, like a good friend.

'I know you are,' I snapped.

I wasn't, though. I wasn't all right at all. The combination of fear, and wanting to kiss Danzel Killick so badly that my mouth kept hanging open, was driving me insane.

DILLY

Have you ever walked into a new place and felt certain you've been there before? Not just because a cupboard looks familiar, or the pantry walls are the same buttery-yellow as the pantry walls at your granny's but because everything about it makes you feel peaceful and happy and safe?

I didn't feel like a trespasser at the old manor house, or even like a visitor. I felt like I'd come home. Even crazier than that, I sensed that the house recognized me too, and was glad that I was there. The walls, I swear, seemed to vibrate towards me, in a welcoming sort of way, and I tingled as I hurried from the kitchen into a passageway, as if I'd just been hugged.

It was pitch black inside, of course, and cold, and damp, and musty—all the things you'd expect in a house that hasn't been lived in for more than fifteen years. Still, it struck me straightaway as being the most amazing place in the kingdom, if not the entire world.

Danzel said he'd seen a toad, and warned us girls to watch out as there were bound to be more of the things plopping around in the dark. Jenna and Maude almost fainted dead away but I didn't even care. I wanted to explore. I wanted to touch things—the curve of the banister, a panelled wall—but Gurnet, as usual, could only think about his stomach.

My mum makes us a Hallowe'en pie every year, out of pumpkins and sugar and honey. She's a good cook; a professional. She married my dad when I was two so I have no trouble calling her 'Mum' or in loving her like she's my own flesh and blood.

My dad was only sixteen when he got landed with newborn me; fifteen (I know, I know!) when he made my real mum pregnant. He wasn't told, he says. He knew nothing about it until he and Grandma and Grandpa Tonkin woke up one bright spring morning to the sound of something screeching on the step.

'That's never a seagull,' Grandma said. And she was right.

My real mother was from Romania, a country of forests and wolves and poverty, according to the inter-telly. She was three years older than my dad, and her name was Aurelia which means 'golden'. She came to England to earn money, and to Port Zannon because she had never been by the sea before, and because a man she met on the aeroplane gave her a ride down in his car. I'm told she had dark hair, like me, but that, unlike me, was the life and soul of the party even though her English wasn't good. She worked every lunchtime at The Crazy Mermaid as well as four evenings a week in the tavern, and lodged, for a while, in Grandma and Grandpa Tonkin's spare room.

My dad says she seduced him on one of her nights off, but that he didn't say no very loudly. It was his first time, he says, and he imagined that Aurelia was too smart to get pregnant—that she was taking a pill to prevent it. Only married women can get those pills now. Single women who fall for a baby have two choices: marriage or a termination. Get wed or get rid. It's hard to believe things were ever any different.

When Aurelia started putting weight on round her middle everyone teased her about eating too much Cornish cream on her puddings. Then she left. To pick daffodils further west, she told my dad (who cried) and then to London, to go shopping and see the sights.

I know about picking daffodils. I researched it, on the inter-telly, when I was nine. My dad had just told me the truth about everything, and I wanted to fill in some gaps. Aurelia would have worn rubber gloves to protect her hands from poisonous sap. She would have worked in a gang of mostly foreign pickers, in all weathers and for long hours at a stretch. She would have snapped the flower stems with both hands and bound them in bunches of ten. The stems had to be at least twenty-eight centimetres long and she would have been paid seven pence a bunch.

More than likely she lived in a caravan, rented from the farmer she was working for. More than likely, that is where I was born. Nobody saw anyone leave the daffodil crate, with me in it, on my grandparents' step, but a neighbour said she heard a car pull up, shortly before dawn and stand for a minute or so, with its engine running, before backing down the alley, onto Fore Street, and away.

My real mother left a photograph of herself (for me, or for my dad, she didn't say, but Dad had it copied, so there's one each and some spares). She had folded that photograph so many times, before tucking it into the crate, that my grandma almost threw it away, assuming it was scrap. It shows Aurelia in a daffodil field, with her hair blowing around, and all the flowers bending towards her like trumpets playing a song. It is a printout of an old-fashioned photograph, taken from somebody's computer. I still wonder, sometimes, whose.

On the back of the photo, in sky blue pencil, were the words: *Barry, this is your little one. I love her but I cannot keep. I go to London now where I stay for maybe two months then back to Romania. It is best all around. Forgive me. Aurelia.*

She wanted to ride on the London Eye. She wanted to buy jeans in Oxford Street and take pictures of the ravens who lived at the Tower of London. I hope she had fun shopping, at least, before she, the Eye, the whole of Oxford Street, the ravens and the Tower were incinerated.

Mum—my living mum—says that Aurelia is always remembered, on Hallowe'en night. The mothers say her name out loud, along with the names of ancestors, stillborn babies, friends gone before their time, and fishermen lost at sea, and then they pass the cider cup and drink a silent sip, to her memory.

'We've got cider,' Danzel announced, in a downstairs room of the manor, where we'd gone to eat our picnic even though there were no tables and only the one old chair.

I'd walked away with Maude, to look at a mural on the wall. The pictures had faded, and the perspective was terrible. My torch picked out grapevines, some kind of a temple and what looked to me like blancmanges with wings.

Maude seemed fascinated—was reaching up to touch—when we heard what Danzel said, about the cider.

'Please tell me you're joking,' I called out. And I swung my torch away from the wall and hurried back across the room, pulling Maude along with me, for moral support.

It's illegal to drink alcohol, even in private, until you're twenty-one. You get a warning if you're caught once, extra community service if the warning doesn't work, and gaol, or a whipping, if you've turned eighteen and are still flouting the law.

Some adults turn a blind eye to their kids, or their neighbours' kids, having an occasional cider at home, even though you're supposed to log straight onto the inter-telly to report them. I've always suspected Danzel's and Gurnet's dads of turning blind eyes on a regular basis, and now I'm certain of it.

I squatted, anxiously, next to Dan and held out my hand for the bottle. 'Give,' I said to him. 'Let me see.'

'Calm down, Dils.' Danzel was taking our old plastic cups from his rucksack and didn't even look up. 'Somehow, I don't think anyone from the authorities is about to storm the building.'

'I thought the cider was just for us two,' Gurnet butted in. 'For later. The girls shouldn't drink it. It'll make 'em puke.'

'I'll drink it,' said Jenna. 'I'll drink anything. Pour it out, Danzo.'

I was beginning to feel stupid with my hand held out like a beggar-girl so I let it drop.

'Jenna . . .' I began and then stopped. She would make herself sick, and be sorry, and that would be her lookout.

Then Maude, in her little mouse-squeak voice, said that she would like to try some cider too. Just a sip, she said, to see what it tasted like—to satisfy her curiosity. Gurnet, Jenna, and I looked at her in amazement, wondering if she was pulling our legs, or running some kind of a fever. But Danzel just chuckled as he arranged our cups in a line along the floorboards: mine (yellow), his (blue), Jenna's (green), Gurnet's (red), and Maude's (white). 'Good for you, Maudie,' he said. 'That's the spirit!'

I stood up. The cups were in the proper order, I noticed, but everything else was . . . *odd*.

'This isn't right,' I said.

'Don't be a smother-all, Dils,' Danzel answered back. He was un-corking one of his bottles and still hadn't looked at me once. 'There's water as well, if you don't want the other stuff. Sit down and eat your pie.'

'No,' I told him, aware, to my shame, that I was right on the edge of tears. 'I'm not hungry. I'm going upstairs to explore.'

Jenna reached up and tugged the sleeve of my oilskin. 'Wait for us,' she said. 'We'll all go, in a minute.'

'No,' I repeated, through the ache in my throat. 'I'm going by myself. I'd rather.'

'OK,' Jenna shrugged, not caring.

Danzel had poured cider into four of the five cups. He passed the white one to Maude and she took it. Surprise dried my tears before they could spill over. 'Have you lost your mind?' I said to Maude. 'You can't, seriously,

69

be about to drink that?' And she told me not to fret, that she felt unusually bold tonight.

I didn't know what else to say. My mouth was like a cod's, opening and shutting. At home Maude would have drunk from a ditch rather than break the law, and she wasn't the only one acting strangely. Jenna—sassy Jenna—was as jumpy as a cat. Really jumpy, not just pretending. And then there was Gurnet, whose attitude, particularly towards Jenna, was especially bad tonight and who might, I realized, be someone to fear—someone we could no longer deal with—if he drank a lot of cider. And Danzel . . . Danzel should have known that, about Gurnet, and left the cider at home. It was stupid of him to have brought it.

Changing. They were all changing—acting out of line.

'You're mad,' Jenna said, as I picked up my torch and began heading for the door. 'Wandering around this old place all by yourself. You're round the flicking bend.'

'You're the mad one,' I snapped back. 'Just don't expect any sympathy from *me* when the room starts spinning round. Or you either, Maude Tremaine.'

'We'll save you some pie, Dilly,' Danzel called as I walked out the door. 'And some cake.'

'Either way,' I called back, coldly. Already I felt separate. No longer part of The Gang. And it was Danzel's behaviour, I realized, that was upsetting me most of all. The bringing of the cider. The way he'd made me feel like a fussy old maid, or a small, silly girl for not wanting to try it.

I had to remind myself, as I headed towards the big old staircase, that Danzel was the idiot here. I had to force myself not to care what he thought about me.

As usual, imagining helped; taking me, as it always does, away from the here and now. I pretended I was living back in the olden days, and that this house was my home. I would have golden hair, I decided, as I walked up the stairs . . . golden hair done in ringlets, with a centre parting. My dress would be silk—hyacinth blue, and full enough to swirl when I waltzed around a room. I would be pretty and witty and loved by everyone. I would drink lemonade, or whatever else I wanted, from a silver goblet decorated with tiny pearls. And my name would not be Daffodil.

What's this?

Lights. Voices. Tension.

A slim slip of a girl is perched on the sage-green chair. She is timid. One nudge from the mouse—awake now, and sniffing, in its nest of shredded upholstery—and she is bound to have hysterics. She is taking small sips from a plastic cup. It is hard to tell, from her face, if she is enjoying whatever it is she is drinking. It could be nectar in that cup, or a dose of stomach medicine. It could be holy wine or horse piss.

She turns her head, as an 'O' of light hits the mural (the tapestry came down in 1901—rotted beyond repair). Her gaze goes straight to the bunch of painted grapes, where a lever is doing an excellent job of looking like a stalk.

Curiosity . . . it's a terrible thing.

A good-looking boy—a god-like boy—is examining the mural by the light of a torch. He is laughing at the cherubs, his head thrown back and his face aglow with health and high spirits. 'Hey, Gurnet,' he calls. 'Take a squint at these weird-looking things.'

The other boy in the room—Gurnet—shambles towards the wall. He does not laugh at the way the cherubs look, for he is no oil painting himself. A blowsy-looking girl watches from the shadows. She is sitting all of a sprawl on the floorboards, among pie crumbs and plastic utensils. Her eyes bore like drills into the spine of the good-looking boy, willing him to turn round and pay her some attention. She wants that boy more than anything else in the world. The wanting makes her dangerous.

When the tapping starts, no one hears it at first. And why would they? It isn't much of a sound. A woodpecker with a rubber beak would be louder. Footsteps in the underworld would echo further into the night.

Then: 'What's that?' says the boy called Gurnet. 'That knocking noise. Listen! It's coming from behind the wall.'

The girls jump to their feet; unsteady, both of them, and uncertain where to go. For want of a better alternative, they run towards each other, meeting in a clumsy embrace that does little to reassure either of them.

The slim girl re-focuses on the wall. She moves, ever so slightly, as if she will go to Gurnet, but the blowsy girl hangs on to her, making her stay. 'Dilly?' the blowsy girl yells, in a voice that would stop a chariot. 'Is that you knocking? Stop messing around.'

The good-looking boy leaves the room. He is only gone a moment. 'There's no one there,' he reports back. 'That noise must be coming from inside the wall. It's probably just an old pipe; a pipe with an airlock in it, making it clank.'

No one points out that the heating isn't on. That it has been a decade and a half since anything flowed through any pipes in this house; that the good-looking boy is talking out of his rear, with his airlocks and his clankings.

Gurnet is down on his knees, his right ear pressed hard against the very bottom of the mural, where painted vine-roots twist, and the artist dared to sign his name. When he leaps to his feet, and starts backing away, the girls jump, hastily, apart.

'For crying out loud, Gurnet!' the blowsy one shouts. 'You almost trod on us. What is it?'

Gurnet doesn't answer. He is staring at the wall. He is thinking that his mind must have played a bad trick on him just now. Either that or . . .

'Danzel Killick,' he growls, clenching both his fists and shaking his big head, like a dog. 'What was in that cider you brought? If you added something . . . some powder, or a herb . . .'

Danzel is immediately concerned.

'Relax,' he says. 'Calm down, my friend. Jenna—fetch my bottle. Not that one, stupid, the one with water in it. Maude? Come away from the wall. Come and help me with Gurnet. It's OK, Gurn. Everything's OK. You want some more pie? Let's see if there's any pie left.'

They move quickly, Danzel and the girls. Like a minder and two nurses they distract and soothe and occupy the one called Gurnet, feeding him pastry and saying 'Come on Gurn, no one's messed with the cider. Look at us—we're all right, aren't we?' Yes, Gurn, think about it, the girls are OK and this is their first time! But no more of the strong stuff for you, my friend. Tell you what, let's go and find Dilly.

They have done this before, clearly—soothed and calmed the one called Gurnet. They have been doing it for years.

The tapping noise has stopped. Nobody mentions it, as they leave the room, and nobody wonders any more (at least not out loud) what in the world it could have been.

Only, in the clatter and chatter of their leaving (the girls are not completely all right; the slim one—Maude—is a little green around the gills and the other one—Jenna—has the hiccups) Gurnet looks, briefly, back over his shoulder and frowns.

His mind, he is certain, was not playing tricks on him just then.

Something—someone—spoke to him. From behind the wall.

He will be back. Later, when the others are asleep, he will camp out beside that mural-thing and get to the bottom of this.

DILLY

There was a lot more to see upstairs. Not just furniture but personal things. It was like whoever cleared the house ran out of time, or energy, or space in their cart after finishing the ground floor.

In one room—the biggest—the bed is a four-poster. The covers and pillows have been taken away but the mattress is still there, and so are the curtains: long heavy drapes of gold-coloured brocade, looped back by tasselled cords. I wanted to clamber up, draw those curtains all around, and stretch myself out. I believed I was entitled, despite it being crazy, and more than a little rude, to go into somebody else's home and lie down on their bed, even a bed that can't have been slept in since I myself was small enough to nap in a daffodil crate.

I made do with pressing my palms, lightly, against the top of the mattress, before stepping away to explore some more. The light from my torch picked out bits and pieces on the dressing table: an old-fashioned brush and comb, a scent bottle with the stopper missing; a green glass tray scattered with hairgrips and pins. I didn't touch those things. They seemed holy to me, like relics, or objects placed in a tomb to keep a dead person company. I didn't open the dressing table drawers either, or look to see if there was anything hanging in the big old wardrobe that loomed up behind me, like a cliff.

I did write my name, though, in the dust on the dressing table mirror, and not in a titchy way either but in great big loops and swirls. 'Daffodil Aurelia Tonkin'.

I wasn't sure, at the time, why I did that. But I'm thinking, now, it had something to do with Danzel—with the way he'd got me wishing, as I walked, alone, up all those stairs, that I was a different kind of girl. I think I needed to remind myself who I really was, after such an intense imagining, and writing my name in the dust was as good a way as any.

I touched window panes like sheets of black ice, and guessed at the view. I trailed my fingers along walls all thready with cobwebs, and when I arrived back at the door, and felt a key in the lock, I did something I should never have done.

I took the key, stepped from the room, and locked the door behind me. Then I slipped the key into the pocket of my oilskin and zipped the pocket up. It was my room now. The others weren't to go in there. No one was. From that moment on it was to be my secret place—somewhere I might be able to escape to, if only once in a while, to be completely alone and away from Port Zannon. Somewhere foreign.

I got out just in time.

'What have you found?' Danzel's voice sounded extra-loud, calling up the stairs, and the light from his torch was bouncing, like a crazy thing, all over the walls. The others were clattering up behind him. I heard one of them trip. Jenna had the hiccups.

'Nothing much,' I lied. 'But I haven't checked the attic yet. I bet there's loads of good stuff up there.'

'Come on then,' said Danzel, happily. 'Lead the way, Dils.'

I was right about the attic. It's big—enormous—and divided into sections. Five small rooms, thinly partitioned, were probably where the servants used to sleep. They were small and bare, like gaol cells, but a big open area, under a long slope of the roof, had been used for storage. The beams from our torches touched chairs, badly stacked as if for a bonfire . . . an old-fashioned washstand with a broken leg . . . a rocking horse, which made Maude shriek when her light hit the whites of its eyes . . . trunks clearly labelled: 'tablecloths', 'beach things', 'glass', 'brass', 'summer wear', and 'hats' . . . crates marked 'baby things', 'Christmas decs', 'children's books', 'photographs', 'fishing tackle', 'crockery' .

Everything was stashed against one wall, leaving more than enough room for all of us to move around in. We could have held a party up there. Half a dozen servants could have slept in that space.

'Nice!' Gurnet made an immediate beeline for the crate marked 'fishing tackle'.

'No you don't,' Danzel scolded, dragging him back by the collar of his coat. 'Let me remind you, Gurn: we don't touch, or take, anything. That way we can't get into any trouble. Got it?'

I looked sternly upon Gurnet, the way Danzel, Maude, and Jenna were doing, and tried not to think about the key in my pocket. I had never stolen anything before in my life—not a sweet from the shop, not a flower from a garden, nothing. I, too, had begun acting out of line, and the knowledge made my face burn.

'We'll camp here,' said Danzel, as if the attic floor was a field, and the slope of the roof a starry sky. 'We'll bring all our stuff up, sort out the sleep bags, and get settled. Then we'll tell ghost stories. All the old ones.'

'Oh please,' Jenna scoffed. 'How old are you?'

Danzel raised his eyebrows at her. 'They're good stories,' he said. 'And I'm feeling nostalgic tonight.'

'You're lashed is all,' said Jenna. 'As drunk as a lord. And I don't want ghost stories told. Not here. Not tonight. It isn't safe. We might raise a spirit.'

'Horse dung.' Danzel was having none of Jenna's nonsense. 'And I'm not as lashed as you are, Jen-Jen. Nowhere near. Your eyes are like kaleidoscopes. And your lip stuff is all smudged. You look like you've been kissing a jelly.'

Maude said she was very sorry but what she needed, just then, was the lavatory.

And: 'I can handle more cider,' said Gurnet. 'I'm not lashed. It takes more than one cup of cider to addle me.'

So much noise . . . the house wasn't used to it. I wanted to tell everyone to shut up; to stop chattering like magpies and go away—to the kitchen, or back to the room with the painted wall. But then Jenna said she too needed the lav, so I went with her and Maude to find one, and we soon realized we would have to go and pee outside, under a bush, because there was no way of flushing and we couldn't—wouldn't—use a lav without flushing.

And that was an expedition and a half, particularly

when Maude declared that the cold night air had woken her up and she wanted to go back to the room with the mural in it. Just for a while, she said, to examine the artwork more closely.

'No you don't.' Jenna told her. 'Time for beddy-byes.' And we marched Maudie between us, up the stairs and back to the attic. Danzel and Gurnet had set everything out so that we could climb straight into our bags and tell stories. So that is what we did. Me, Danzel, Jenna, Gurnet, and Maude, cocooned and snug enough, despite the draught whistling in through the roof slates and the darkness that, as soon as we switched off our torches, was complete.

'Dan,' hissed Jenna. 'Hold my hand. I don't like the dark.'

'Since when?' said Danzel. He was sitting bolt upright in his sleep bag and finishing off his cider—drinking it straight from the bottle. The sour-apple smell wasn't pleasant and he'd burped, twice, between swigs.

'Since today. Since coming here. I told you . . . there's something about this place that isn't right. Something *beyond scary*.'

'Oooooh.' I heard the tip and glug of more cider being swallowed, just above my right ear. 'Hark at gypsy Jenna Rosdew, Port Zannon's very own psychic. Who is it, Jen? Who's haunting the place? A plague victim? A murdered bride? You'll be telling me next that the knocking noise we heard downstairs was a raving lunatic, bricked up hundreds of years ago for being an embarrassment to his family.'

'What knocking noise?' I asked.

Nobody bothered to enlighten me.

Danzel told the stories. He remembered them well, considering the state of him, almost word for word, and when he came to the one about the ghostly rider he waved his bottle around in time to the chant:

'That footman he rode like a bat out of hell, lickety-lickety-split, but the imp bit his throat and down he fell, lickety-lickety-split.'

Luckily he'd drained the bottle by then, otherwise my sleep bag might have got splattered. I don't know if alcohol burns, or stains, but I do know it stinks and no way did I want Dad, or my mum, smelling it on my stuff.

'Any cider left in your bottle, my friend?' Danzel called out to Gurnet.

'Nope,' said Gurnet.

He was fibbing, I could tell. I could also tell that he was nowhere near as lashed as Danzel which meant he'd been abstaining. I was glad about that. Danzel, drunk, was still Danzel, only louder, and I wasn't afraid of him, only more on my guard than I would normally have been in case he rolled onto me by accident, or threw up into my hair.

Gurnet though . . . Gurnet was a horse of a different colour. I would not have wanted to be next to Gurnet after he'd been drinking heavily. I would not have wanted him in the same room, even, and that was a new and disturbing thought to be having about one of my closest friends.

Maude was the first of us to go quiet, followed by Jenna. I went quiet, too, not wanting to talk any more, and only dimly aware of Danzel burbling on and Gurnet's occasional grunt.

Eventually the burbling stopped and Danzel began to snore.

I listened to the others breathing. I know how they breathe, when they're asleep, just as I know how they cough, or sing; and how their feet sound on floorboards or cobbles or stairs. Maude breathes apologetically, like she doesn't deserve the oxygen; Jenna huffs and puffs like a stroppy kid; and Gurnet sounds like he has bronchitis, even when he hasn't.

They were awake, all three of them. As wide awake as I was, but pretending not to be.

I thought about the key in my pocket. And then, to ease the guilt of having taken it, I imagined myself back in 'my' bedroom, fast asleep on the four-poster bed just like the Sleeping Beauty.

A prince. I was waiting for my prince to come. But what would he look like, I wondered, and where would he be from?

I began to invent a prince for myself, starting with his shoes and moving up. I'd got as far as his eyes (blue . . . brown . . . ? I couldn't decide . . .) when I must have dozed off. I don't know how I sound when I'm asleep. One of these days, I will have to ask someone.

JENNA

I heard them leave the attic—Gurnet first, then Maude—
and even though I was scared out of my wits I knew I
had to follow, to check what they were up to. I'd been
pretending, for hours, to be asleep, thinking (hoping)
that if I pretended for long enough I'd eventually drop
off.

Fat chance.

Danzel had turned his back on me. If he hadn't, I might
have accidentally-on-purpose laid my head against his
shoulder and pretended we were married.

I needed a hug. I needed Danzel Killick to wake up
and kiss my face off to take my mind away from where
we were and what night it was. I didn't care that he was
lashed. I was, too, a bit. Well, more than a bit, if I'm
honest, because the longer I lay there, unable to sleep,
the more seriously I considered taking my pyjama top
off and snuggling my naked thingies up against Danzel's
spine.

If Gurnet had been asleep I might have dared do it, but
Gurnet just lay there on the other side of me, brooding.
He hadn't even closed his eyes, the splat-brain. When
he suddenly got up, and went clumping down the stairs,
I assumed he needed to pee. I guessed he wouldn't be

83

gone for long (not long enough, anyway, for me to get semi-naked and for Dan to get the message) and besides, what if he shone his torch on us on the way back to his bag? He's the last boy on earth, believe you me, I'd want ogling my bare thingies.

When he didn't come back at all I got anxious. Not over his safety (Gurnet can look after himself) but about what on earth he thought he was doing, sneaking around the house at what—three, four o'clock in the morning?

I considered waking Danzel, to warn him that Gurnet might be stealing stuff, or trashing one of the rooms. But whatever Gurnet was up to, Danzel would, I had to admit it, be horrible about being disturbed. Not because he likes his sleep, but because it would be me doing the disturbing. Even if I dared to take my top off, and do a jiggle above his face, he would still, I knew, be more annoyed than flattered. 'Jenna,' he would say, 'you're as lashed as a herring in brandy butter sauce,' or 'Put them away, Jen-Jen, before you catch your death.' And yet, he would treat that splat-brain Gurnet kindly even if he'd plundered a jewellery box or set the flicking staircase alight.

I knew all of this, in my heart of hearts, just as surely as I know my own name, and how to make the very most of my height, weight, and colouring.

I'll get you one day, Danzel Killick, I thought to myself. *You reckon you're too good for me—too good for any maid in Port Zannon—but I'll win you round, just you wait and see.*

Then Maude got out of her bag. She was ultra quiet about it—stealthy is the word—and something told me that she, like Gurnet Carthew, had a lot more on her mind than needing the lav.

'Let. Me. Out.'

The voice is bleak. A sandpaper rasp. Not a bit like Hope's.

Young Gurnet presses one side of his head so hard against the mural that his right cheek goes numb and his right ear starts to ring.

'Who are you?' he asks, sternly. 'And what are you doing in there?'

Fair questions.

'Out. Out.'

Gurnet moves away. Frowning, he considers the panelling, concentrating the beam of his torch on the line where it joins the floor. His bottom lip juts out and he chews on it, thoughtfully. Then he presses the wall to see how much give there is to the wood. Not much, he realizes. Not enough for a person to knock a hole through and then pretend it was an accident.

He is wearing a heavy black coat over his night things. He takes something from one of its pockets: a knife (a sharp one) which he uses for a while to chip and jab and worry away at the join between the panelling and the floor. It's no use though. No use at all. When the girl appears in the doorway his hand slips and he almost takes a slice out of his own meaty thigh.

'Go away, Maude,' he says. 'Get back upstairs.'

Maude moves in closer. The beam of her torch, on the blade

of the knife, is steadier than an angel's gaze. She asks Gurnet what he thinks he is up to, her voice as unwavering as her light. She reminds him that he's not supposed to wreck anything.

'I'm not. I haven't.' Gurnet is indignant, and rightly so. He tells the girl that the knocking noise they heard earlier has started up again; that something is trapped behind the wall. A little bird maybe. He doesn't mention a voice—doesn't want her to think he's crazy, or drunk, or both—and he puts a lot of stress on the word 'little' even though he has no idea, really, how big or small the thing behind the wall might be. It could be colossal: as big as a genie and as weighty as a bull. It could fall through the panelling any second now and squash him flat. He doesn't know. He is intrigued.

'I'm not kidding,' he says, glowering at the girl as if daring her to call him a liar. 'There's something there. You believe me, Maudie, don't you?'

Maude tells him yes. And it is clear that she does believe. That she isn't just saying so because friend Gurnet is a few waves short of a shipwreck, and clutching an extremely sharp knife.

Beyond the drawing room windows—curtainless these many years—something is happening to the sky. Is it dawn? It could be dawn. But the light seeping in has an odd quality about it: syrupy, as if filtered through amber. It makes the drawing room like a stage set, the boy and the girl other-worldly.

The mural doesn't look half so bad, in this strange nicotine-light. And the girl is staring at it as if she knows the cherubs personally, or once walked in the hills, and tended the vines, depicted by the artist. In her silvery-coloured nightgown, with some woollen thing flung over it, she has the appearance, certainly, of one who might have stepped out of the painting, one charmed night, and is about to step back in.

'I might have to bash a panel down,' says Gurnet.

No, the girl tells him. You won't. And she walks, very slowly, across the room, her gaze fixed on the mural. She moves like a wraith, barefoot in her silver and grey; her face pale and her eyes huge.

She knows. When she reaches the wall, she knows exactly what to do.

Up on tiptoe she goes, her fingers reaching, unerringly, for a particular bunch of grapes . . . She is almost there, about to touch the lever, when somebody else rushes into the room: Jenna, the blowsy one, all straggling hair and pink silk pyjamas (no woollen over-garments keeping this girl modest and warm).

'Stop it!' she shrieks, pointing at the tiptoeing, reaching, girl with a finger that jerks like a crone's. 'Don't do it!'

She has no idea what 'it' is; only a powerful conviction that she has interrupted something so dangerous . . . so potentially catastrophic . . . that she must stop it at all costs.

Maude keeps her eyes on the wall. Her fingertips tremble, a hair's breadth from the lever. Is she aware, as Pandora was, that she is on the verge of something momentous? Does she feel manipulated, at all, by some higher power? Probably not. These are modern times and it is rare, among the young, for the notion of a higher power—any higher power—to hold water.

Puzzled. That's probably all she is. Like a sleepwalker, partially roused.

'Do it, Maude,' says Gurnet, his voice low and urgent. 'Let the poor little creature out.'

No Epimetheus he. And there's that word 'little' again, tugging at the heartstrings.

Jenna takes one . . . two . . . steps, closer. 'Don't,' she begs. 'I'm telling you, Maude . . . Don't.'

Gurnet's right hand tightens on the handle of his knife. The blade flashes a warning.

'Shut your mouth, Jenna. Nobody asked you to interfere. Shut your big wobbly mouth or . . . '

'Or what, splat-brain? Or WHAT?'

Gurnet lowers his head. Poised to charge, he raises high his right fist and Jenna sees the knife, pointing straight at her heart. Maude, turning, sees it too. It decides her. It tips the balance.

DANZEL

My friends, I shouldn't drink. I don't need to drink. I have no sorrows to drown and, unlike my best-buddy Gurnet Carthew, am amiable enough without a cup of alcohol singing through my veins. I don't mean to boast; it's the truth, is all.

I took to cider out of boredom, and because my parents were radical enough, last Christmas, to let me have a sip (just the one, mind) with my dinner. I think they hoped I would gag on it, the way my brother Michael did when he turned fourteen and was offered his first sip. They might even have added something to the cup, to put me off strong drink for good (I swear there was a chalky undertaste that hadn't come from apples) but, whatever the case, I got a nice little buzz from that first ripe mouthful.

One sip does not a sinner make, nor has it turned me into a hopeless drunk, like Gurnet's old man. And, because of the laws, I'm careful. I don't take the stuff to school, nor do I swill it in public. I steal a dribble at a time, from the family barrel, so nobody catches on, and, unless I'm so bored that I might as well be turning into stone, I save what I take for special occasions—for high days and holidays.

It was my idea to spend Hallowe'en at the old manor house, and my fault, once we got there, that the girls found out that Gurn and I had cider with us. Why I felt the need to announce the evil fact—the words 'we've got cider' falling from my mouth as heedlessly as 'we've forgotten the salt' or 'the cake has cherries in it' I do not know. Jenna wanted some (I knew she would). Dilly got sniffy and gave me a hard time (I knew she would). And Maude? Well, Maude surprised the stuffing out of me, actually, by going not just for a teeny-tiny doll's sip, but for a whole cupful. And she handled it well, too, better than Gurnet who, despite being a seasoned quaffer, went off on one of his Gurny-turns after only a couple of swigs.

I sleep well after a few ciders. I sleep like I'm in a field full of poppies. I would have slept until way past dawn, in the attic of the old manor house, if Dilly hadn't shaken me awake.

'They're gone!'

It took a good few moments before I understood what she was on about. Then: 'They'll be finishing the pie,' I mumbled. 'Or peeing in the bushes. *I* don't know, Dils. Go back to your bag, can't you? They won't have gone far.'

But: 'I heard Jenna scream,' she insisted, clutching my arm like she might drag me, forcibly, to the top of the stairs. 'It woke me up—Jenna screaming. She was shouting "Stop it! . . . Don't do it!" and she sounded really scared. What if . . . what if Gurnet . . . '

Her voice trailed away, but I knew what she was thinking.

'All right,' I said, beginning to move. 'All right, all right, all right . . . I'll go and find out what's happening. Are you coming or staying?'

She said she would come, and went to fetch her torch.

I don't do hangovers, at least not the kind that give you hammers in your head and a mouth like an un-scrubbed dinner pot. I go a bit vague sometimes; a bit fuzzy round the edges, but that's all. I felt steady enough, anyhow, as I went down the stairs of the old manor house, shining my torch so I wouldn't do a header, and croaking at Dilly to watch out for the toad.

I was kidding. There was never any toad. She's so easy to kid, is Dilly . . .

'Jeeenna?' I called, as we reached the ground floor. 'Maudie? Guurnet? Where aaaare you?' I'd made my voice go all high and silly, as if we were little kids again, playing hide and seek. I told myself it was to reassure Dilly.

A light was shining. Not in the hall, but in the room where we'd had our picnic. I could see a yellowish glow spilling out of there, as if a switch had been flicked or a generator kicked into action. It should have struck me as peculiar, that spill of light, but it didn't. Not then.

'We're coming to fiiiiiiind you . . . '

When Jenna stumbled out of the room and came running, dazzled, straight into the beam of my torch, I dodged, automatically, and flicked the light sideways. Don't read me wrong. I love Jen to bits, but not in the way I'm starting to think she wants me to. Not in a lusty way. I mean . . . we did potty training together, for crying out loud; side by side, grunting, and comparing!

91

I remember when she took her first steps (later than the rest of us, like she couldn't be bothered to get up off her bum) and how she and I once spent a whole week-end doing a jigsaw of the world, becoming so absorbed as it spread slowly across my parlour table that we wouldn't go to bed, or eat anything except fudge-sweets and apples until it was all finished.

I can look at Jenna nowadays, knowing she's got huge breasts and things, but it doesn't do anything for me. It doesn't float my boat. Because, to my mind, she's also still baby Jenna, and toddler Jenna, and little girl Jenna; and all the Jennas I've ever known up until this point. And there's no fancying those Jennas, my friends. That would be perverted and a criminal offence.

Anyway, that was my reason—my understandable excuse—for skipping out of Jen's way quick smart. I wasn't about to lead her on with hugs and so on, for that would only have made her more leery, and harder to discourage. The closer she got, though, the more obvious it became that she wasn't—she really wasn't—over-reacting to something as an excuse to wrap herself around my irresistible torso. She was in genuine shock. She could barely string two words together.

'Evil,' she gasped, eventually, and then 'ugly' and then 'thing'. And then, after a long shuddering pause: 'Gurnet . . . was going . . . to kill me.'

Dilly and I said nothing; we just looked at one another over Jenna's head, not in disbelief (Jen clearly wasn't lying) but in a sad and sorry way. Gurnet, as we've all always known, has the potential to end up in deep dark dung, but for him to have crossed the line with one of us . . . with one of his closest friends . . . well, it wasn't just a shame, it was tragic.

I was off down the passageway before you could say 'life sentence', fully prepared to take old Gurn on even though he is as strong as an ox and had no doubt been driven to the very end of his rope by Jenna's taunts. Had she called him an evil, ugly thing to his face? I wondered. Probably. She was lashed enough to be more than usually cruel.

For crying out loud, Jen, I thought, before admitting to myself that whatever the girl had said or done to bring on an especially violent Gurny-turn, I was partly to blame for having been so free and easy with the cider.

I expected to find Gurnet curled up like a hedgehog, and rocking on his heels (which is what he does when he knows he's in the dung), with Maude doing her best to soothe him, just as Dilly was doing her best, back in the hall, to soothe and calm Jenna.

What I actually saw stopped me dead in my tracks.

I dropped my torch, but it didn't matter. The room was bathed in its own peculiar light which, because it didn't seem to be coming from anywhere, was enough, all by itself, to make my blood run cold.

'Stay there,' said Gurnet, looking briefly up at me, and then away. 'Don't frighten it.'

I could not have said, at that precise moment, whether 'it' was a bird, a beast, or a very small piece of litter that Gurnet was examining, down on his knees with his rear in the air and his nose almost touching the thing. *To be frank, I'm still puzzled.*

Maude was keeping very still, on the other side of the

room, and part of the wall she was standing by had come away—opened out, to reveal some sort of a cubby hole.

'What,' I said (quietly, so as not to startle the object that was too close for comfort to my own bare toes, never mind Gurnet's face), 'have you DONE?' My voice soared about three octaves on that last word. I couldn't help it. I was freaked.

'It's all right, Danzel,' Gurnet replied, keeping his own voice low and his eyes on the splat on the floor. 'We haven't wrecked anything. Show him, Maude, how it goes.'

Maude reached up and touched the mural. The opened-out bit of wall swung back into place, like a carnival trick, only louder.

'See?' Gurnet said. 'No harm done.'

Then the thing in front of him wheezed, as if the bumping-shut of the wall had been a signal of some sort and it was preparing, now, to fly or crawl or jump—to do whatever passed for movement, anyway, among its own revolting kind.

'Move away from it,' I called across to Gurnet, but Gurnet stayed where he was, not even flinching when a trickle of slime came from what might have been the creature's mouth, or might have been its rear, but either way was not a pretty sight.

'Maude!' I pleaded, as the creature continued to wheeze; not shifting yet but building up to it, I could tell, and leaking like a blister. 'Tell him, will you? Help me out here.'

But Maude just shook her head, dazed.

So I glared my hardest at the thing on the floor, willing

it not to move. Like, ever. I wanted it dead, it unsettled me that much. If I'd had my boots on, and hadn't been so spun out already by the odd light and the goings-on with the wall, I might have gone right over and stamped upon its head (supposing, of course, I'd been able to tell its horrible head from its equally horrible tailbone).

Again, don't read me wrong, I love animals. Horses, dogs, cats . . . I love all of those creatures. This thing, though, wasn't a proper animal. It was . . . it was an abomination.

'Are you hungry, mate?' I heard Gurnet ask it. 'Do you like pie, or would you rather have a worm?'

'For crying out loud, Gurnet . . . ' I began.

Then the thing started to move.

Hopelessness is out.

Too weak to fly, it can only lie still to start with. Pulsating.
Catching its breath.

It hears itself being asked a question—something about food.
Up yours, it thinks.

GURNET

I've never owned a pet before, except a crab, once, which I kept in a bucket, out in the yard, until it died of natural causes. Houses are for people to live in; for parents and their kids. Fish, birds, and all the beasts belong outdoors. They come in to be cooked and eaten and that's how things should be.

I found Laurence though. I rescued him. He spoke to me, and then he came to me, and I was the only one, out of all of us, who didn't want to put him out of his misery, or back behind the wall. He was only little—no bigger than a sparrow or a baby vole, although he isn't either of those things—and he was helpless.

'What misery?' I argued, holding Laurence carefully in both of my hands, which is where he'd jumped, using all his energy, like they were somewhere he knew he'd be safe. 'Who says he's in any misery?'

'It's a mess,' Danzel replied, keeping his distance and eyeing my fingers like they had sticks of dynamite in them, ready to go off. 'It's barely breathing. And who say's it's a "he"? I can't see its eyes, never mind anything else.'

Laurence has eyes. They just weren't fully open at the time. He has eyes, and a mouth, and what look like they

97

might be wings, only they're flat against his body, like little squashed umbrellas, and he hasn't flapped them yet. He has black hair—or it might be fur, I'll know better when it grows some more—and *hands*. Laurence has tiny hands, like a person.

There was a cat carrier up in the attic. I'd seen it earlier. I took Laurence up the stairs and put him inside it, with my under-vest for some bedding. Then I came back down to find food for him and a utensil to put his water in. I hadn't named him then. That came later.

There were a few odd bits of china in the kitchen; all chipped or cracked and worth diddly squat. I took a saucer and told Danzel to shut it when he saw. Then I went outside and picked a bit of grass. It was almost properly light by then so I found a patch of earth and scrabbled about for worms. Too cold though. None to be had.

Back in the room with the painted wall, my Dilly and Jenna were packing away the picnic things. I told them that if there was any pie left I would take a few crumbs for my new pet. Not a whole crust, just the crumbs, because when something has been starving it does more harm than good for it to gorge. I know that from The Terrible Death Camps—from stuff on the inter-telly about how, many years ago, the Russians gave food to some people they rescued from The Terrible Death Camps and how the food was too much for those people's shrunken digestions. It killed them with kindness, that food, which seems a very dark and unfair thing to me, after all the hardships those people had been through, up until that point.

My Dilly's share of the pie was still in the dish, so she

broke a piece off and passed it to me, before putting the dish away in Danzel's rucksack.

'You owe Jenna an apology, Gurnet,' she said, sternly. 'And some reassurance.'

Jenna wasn't looking at me. She was dressed in all her clothes, including her oilskin and her boots, and gathering up our picnic cups. She was in a big hurry to leave the house, I could tell. My red cup was over by the wall, where I'd left it the night before. I saw how Jenna's face went, when she picked it up, and it would have made me angry if I hadn't been thinking so hard about keeping Laurence alive and getting him home.

'Gurnet?' said Dilly. 'Are you listening? We know you didn't really mean it, threatening Jen the way you did. You were upset, is all. And you won't ever do anything like it again, will you?'

What she said confused me. I looked into her eyes, needing more information. Dilly's eyes are dark grey, like the sea goes in December. She has the prettiest eyes of all three of my girls, but I don't think she knows it or has ever been told.

'The knife, Gurnet,' she added after a while, in a voice that said I shouldn't need reminding. 'You threatened Jenna with your fishing knife. Right here in this room, less than an hour ago. You said you would kill her if she didn't shut up.'

'I never,' I told her. 'I never did that, Dilly.'

In my mind, I was thinking backwards; trying to remember. I got as far as the wall opening up, and Laurence coming out of it, but everything before that was muzzy, like a dream can sometimes be.

Dilly looked at me sadly. 'Maude was here,' she said. 'Maude will back Jenna up.'

'Leave it, Dilly. He's not sorry—he's not even listening to you.'

Jenna came stomp-stomping across the room, holding my mug out in front of her, like it was a fish gone bad. There was some cider left in it, which she threw into the fireplace. Then she hurled that mug of mine so hard into the rucksack that I was lucky it didn't crack.

'Hey,' I said. 'Watch what you're doing with my stuff, Jenna Rosdew.' I was full of anger but didn't want to show it, not after what Dilly had just said about me and my knife. It bothered me that I couldn't remember whether I'd really done that thing to Jenna or not. But if I did do it (and I'm not saying it's the truth) at least I never sliced that girl. I only did a threat.

'Be more careful from now on, you,' I said to Jenna, so she would know I'd meant it, about her not throwing my stuff around. Then I left her and Dilly alone. I had my new pet to look after, and that is a big responsibility.

DILLY

All I wanted to do, when we got back to the port, was write in my book and then sleep. I slept for so long— all afternoon, right through the night and on into the morning—that Mum got worried, thinking I might be sickening for something.

I wasn't sick though. I just felt drained, wrung out physically and mentally, as if I'd walked a hundred miles to sit a twenty hour exam. Luckily today was a Monday, Community Service day, so I wasn't expected at school, only at The Crazy Mermaid, to help my mum (not that she ever needs much help during the dark time of the year. I usually end up dusting the mermaids or going home to look up new recipes on the inter-telly).

'I'm all right,' I told Mum, when she tiptoed into my room, just before ten. 'Go back to the café. I'll be there in a bit.'

'Are you sure?' She perched on the edge of my bed and peered anxiously into my face. 'I'd be glad if you would. We've a big booking for lunch today—a party of seven from the Council's NIT department. I'm doing individual pilchard pies and a figgie hobbin.'

I said I was sure, although my heart sank at the thought of having to wait on a table of po-faced officials who were bound to want big second helpings, for free, and might quiz me about the school, and what I'm planning to do with the rest of my life.

Why would councillors bother coming to Port Zannon for their lunches anyway, I wondered. It's one heck of a ride. It crossed my mind that The Crazy Mermaid might be in trouble. But if it had been a check for health and hygiene, or something to do with taxes, the councillors would have come in secret, and from a different department.

And anyway, Mum is an honest trader, and that place is as clean as a bone, despite being stuffed full of all-things mermaid.

So maybe, I decided, there was a positive reason for the visit. Maybe the Council's New Initiatives in Tourism department was planning to give us a grant, to tide us over until next summer. I hoped so, for my mum's sake.

'Your dad's up at the farm,' Mum said. 'He won't be back until sunslide otherwise he could have helped me out, and you could have had a rest day.'

My dad works the land. It's what most of the men round here do, if they don't work the sea. He can handle a boat as well though—a Jack of all trades, he calls himself—and will wait on tables too, if he's free and there's a rush on. He has his own apron with 'Catch of the Day' on the bib in big red letters. People—women, anyway—think it's funny.

Mum leaned forward, to smooth my hair away from my face. 'You're looking peaky,' she said. 'I could always track Jenna down and ask her to cover lunchtime. She's only beachcombing—I saw her earlier. She'll be done by twelve. It's not like she's thorough.'

'Mum,' I said, moving my head away and trying not to sound too impatient. 'I'll be there, OK? Just give me ten minutes to have a wash and get dressed.'

'All right,' she agreed. 'But don't push yourself, and go straight back to bed if you go wobbly in the wet room. I'll cope, or I'll find Jenna. Maybe I'll grill some mackerel. It'll be quicker than doing pies, but not as fancy . . . No. I'll do pies. Definitely, pies. The mackerel are biting again, did Gurnet say? His dad'll be relieved. Maybe he'll stop droning on, now, about the plankton dying, or whatever . . . '

She left, at last, and I closed my eyes. I didn't mean to go back to sleep. I just needed to lie quiet and still for a while, to gather my thoughts and ease myself into the day.

The key from the old manor house was underneath my mattress. I could feel it, I swear, through all the wadding and the feathers.

I knew I should get up. Get washed. Get dressed. Get a move on. But I wanted, so badly, to go back to the manor that I stayed where I was, imagining the way . . . the climb from the harbour . . . the zigzag walk across the cliffs . . . the gap in the wall . . . the path behind the brambles . . .

The house is waiting for me. I don't care how daft that sounds, it's true. And I'm not afraid to go back to it alone. The rest of The Gang would only spoil the magic—the perfect peace of the place—and I don't want a single one of them in the bedroom where I wrote my name.

When though? When can I go back there? Everyone's used to me going off by myself, just to walk, or sit somewhere and read. But not in winter, and not for as long as it would take to get to the manor and back. I could borrow the horse, but Dad needs it for work and, anyway, he doesn't like me riding—says I've got two long strong legs, to get from A to B, and should use them.

No. My only chance to go back, this side of springtime, would be if we all went: me, Danzel, Jenna, Gurnet, and Maude. We could pretend to go camping again; no one would mind, or suspect anything. We've been camping together since we were old enough to hammer tent pegs into the turf—in Grandpa Tonkin's garden, to start with, then overnight, within sight of the harbour, then further and further afield. The grownups think it's healthy. They trust us not to break any laws, and to be back in the port when they say. They believe in allowing us the freedom to roam. Safely, in a pack.

The house needs looking after. It needs someone (me) to be there, cherishing it a bit; letting fresh air in, and mustiness out.

There was a creature trapped in one of the downstairs rooms. We have no idea what kind of animal it is, or how it got itself stuck in a funny little cupboard-space behind the wall. But Gurnet heard it scrabbling, and Maude worked out how to free it.

It is a sorry looking thing. Danzel says it's not long for this world but Gurnet took a fancy to it and has taken it home.

I was thinking of Gurnet, and of how I would call on

him, as soon as I could, when I fell right back to sleep.

I slept like I'd taken a herb or something, and dreamed I was back at the old manor house; dancing through doorways in a blue silk dress and completely and utterly at peace.

Laurence? Please! It's hardly mythological. As for that help-ing of leaves and worm, with a sardine on top for good meas-ure: Hopelessness can do without any of it. It can survive—has survived—on absolutely nothing.

Gurnet is worried. He has fashioned a cage out of a lobster crate and chicken wire and has settled Hopelessness into it as best he can. The cage is in his bedroom, where no one will ever see it unless he invites them in. Gurnet's bedroom is a lair. The walls and ceiling are painted black. The window looks out onto a blank brick wall. The whole room smells, miserably, of socks, sweat, and the unwanted sardine. It suits Hopelessness very nicely, for now.

'Come on, mate.' Gurnet raises the chicken wire frame and nudges the little pile of victuals closer to where he believes his new pet's mouth is. 'Eat something.'

Hopelessness stirs. It is as weak as a newborn for all it is so ancient.

'Have a drink then. Just a drop or two, so you don't dehydrate.'

Gurnet dabbles his fingers in a saucer of water and offers them, like teats. He has been swabbing the deck of his father's boat and his hands are all crusty with salt from the sea.

Hopelessness opens one eye, then the other. It considers a series of options (speak, bite, ooze, spit, ignore) then starts, very slowly, to move. Gurnet's fingers drip. He dabbles them again in the saucer and leans further into the cage, murmuring encouragement.

'Good boy,' he says, delighted now, as the tips of two of his fingers are clamped onto, held fast, and sucked. 'Good boy, Laurence.'

Hopelessness can take or leave most kinds of water. The liquid dripping from Gurnet's fingers, though, is like nectar on its tongue. It resembles the salty drip of teardrops, and Hopelessness thrives on tears.

JENNA

'What's in it for me?' I wanted to know, when Dilly's mum asked me to help out at The Crazy Mermaid. 'I'm on beachcombing duty, Mrs Tonkin, and I haven't finished yet.'

'No pay, I'm afraid,' she answered. 'But the Council's NIT department, so I've heard, has a higher than average quota of handsome young lads on its training scheme. Seven for lunch? The odds are good, Jen.'

She knows me so well.

I went home first, to get changed and put some make-up on. My mum lets me use her stuff, but only on special occasions and only if I ask. She orders it off the inter-telly, from somewhere over in France, and it takes so long to be shipped that we have to put in a request for a new mascara about three months before we need one.

Old Mrs Tweedy, in Dolphin Street, makes lipstick out of beeswax and berries but the colour only lasts about two minutes. A light breeze could wipe it off. Mum and I both favour a bold shade of red, and I don't ever want my kisses to taste like a bee's bum, thank you very much.

'Mum,' I called out, as I headed for our wet room. 'I'm using the lipstick, OK?'

'Not for picking up fishing wire and bits of dead coral

you're not,' she yelled back from the kitchen.

'I'm not beachcombing any more. I'm helping Mrs Tonkin. There are councillors coming from Truro. Seven of them, for lunch.'

'From Truro?' My mum came in behind me, wiping her hands on her apron. 'Are you sure they're coming from Truro, Jen, not the regional office in Bodmin?'

'Truro,' I said, putting the top back on the lipstick. 'Definitely. Have we got any eyebright?' The whites of my eyes were dull and in need of pepping up—much like the rest of me if the truth be told. I've been down in the dumps since Hallowe'en and that's not like me at all. True, I didn't get to have my wicked way with Danzel Killick, but there'll be other opportunities. It's not that big a deal. It's not breaking my heart.

Mum found the eyebright and held my head, tipped back and steady, while she used the dropper. She would say it's the time of the month, making me so mopey. She blames everything on that, including her own behaviour (which is embarrassing every single day of every single week, so fat limpets to the menstrual theory . . .).

'I might pop into The Crazy Mermaid myself at lunch-time,' she said. 'Just for a milk-shot or something.'

I'd been holding my breath, in case it still smelt of cider, but I let it out into her face when she said that, and told her not to bother.

'Why not? I can if I want.' She let go of my head and opened the cabinet, to put the bottle of eyebright away. The cabinet door is all mirror, and I caught the way she checked herself out in it—slyly, and with purpose.

'Just because,' I said, scowling at the back of her head.

She would make herself up, I knew, like an old-fashioned night walker. A harlot. She would lard on the lipstick, do her eyes like a panda's, and put on a top cut so low that she would be in danger of plopping out of it. She might even turn up wearing something of mine, which would really raise my hackles.

One sniff of a man—a visitor, a stranger, someone she might like to know—and this is how she is. It's five years since my dad left us, to live for ever away, with another woman, so I can't blame her for being desperate. But it's hard on me having my own mum trying (and failing) to be a man magnet right under my nose.

'Because what?'

'Because I'll be working,' I snapped. 'And you'll distract me.'

'Promise I won't,' she replied, pouting like a kid. 'I'll sit in a corner, minding my own business, and won't say a single word to anyone—unless I'm spoken to, of course.'

Beyond annoyed, I checked my watch. I had to go.

'Just don't embarrass me in front of all those councillors,' I warned her. 'Just don't, that's all.'

I might as well have told a wave not to crash on the beach. I might as well have saved my breath to cool the figgie hobbin.

DANZEL

I was on my way home from the farm when I heard the noise: a deep steady rumble coming closer, growing louder . . . I had a split second's unease (what is this—a freak storm? A rock fall? Another Attack?) before I recognized the sound. And when the vehicle zipped past me, heading for the port, I started to run.

It was a big vehicle—a van—painted dark green, with the Council's logo on the side. It passed too quickly for me to count the people in it but I was kicking myself, as I ran, for not sticking my hand out to stop the thing and ask (all right then, beg) for a ride.

As soon as I turn twenty-one I'm going to learn to drive. I'll kid on that I want to work for the National Summer Bus Corporation (John, my cousin, will put in a good word for me) but I won't. No one will ever catch Danzel Killick going up and down the old motorway routes, fetching and carrying inlanders who want their ten days by the sea. I couldn't handle the jolliness—not in a confined space—or the constant vomiting. (John says they spew like gargoyles, particularly the kids. It takes them a while, he says, to get used to being inside a moving object.)

I have big plans, my friends. Ambitions. I'll make a tidy

fortune somehow, well away from Port Zannon. Abroad, perhaps, where I'll rip through cities in the smartest, sleekest vehicle money can buy. No rush. I'll get there. I just need to stay sharp, is all. Stay sharp, study hard, and keep my eye on the prize in case my big opportunity comes sooner rather than later.

I don't want to miss the boat.

By the time I reached the harbour I was whacked (fair trial, I'd been digging all morning, up at the farm, and it's hard work). The Council's van was parked outside The Crazy Mermaid and a small crowd had gathered to admire it. I saw my niece, Sheila, go to touch the wheels, only Nancy, my brother's wife, yanked her away— yanked her so hard, by the hood of her coat, that she fell over backwards and started to howl.

Nancy looked done in. She looked like she was about to start bawling herself as she hauled Sheila to her feet, and the way she began brushing dirt off the back of that child's coat looked more like a beating to me. It's not easy raising a kid like Sheila but all the same . . .

'Hey, Nance, hey, Sheila,' I called out. 'How about a milk-shot? My treat.'

Sheila stopped crying and reached up, as I got closer, for a hug and a carry. She loves everyone, that kid; will sit on anyone's lap—her dad's, the physician's, a summer visitor's—and slobber them with kisses. It's cute at the moment, because she's only six, but will look dodgy by the time she's in her twenties.

Nancy shoved Sheila towards me like a charity par-cel. 'Just take her, will you,' she begged, her voice all strained and teary. 'Just for half an hour while I peg the washing out. She's driving me insane.'

''Course,' I said, and then: 'Are you all right?'

'No,' she answered. 'Not really, no . . .'

Nance is on tablets: herbal ones from Mrs Tweedy in Dolphin Street and serious ones from the physician. They're for depression, or nerves, or hormones—maybe all three, who knows—and I could only assume, as I piggy-backed our Sheila into The Crazy Mermaid, that Nance had run out of the things, or forgotten to take one.

The councillors were sitting at a table in the window: five men and two women, all as smart as paint in their dark green suits with logos on the jackets, same as the van. The view across the harbour seemed to be interesting them a whole lot more than the little fishies on their plates. Anyone would think they'd never seen the sea before. They were drinking that view down; feasting on it.

One of the men had a seriously smart piece of recording equipment next to his plate. As Sheila and I went past he picked it up and pressed a button. 'It's perfect,' I heard him say into it. 'No wires. No street signs. No ice-cream kiosks or fish and chip stalls. Just cobbles and shingle and the murderous sea. Exactly what the doctor—sorry, Hollywood—ordered.'

The other councillors chuckled and clinked their cups in a toast to something. *To what?* I wondered. *To what, exactly?*

'Hey, Danzel—over here, sweetling.'

It was Mrs Rosdew—Jenna's mum—sitting by herself at an almost-but-not-quite discreet distance from the councillors. Her mouth was like a clown's and you could have parked your bike in the amount of cleavage she had on show. If you want to know where Jenna gets her sass from, you only have to look at her mum, and maybe times it by ten . . .

Sheila started scrabbling, so I put her down, and she went, straightaway, to Mrs Rosdew, leaving me no choice but to follow, ducking my head to avoid being whacked by a shoal of plastic mermaids.

Other folk, I noticed, had bagged most of the other tables—Mrs Tweedy, with her grandchildren; Dilly's grandpa and Gurnet's uncle; Maude's aunt Jane and her baby twins; Mrs Janson from the tavern and Mrs Daniels from the shop.

None of them were eating, only making a milk-shot last, or eking out a jug of lemonade. And although the little Tweedys all clamoured hello, and came to cuddle Sheila, the grown ones simply nodded. Like me they had their ears fine-tuned to the visitors, curious to know what had brought them to our café—brought them out of season, and in a high old mood to party, like it was the king's birthday or something.

Like me, they had all caught that magical word 'Hollywood' and were wondering *what the—?*

JENNA

Oh, brilliant, I thought, when I stepped out of the kitchen, and saw half the flicking port sitting around. *Just brilliant . . .* As if my mum wasn't shaming enough, I had to have old Mrs Tweedy and her cronies cackling like night-frights, and Dilly's grandpa banging on, to anyone who'll listen, about his marrows, or his lemons, or whatever . . .

For once, though, they were all being quiet; unusually so, like they were waiting for some kind of announcement.

I served them all quickly (they didn't want much) while the visitors from Truro ate their starters. Mrs Tonkin had got me there under false pretences. Not one of those councillors was going to see thirty again and two of them were women.

I tried to ignore my mum, as I passed by her table, but she had taken her jotter-slate out of her bag and written on it, in capital letters: THE ONE WITH THE RED HAIR IS TASTY.

Mortified, I stopped on my way back to the kitchen and used the hem of my apron to scrub the slate clean.

'Well he is!' Mum insisted, loud enough for the whole café to hear. 'And I'm getting, you know . . . ' she lowered her voice to just above a whisper: *'a reciprocal vibe.'*

'*Stop it!*' I hissed. '*Stop it, Mum. I mean it.*'

I stayed in the kitchen after that, until it was time to wait on the councillors again. Mrs Tonkin was being a slave to her oven, testing pies with a skewer and hoping that our visitors wouldn't think she'd been mean with the pilchards.

' "Sustainable fishing" and "frugal usage", my ankle . . . ' she muttered, crossly. 'Whichever eco-minister made the "no more than three pilchards to pies of less than fifteen centimetres diameter" rule was a po-face, is all. . . . Cheer up, Jen,' she added, as I squeezed past. 'And help yourself to a milk-shot if you want one.'

Big deal, I thought. *Lucky old me.*

Danzel had come in, and was sitting with my mum. He had his niece with him; the defective one who needs masses of attention and won't ever be going to the school. She was on his lap (the niece, not my mum, although I wouldn't have put it past my mum to try . . .) and he was spooning blackberry milk into her mouth.

He smiled at me, and even winked, as if we shared an understanding, and the way he was minding that kid made him even sexier, in a saintly sort of way (not that saints are supposed to be sexy, but you know what I mean . . .).

Just the sight of him, there in the café, should have raised my spirits. The smile and the wink should have sent me straight to Cloud Nine. A couple of days earlier they would have done exactly that, and I wondered what had changed; what switch had tripped in my head to make me feel as if wanting Danzel Killick had suddenly become a hopeless waste of my time.

116

THAT REDHEAD IS GIVING ME THE EYE

I knocked Mum's jotter-slate clean off her table, not caring if it broke.

'Put it away,' I whispered, fiercely, as she bent, protesting, to pick it up. 'Or I'll stamp on it.'

'Cheer up, young girl,' one of the councillors said, as I cleared away his starter plate. I flinched, not wanting to reply. I'd held my breath as I leaned over him because heaven forbid that a councillor, of all people, should smell stale cider on me. But not replying, I realized, looked even more suspicious than not breathing so I took a step backwards, said 'I'm sorry, sir,' and beamed.

'That's better,' the councillor said, smiling, tightly, back at me. 'You turn it on well, young girl. I bet you're the star of every show and service, up at the school. You are still at the school, aren't you?'

I told him I was, but that today was our Community Service day.

'Mrs Tonkin will tell you, sir,' I said, starting to panic even though I'd told the truth. 'She'll confirm it. I was on beachcombing duty until . . . '

He flapped his hand, to shut me up. Then he beckoned me closer, so I took another deep breath, held it in, and went.

Closer and closer he beckoned me, and then lower, until his mouth was so close to my right ear that he could have bitten it off, and his fingers were clamped on my arm, keeping me bent over and attentive.

'Keep an eye on the inter-telly, young girl,' he whispered, and his horrible hot breath seemed to enter right into my brain. 'The local site. It hasn't been announced yet, and won't be for a while, but we're working on something—something big—that's to happen right here in Port Zannon. And the people involved are bound to want extras. There. I've given you a clue . . . '

He let go of my arm then so I straightened up and backed away. Still smiling, though . . . smiling like a good young girl . . . like the cluster of pink and silver mermaids swinging above my head.

'So . . . another jug of cider I think,' the councillor said, all loud and hearty this time, for everyone to hear. 'To drink a toast to Port Zannon and its many and varied attractions.'

Then he winked at me; an old man's wink that left me as cold as the fish eyes he'd left staring up from his plate.

URGENT GANG MEETING TONIGHT. YOUR PARLOUR. 7PM!!

The new message fuddled me until I realized that Mum had lent Danzel the slate and it was he, not her, who had written on it.

'Fine,' I said as I passed him. But *Gang meeting?* I thought, as I thumped hot pies straight from the oven onto my tray. *Grow up, Danzel. We're not five years old any more . . .*

Somehow, I carried on smiling as I served those councillors their mains. I did OK with the puddings as well, and didn't even scowl when the councillors asked for their coats, even though it was blindingly obvious to anyone with a clear view of the table that they hadn't left me a tip.

Extras is it? The flicking nerve . . . I may still be at the school, but I know what that old councillor was hinting at. Was it my make-up that made him write me off as a bad girl? Or was it something else . . . something in me that he saw and didn't like? Or had he liked it, the saggy old fright? Had he intended to shame me, with what he'd said, or did he actually mean it—that there's to be some big event, here at the port, and, if I want, I can provide a few extras?

And what did he mean by 'extras', as if I didn't know? Waiting on tables without my top on? A kiss and a cuddle between courses, with other pervy officials like him? Or something worse . . . something truly disgusting?

There are laws—strict laws—to stop men being lewd with girls my age. But maybe councillors are above all those laws. Maybe they get away with all kinds.

'Are you all right, Jen?' Mrs Tonkin said to me, as I scraped leftovers into the pig bin and struggled not to cry.

I said I was tired is all; that I'd forgotten what hard work waiting on tables can be when there's a rush on.

'Yes,' she sighed. 'We get used to it, don't we, being so quiet here during the dark time? Having strangers drop by in November is unsettling, like a snowstorm in May. It's a bigger deal to you kids, of course, because you've never known things any other way. I forget that, sometimes.'

I nodded, and kept on scraping.

Beyond the kitchen door I heard my mother laugh. I hoped it was over something Mrs Tweedy or old Mr Tonkin had said, and not because she had cornered the red-haired councillor before he could get away.

I really did feel tired. Drained, like an old woman. I

would go home and have a sleep, I decided, and to merry hell with combing the rest of the beach. No one would notice. We don't get half so much dross thrown up since the eco-laws took effect and, anyway, the tide was coming up so would take whatever I'd missed. I wished it would take that old councillor. He deserved to be dragged out to sea—dragged out and bitten in half by a ravenous basking shark.

Mrs Tonkin brought me a milk-shot: strawberry, my favourite, and a special treat at this time of year. 'It's all right,' she said as I hesitated over accepting it. 'We had a strawberry glut this year. I managed to preserve some. And, anyway, you've earned it.'

I drank the milk-shot slowly. It reminded me of warm evenings, and of being little. I had a yearning, suddenly, to be a small child again; to be sitting, like Danzel's niece, on a kind man's knee, being fed from a spoon, and kept safe.

It was a daft thing to be wanting, and it gave me no comfort at all.

DILLY

I can't believe it. I'm having trouble wrapping my mind around the most incredible piece of news. But Danzel says it's true. Danzel says he heard one of the councillors drop a hint about it, in The Crazy Mermaid, then got his brother Ned's girlfriend to tell him more.

People are coming here from America—from HOLLYWOOD, no less—to make a film about the Port Zannon wreckers. Not a docu-clip for the inter-telly either but a proper movie, with real stars acting in it, and a real director shouting 'action!' and 'cut!' and all of that.

It has taken months and months to organize, according to Danzel's brother's girlfriend. Everyone who'll be coming has had to go through the strictest of security checks known to man, and the king changed his mind at least three times before the film people made an offer for the treasury that he Absolutely Could Not Refuse.

'It's the start of a whole new era!' Danzel marvelled, at a hastily-called Gang meeting in Jenna's parlour. 'It's the king seeing sense at last and letting people in. And it'll be happening right here, my friends. Not at Porthleven or Lizard Point, but *here* on our very own doorsteps . . . How absolutely sing-song is that?'

'When?' Gurnet wanted to know. He didn't sound

happy, but then he wouldn't. Gurnet hates it when strangers come. In the summer, if he's not out fishing, he hides, or wears a hood.

'Late spring,' Danzel said. 'Or early summer. Before visiting season anyway. It's going to be *incredible*!' He turned to Jenna, who was sitting on a stool beside the grate, looking surprisingly uninterested for a girl who has dreamt, since she was little, of being a world-famous actress one day.

'Maybe they'll give you a walk-on part, Jen,' Danzel said. 'Think of that! It'll be a start, won't it—an amazing start—being an extra in a *Hollywood movie* of all things?'

'Being a what?' Jenna lifted her head, as if from a stupor.

'An extra. In *Wreckers*—the film. For crying out loud! Am I the only one dancing a jig over this? Don't you see? This is going to be the most amazing thing that's ever happened—not just here but in the *whole kingdom*— since . . . since before . . . ' He waved both his hands dismissively, as if we didn't deserve to have the sentence finished; weren't worthy of hearing the last two words spoken aloud, we were all such mopes.

'The Attack,' I said for him.

'Yes,' he agreed, humbly. 'Since then.'

I considered the movie, trying to imagine how it would go; what the storyline might be. 'Our ancestors were wreckers,' I said. 'All of ours. My grandpa told me.'

'Then maybe they'll let us *all* be in it,' said Danzel, his eyes shining brighter than ever. 'Maybe we'll even get *speaking parts*, for being linked *by blood* to the original families.'

I wasn't sure. Something was troubling me although I couldn't quite pin it down.

Maude said she was surprised the king had agreed to a film being made about the wreckers.

Why? the others asked. Why wouldn't the king agree if it's going to add a fortune to the treasury and he's sure it's a safe thing to do? That it's not some plot for people to infiltrate our kingdom and blow some more of it sky high?

'Because,' I chipped in, understanding straightaway what Maude was trying to say, 'it's not going to show the kingdom—our part of it, anyway, and especially our ancestors—in a very good light, is it? Unless . . . unless the Hollywood people have agreed to be kind. To turn it all into a beautiful romance, or something.'

'What,' scoffed Danzel, 'are you on about?'

He didn't get it. My grandad would have done, though. My grandad is going to be the first to object if Hollywood makes its actors shine false lights from our cliffs, as if luring storm-tossed ships onto the rocks. Because nobody has ever proved that that's what really happened here. Not in real life. And if those actors pretend to kill people as well—are filmed battering or drowning the survivors of a wreck—well! My grandad will be livid.

Nothing was going to burst Danzel's bubble though, least of all a lesson in local history from me. He was practically hopping up and down with excitement, the way he used to do on Christmas Eve.

Then something else—something far more troubling than having the old ones of Port Zannon shown up as murderous thugs—dawned on me. These people coming from Hollywood. The film crew. What if they want to use the old manor house, as a set or something?

I've learned enough from the inter-telly, to know that camera people, make-up people, canteen people, wardrobe people and goodness knows how many hangers-on will take a set over like ants. And the very thought of all those strangers swarming around our—my—special place appalled me.

'I'll fetch us some lemonade, shall I?' said Jenna. She had cheered up, dramatically, after what Danzel had said about her being an extra. 'And then,' she added, 'we girls can log onto the inter-telly, to see if it says, yet, who's coming. Which big star, I mean. If it's Connor Blue I'll just *melt*.'

Maude and I had never heard of Connor Blue, but then we're not obsessed with foreign celebrities, the way Jenna is. Gurnet said he needed to get home. Danzel said he'd go with him, but only if Gurnet's new pet was securely caged, not roaming around like some ugly mutant recently escaped from the sewers.

'How is Laurence?' I asked, quickly, before Jenna could say anything mean, or start on about how Gurn threatened her with his knife, on Hallowe'en night, which he can't remember doing, and Maude can't recall seeing, so we're starting to think is just one of Jenna's Things, and part of the reason why she'd make a wonderful actress.

'He sleeps a lot,' Gurnet answered. 'And he doesn't seem to want to eat. But his hair's growing, and he knows his name. He comes to me when I call him and he likes to suck my fingers.'

'Oh, *please* . . . ' Jenna pretended to retch. 'Spare us.'

And off she flounced to fetch lemonade, leaving the rest of us to carry on marvelling (Danzel), dreading (Gurnet), worrying (Maude), and part-marvelling-part-dreading-and-part-worrying (me) about how this huge and glamorous event—the coming of Hollywood to Port Zannon—might change our lives.

*When winter comes to this coastline it does so with a vengeance.
The wind flays you and the nights seem everlasting. Before The
Attack, November had much less bite. On any bleak afternoon
you could drive to a city and spend hours in a shopping mall,
basking in artificial light and warmth. The big supermarkets
sold strawberries and roses all year round. And in the evenings,
with the central heating on full blast, you could sit at home in
your scanties, as if England was in the tropics and you, yourself,
about to take a midnight dip in the sea.*

*In the fifteen years since the borders were closed, families in
Port Zannon have Battened Down The Hatches and sat the winters out. They have used power frugally, like good citizens, and
eaten a lot of thick soup, made from parsnips and other roots.*

*Many older residents have come to prefer this way of life—this
virtual hibernation—to the way things were before. They feel
more in tune with the seasons and much closer to their neighbours (with whom they share everything, from childcare to firewood). The children, of course, have never known any different.*

*Quiet. Predictable. Safe. That's how Port Zannon has come
to be as November turns to December, the shortest day comes
and goes, and light returns to the land.*

*But that's without Hopelessness, grown as big as a man's
head on its salt-water diet, and ready, as the New Year chimes,
to get down to some serious work.*

DILLY

'Have you started your new book yet?' my grandpa Tonkin asked me today. He meant my diary. Ever since I began forming sentences, Grandpa has given me a blank exercise book for Christmas with 'DILLY'S DAILY DOINGS' written on the front in thick black ink.

This year's book is bright yellow. I had hoped Grandpa would leave off writing on the cover, or put something less childish now that I'm almost sixteen. Plain old 'Diary' would have done. 'Dilly's Diary' if he absolutely had to keep it cute.

But no. Dilly's Daily Doings it is and always will be, I suspect, until my daily doings involve washing babies' nappies and tending my own allotment.

'Not yet,' I told him. 'There's been nothing to write about yet.'

'What?' he replied. 'No thoughts about the movie people coming? No new theories about why everyone's so down in the dumps right now when they ought to be getting excited? That's not like you, Dilly Tonkin.'

He wasn't being sarcastic, my grandpa, or even a bit of a tease. He knows I've been waiting, all my life, for something incredible to write about. He has no idea, of course, that I've been to the manor house. So far as he's aware, this movie is the most thrilling thing, ever, to have touched my life. And the movie *is* thrilling. Of course it is. And Grandpa is right. Nobody—apart from Jenna, I suppose—is getting properly excited about it.

I don't know why this is. Certainly, I've got nothing to be especially anxious about since, according to Danzel's brother's girlfriend, the movie people haven't even asked about the old manor house. The harbour. The cove. The tavern. Squeeze Belly Alley, where Gurnet lives. The church. The fish sheds and maybe one or two of the cottages. Those are the places they're wanting to film, for *Wreckers.*

It's normal to feel fed up in January. The post-Christmas blues, my mum calls it. Seasonal Affective Disorder the physician says. But the way some people around here are moaning on and on, you'd think springtime, and all those glamorous people from Hollywood, were never going to come.

'To be honest,' I said to Grandpa, 'I haven't felt like writing anything much, lately. Maybe I'm down in the dumps too, like everyone else.'

'Ah, you're entitled,' he said. 'At your age, you're entitled to mood swings. Here—have a lemon. Take it home with you, for the vitamins.'

He reached out, then, tugged the biggest fruit from the tallest tree, and placed it, warm as a new-laid egg, in my hands. My grandad's garden looks wild, from a distance, but there's method to it. It's on three steep terraces, with the citrus trees right up on the top level, where they get the best of the sun all year round.

When I was little, before Dad and Mum and I moved

to our own cottage, I used to toddle out of Grandma and Grandpa's front door and scramble up all the terraces, to sit among the lemon trees and look out across the port.

Somewhere on the inter-telly, in one of our family files, is a photograph of me, aged two, doing exactly that— sitting on my backside in the dirt and gazing, hopefully, out to sea as if someone I loved and missed was about to come sailing into port. 'Daffodil among the lemons', Grandpa labelled it. He entered it in one of the 'Happy Snaps of England' competitions that were popular after The Attack. It didn't win anything though. *Where's the flower?* the judges probably thought. *Has the child eaten it? Where exactly is the daffodil in this happy snap of England?*

I put my lemon in my pocket. It was the best of a bad crop—the worst in living memory, Grandpa told me, even though the flowers had been thick and sweet.

Could the sun be losing its strength? I wondered, bleakly. Could Gurnet's dad be right, about other countries ignoring the eco laws and fouling up the planet all over again? Could the seas still be boiling, and the plankton dying, and the oxygen running low? Might we all have trouble breathing soon?

'Hmmm,' he said. And then: 'You really are in the doldrums, aren't you, Dilly Tonkin?'

This evening, after supper, I went round to call on Jenna. I'm longing—*yearning*—to go back to the manor house, now that the days are getting longer, but persuading the others to go with me is like trying to pull four limpets off a rock.

Jenna is proving the hardest one of all to motivate. She says wild horses wouldn't drag her back to the manor. She says a tidal wave could be sweeping towards the port, with everyone yelling 'Quick! Head for higher ground!' and still she wouldn't go within a mile of the place.

I'm worried about Jenna. Maude says she's losing her sass—the raunchiness that can be *so annoying* but is as much a part of Jen as her fingerprints and foghorn voice. Danzel says she's no fun and needs to pull herself together. But he's just peeved, I reckon, because Jenna doesn't flirt with him any more.

'Maybe it's a tactical thing,' I told him the other afternoon. 'Maybe Jenna's hoping you'll start flirting with her, now that she's stopped flirting with you.'

'Horse dung,' he replied. 'You know that's not true.'

'Does it bother you,' I wondered, 'that Jen doesn't feel . . . you know . . . *special* . . . about you any more?'

'Special? *Special?* . . . ' He'd laughed, and I'd smelt the sour apples on his breath. 'Oh Dilly . . . ' he said, almost choking on the laughs, 'you are so . . . ' He'd paused, then, like he had a very long list of Dilly-adjectives filed away in his head, and was mentally flipping through.

'So *what?*'

'So . . . I don't know . . . quaint. The Americans are going to love you. Seriously—don't look at me like that—they are.'

That boy should stop helping himself to his family's cider. It makes him ridiculous and, if he doesn't watch out, someone—a grown-up—is going to catch on soon and report him. And if that happens he'll be in serious trouble and I . . . I will be more disappointed in him than I can possibly say.

I took my lemon, to give to Jenna. She reckons her hair is getting darker—is paranoid about going from blonde to mouse before she's out of her teens—and has read somewhere, or been told by Mrs Tweedy, that a lemon rinse will help. I don't get why she's fussing. Her hair's as blonde now as it was when she was three, just less like a dandelion clock is all.

'Thanks,' she said, putting the lemon carefully on the mantelpiece, between a candlestick and a framed photo of her dad. 'Now come and look at this!'

She seemed excited; more like her old self, yet there was an edge to it, something desperate that I'd never sensed in her before. I watched, warily, as she flicked on the inter-telly, hit 'I' for international and began scrolling through the options.

'There!' She hit the 'freeze' button. 'I guessed right. He's the one—the star of the movie. Just look at him, Dils. Isn't he divine? Isn't he the most heart-stoppingly gorgeous being you've ever seen in your life?'

I looked at Connor Blue and he didn't seem real.

'How old is he?' I wondered.

'Twenty,' Jenna replied. 'He's twenty years old, lives in Laurel Canyon, enjoys horse riding and Mexican food, and likes girls with inner beauty and a strong sense of faith.'

She was quoting, like a parrot, but it must have been from memory because I couldn't see any of those facts in front of us, on the screen.

'Faith in what?' I wanted to know.

'Dunno,' Jenna admitted. 'Isn't he beautiful though? Look at those eyes . . . and his *teeth*. Have you ever seen teeth so white?'

I said I hadn't. Except on some of the mermaid dolls, hanging in Mum's café. And on a shark. A toy shark I used to own, and played with in the bath.

'You can have that done, cosmetically,' Jenna said, with a sigh. 'It isn't even all that expensive. You can have your teeth whitened anywhere in the world—except right here in this stupid kingdom, of course.'

'Shush,' I said, because it's said that the authorities eavesdrop on people through the inter-telly, and report what they see and hear to the Minister for Social Control.

Jenna shrugged, like she didn't care who might be watching us, or listening in. Then she carried on drooling over the picture of Connor Blue while I read the news bulletin that had come up underneath it:

'BLUE TO STAR IN THIS YEAR'S MOST TALKED-ABOUT MOVIE'

The story said how much Hollywood's hottest young actor was looking forward to being in England . . . how privileged he felt to have been chosen for the leading role in *Wreckers* . . . how seriously he viewed the honour, and responsibility, of becoming the first foreign celebrity to set foot on English soil since The Attack.

'Scroll down,' I said to Jenna. 'I want to see what else it says.'

But that was it. Short and sweet.

'Well?' Jenna asked. 'Is he sex on legs or *what*?'

I said he was. I said it in the same kind of voice Jenna was using, like Connor Blue was a dish of well-sugared strawberries that I couldn't wait to gobble down. But, really, I was shamming . . . agreeing with my friend so I wouldn't look like a smother-all or a complete and utter child.

'Do you like him more than Danzel, then?' I asked.

Her laughter made me squirm.

'Dilly,' she said. 'Open your eyes. There's no contest, is there?'

'No,' I agreed. But privately, I knew that there was, or that there had been, and that, so far as Jenna was concerned, Connor Blue had won, even though Dan is as handsome as any movie star, and fun as well, usually, for all he's only sixteen and wouldn't know Mexican food from a barrel of bait.

As soon as I got home, I called the same international news file up on our inter-telly for a better, closer look at Connor Blue. Mum and Dad were in the parlour, playing Scrabble, so they looked too.

'What amazing teeth that boy has,' said Mum. 'I hope he eats fish. I hope he likes crab sandwiches and pilchard pie.'

'I hope he's wed,' said Dad. 'And I hope his missus comes along to keep an eye on him. Otherwise there are plenty of young maids in this port—grown women too— who'll be after him like wasps to a plum.'

'He's single,' I said. 'And he likes Mexican food, and girls with inner beauty.'

'Not on the same plate I hope,' Dad replied, adding, 'What? *What?* Only joking,' as Mum cuffed him lightly round the head.

I had homework to finish, which didn't take long, and then I went to bed. My dream must have been ready and waiting in my head, because I woke up from it less than half an hour ago and it's only five minutes to midnight.

I dreamed I was back at the manor house, sitting sideways on the edge of the four-poster bed, while Connor Blue brushed my hair. He was using the antique brush from the dressing table, and being very gentle.

'Do *I* have inner beauty?' I asked him, in the dream.

'Of course,' he replied. 'Of course you do, Daffy . . . ' And his voice was gentle too, and so full of love for me that I wanted to curl up against him and just rest.

Daffy.

Nobody has ever called me that before. It can, I know, mean stupid. Away with the fairies. Daft as a brush. But in the dream-voice of Connor Blue it sounded like the loveliest name in the world.

GURNET

Mum says she can't be bothered with the spring-cleaning this year. Dad says it's because she's turning into a fat lazy cow before our very eyes—meaning his eyes and mine—and she needs to buck her ideas up before it's too late.

'Too late for what?' you might expect a woman to wonder.

But Mum never asks that question.

Things have slid a lot these last few months. Since New Year, to be precise. Monday, for instance, used to be wash day but now it's a sit-in-front-of-the-inter-telly-in-a-dressing-gown-day, like most days have become so far as Mum is concerned.

Yesterday was a Monday and I had to wash my own stuff, and some of Dad's as well, otherwise we would have had to start wearing things that stank. I gave Mum merry hell for that, but I don't think she was bothered. Maybe she is suffering from Seasonal Affective Disorder. There is a lot of it about.

That is sing-song news, though, about no spring cleaning because it means I will not have to unlock my bedroom door. The last thing I want, at this point in time, is anyone fussing around Laurence's cage with mops and dusters and that vinegar-stuff Mum uses—or used to use, anyway—to get germs off our surfaces.

Laurence has grown. He was like a squished tomato when I found him; now he is the size and shape of a good-sized pumpkin. I still do not know what kind of a creature he is, despite all the checks I have run on the inter-telly, but he has started—just started—to stretch his wings, which makes him some sort of a bird, I suppose. A hairy bird with fingers instead of claws and two flat feet that he uses to hop around on, or to swivel, in his cage.

Not knowing for certain what species Laurence comes from does not bother me unduly. My Danzel says he is a mutant—the spawn of two creatures that should never have reproduced—but I stopped listening weeks ago to what Danzel Killick has to say. It's mostly babble now-adays; the cider talking, as my dad would say, and he should know.

I have sworn The Gang to secrecy where Laurence is concerned. I am beginning to think, though, that they have forgotten all about him. My Dilly used to ask how he is getting on, but she is preoccupied, now, with the movie that is going to be made here about fishermen from this port who used to filch things from shipwrecks but were never punished for it because a) they were too smart and b) everyone who knew about it, including the lord of the manor, thought it was acceptable behaviour.

Jenna is preoccupied with the movie too. There is a famous actor coming to be the star of it, and she is deter-mined to make him love her. That actor had better watch out is all I can say. That actor had better know how to run.

I don't know if my Maude is preoccupied with the movie coming or not. She doesn't go to the café after school any more, nor does she sit around with us in the harbour, or up on the cliff. I must go and see my Maude, and make sure she is all right. If anyone is going to get Seasonal Affective Disorder so bad they can't even leave their house it is going to be her.

I will go and see Maude later and remind her not to say a single thing to anyone about Laurence. I don't think she will. It was her, after all, who opened up the wall and let my Laurence out, so she has a responsibilty, like I do, to look after him. I'll remind her all the same, though, because if anyone outside The Gang finds out there will be serious strife. My mum, I know for certain, would not want my pet in the house. She would make me set him loose or—worse—hand him over to my dad.

I don't like to think about what might happen after that. I see black when I have those thoughts.

DANZEL

The fat, my friends, is in the fire. Nance, my brother's wife, has vanished. No note. No goodbyes-and-see-you-laters. She has simply disappeared.

Brother Michael went frantic at first, thinking she might have jumped clean off a cliff, she's been that depressed since Christmas. But their horse has gone, and so have Nance's clothes, and ditto all the money she and Michael had been hoarding to send Sheila to the County Care School by and by.

Sheila won't stop screaming. She wants her mum and doesn't understand why she's not around.

'Get straight on to the authorities,' Mum told Michael, this morning. 'File a red alert. Nance can't have got far, not on that old nag of yours. And where would she go to anyway? Who does she know outside of Port Zannon? No one.' But Michael doesn't want the authorities involved. Not yet. He's hanging on to the possibility that that horse of his will come trotting along Fore Street any minute now, with Nance drooping in the saddle, all pale and contrite and ready to make amends.

He says Nance would never leave him; not properly and for good. He says Nance didn't take her silver locket —the one with the fingernail-sized pictures inside it of him, smiling, and Sheila, laughing—and that this is a sign, should anyone need one, that she won't be gone for long. He says he trusts her to stay safe and to do the right thing. Each time he opens his mouth to say all this to someone who hasn't heard it yet, he sounds less and less convinced.

Personally, I'm thinking *Nance, how sing-song are you for getting away from here. For grabbing your chance to go.* I've come up on the cliff this evening, with a helping or two of cider, and I'm hurling pebbles down into the sea and willing Nance on as far as my brother's nag and Sheila's funds will take her.

Tomorrow is Remembrance Day. March 20th. There will be no school (good call, since my science assignment might as well be the latest edition of *Ecological Theology: A Turning of the Tides* for all I've bothered looking at it).

I'm getting a bit lashed, up here on the cliff.

According to the inter-telly the film crew from Hollywood will be docking at Falmouth early next week. They'll rest up there awhile, until Security has finished with them, then they'll be here, with us.

I have a strong hunch, my friends, that my own chance to go—to leave Port Zannon for ever, and really start to live—will come sailing in with those people. I have no idea what shape this chance will take, but it is *of paramount importance* that I recognize it, and grab it with both hands.

It is beautiful up here. For all I know, Port Zannon is the most beautiful place in the world. The gorse is starting to flower. When Dilly was little she used to pick the buds and put them on dolls' plates with bits of grass and daisy heads. Poached eggs, she called the daisies and the grass was a dolly salad. I forget what the gorse buds were. Potatoes? More egg?

As if it matters. As if I care.

I need to stay focused, and I will. Right now, though, I'm going to hurl a few more stones and have another drink.

GURNET

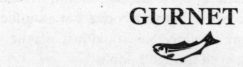

I have been waiting for my Laurence to speak. When he was trapped he spoke. 'Let me out,' he said. 'Out!Out!' But since Maude and I rescued him he hasn't said a thing—until today.

There was no school this morning, and no overnight fishing either, because today is the anniversary of The Attack. I meant to have a lie in but didn't get one.

Laurence sleeps on my windowsill now. He likes it there. I was worried, at first, that someone might spot him from the alley and be alarmed. I was so anxious about this that I went to put him back in his cage. But he cried, and wrung his hands, like it was the end of his world.

I told him I would do a compromise. I said he could sleep on the windowsill if he wanted to, so long as he stayed very still—as still as my radio, which is also on there—and kept off it during the day. Laurence is smart. He understood. I've tested him seventeen times now and he hasn't let me down. Coming back from fishing, at four or five in the morning, I entered the alley quietly and looked up at my bedroom window.

To date, I have yet to catch my Laurence dancing a jig or scrambling up the curtains, or doing anything at all that might attract someone's attention. From down in the alley he looks like a coconut, or a stuffed toy of some kind, and it doesn't matter if he blinks because he is too high up for that to notice. Also, there are no windows on the opposite side of the alley, only a brick wall, so that is in his favour. Dad never looks up and, even if he did, he wouldn't think to wonder what a coconut or a stuffed toy were doing in my window. He would just assume I owned those things, even though I don't.

My first thoughts this morning were: 'No school. Perfection!' My second thoughts, as I closed my eyes again, were: 'Got to be in church for twelve. Can't miss The Remembrance.'

Then I felt a weight land, thump, on my chest.

Laurence.

He had jumped onto me from the windowsill and was staring, without blinking, right into my face, and holding both of his hands out like he wanted something, badly.

'What is it, mate?' I said. 'What's up?'

I did not expect an answer. I expected that pet of mine to go back to the windowsill, or over to his cage where he had, I knew, plenty of water to drink and a choice of flesh (worm), fish (pilchard head), and fruit (orange slice) to eat up should he feel an urge, ever, to do more than sniff and nibble.

His mouth made a tearing sound when he opened it, like it had been glued or sewn tight shut. It wasn't nice to hear. It made me wonder if I should have been washing his face for him, these past few months, and checking his teeth and his gums.

'Take me to the church, Gary,' he said, his voice all raspy, like an ancient man's. 'At midday. Take me.'

There was little talk of retaliation, after The Attack. The piling of death upon death, the tit for tat of it, the expense and the horror and the waste . . . where had it ever got the world? What lessons had ever been learned?

No.

It stops here, the new king decreed. It stops now.

Church-attendance was one of the first things to be made compulsory, in the new scheme of things. Once the massive upheaval of deportation and voluntary emigration was over and the borders officially closed . . . once the dust had settled (literally—horribly . . .) the new king took stock and decided that the time was right to unite what remained of the country, faith-wise.

The Muslims had nearly all gone, by then, willingly or otherwise. So, too, had tens of thousands of Sikhs, Buddhists, and Hindus. So much for so-called tolerance. Whoopee for integration.

One culture. One language. One unifying faith. That's what the new king envisaged, meaning, of course, a predominantly white culture; the English language and the orthodox Christian faith—none of your new-fangled Eco-Christianity; too much like paganism, in the king's opinion.

'We are going back to our roots,' he announced to his subjects,

via the inter-telly. 'Back to a simpler time.' And if anyone wondered precisely how deep this new monarch intended going, roots wise (The Second World War? The First? Victorian England with its appalling hypocrisy and terrible smogs? The Civil War? The religious persecutions of Tudor times? The Dark Ages? The Roman occupation?) nobody said, at least not for the record.

Compulsory church attendance, though, went down like an iron balloon. The king, it seemed, could phase out cars, ration food, and re-structure the entire labour force without too much of a backlash from his traumatized and largely biddable subjects. But laying down the law where religion was concerned was seen as a step too far. The trouble was—and the king knew this as well as anyone—churches had been struggling, for years, to stay in business. In a land that claimed to embrace multi-culturalism and any number of faiths (but had failed, spectacularly, to do either) the Church of England had floundered. Lost its clout. Been pushed out of the game like a kid who keeps insisting that he, and he alone, has all the right answers, until it becomes just too annoying.

Ecological theologians have changed all of that. Making the continuing destruction of the rainforest a sin, as well as a crime, and ditto the polluting and over-fishing of the seas, has united faiths, healed all kinds of rifts and done wonders for the quality of the air.

The king, though, was thinking personally rather than globally when he dreamed, in those first raw weeks, after The Attack, of church bells ringing the length and breadth of the country, summoning the faithful to prayer. Men loyal to God would, he knew, be loyal to their King. English monarchs have always known this—have relied upon it, and milked it for centuries—and loyalty, after The Attack, was what the king wanted most (actually, no, he wanted his wife back, and his father, and most members of parliament, but that would have taken a miracle).

Get to church on Sunday, this new monarch ordered his subjects, with the earth still cooling, from Uxbridge across to Dagenham and Enfield down to Croydon and St Paul's Cathedral gone, likewise the abbey at Westminster. Get to church and pray for this country, like the good citizens you are, or ought to be, and will be from now on.

Protest groups sprang up. They tried—and failed—to infiltrate the inter-telly; tried—and failed—to organize a rally; tried—and failed—to get a message out to the rest of the world that the new king of England had overstepped the mark.

The protestors were soon silenced. But the king, who is no fool, saw the error of his judgement and made church attendance, once again, a matter of personal choice. Except on March 20th when bells across the land begin tolling at 10a.m., summoning every able-bodied man, woman, and child to their nearest place of worship. To remember. To mourn. To observe the midday silence and to sing a song of hope.

Hope . . .

That's right.

For the future of mankind.

JENNA

The church smelt disgusting, like all its drains were blocked, or someone had left a bucket of starfish, rotting under a chair. Mum whispered that it was probably the vases; that the insides of the vases hadn't been scoured for years.

It was certainly stagnant, that smell, but way too strong to be coming from any vase. I couldn't understand why other people weren't complaining, if only among themselves. I supposed they were trying to ignore it, out of respect for the occasion.

We found places to sit behind the Carthews and then I realized: that smell was coming from Gurnet. He was wearing his stupid black coat, all buttoned up like it was the middle of winter and he kept wriggling, and hunching over, as if his armpits were itching, which no doubt they were.

I wanted to move. The church was packed though, and we were stuck. I told myself that at least I was behind Gurnet, not in front of him, because having that splat-brain looking at the back of *my* head, and maybe fingering that knife of his, would have really spooked me out.

Maude's mum and dad came in and managed to squeeze onto seats next to Mum and me.

'Where's Maude?' Mum wanted to know.

Maude's dad shot her a look that said *keep-your-voice-down-woman* and Maude's mum just shook her head.

It's a big deal if you don't do Remembrance. They take a register at the church door and you have to be practically dying, or two seconds away from having a baby, not to come. I'd been wondering how Michael Killick was going to explain Nancy's absence because you can bet your life that whatever he tells them, they'll check.

Maude is turning into a total recluse, like a nun or a mad girl. Mind you, I haven't been out myself much lately, what with Danzel no longer floating my boat, so to speak. I am saving myself (sigh) for Connor Blue. I am treating my face every evening with one of Mrs Tweedy's oatmeal and lavender skin scrubs, making myself a new summer dress, and reading a brilliant book on the inter-telly called *Men: How to Catch and Keep One*.

I'm going to need a pink lipstick to go with my new dress. Hot pink, not pale. I was thinking about that; and wondering whether it would be worth asking Mum to order us one—whether it would actually get here before Christmas, never mind in time to leave kiss-shapes on Connor Blue—when the clergyman appeared and everyone who wasn't already standing up rose to their feet.

People were crying, already. People like Danzel's mum who lost an aunt and three cousins in The Attack, and Mrs Daniels, from the shop, whose best friend had been doing a degree course at the London School of Economics. I looked all around until I found Dilly. She was staring straight ahead, her eyes fixed on a big display of daffodils as if they, not the clergyman, were about to say something profound.

Dilly lost her mum—her biological mum, that is—although, since her biological mum never actually wanted her, and abandoned her the first chance she got, you could argue that poor Dilly would never have seen or heard from the selfish cow again anyway.

I felt my own mum take my hand, and squeeze it. I squeezed back, and made a big effort to concentrate. Seven million dead is a lot of dead. You don't think about pink lipstick—at least, you shouldn't—when you're remembering that many people, gone before their time.

The clergyman wasn't one I recognized. They come here on a rota, never the same one twice. He wasn't as gnarled and ancient as others have been, in the past, and I had a silent bet with myself that, when the service was over, my mum would undo at least three buttons on her blouse and make a beeline for him, down the aisle.

The crying got louder. Ridiculously loud. It would have drowned the clergyman out, had he not had a microphone clipped to his robe. In front of me, Mrs Carthew began gulping and shuddering like The Attack had happened yesterday and she had just been plunged into mourning for her own flesh and blood.

The clergyman blessed us, and made a start on his sermon, but after a while, as the weeping and wailing continued, and Mrs Carthew's gulps turned to loud hacking sobs, he stopped, mid sentence, and waited. It's what instructors at the school do when a class gets too rowdy. They stand very still, with this *look* on their faces, until whoever's making a noise gets the message and shuts up.

The clergyman was looking more baffled than annoyed but I wondered, all the same, how long he would give it before telling the weepers and wailers to shut up and pay attention.

'Hey, Mum,' I heard Gurnet say, in a growly whisper. 'Calm down. You're upsetting . . . people. Me. You're upsetting me.'

He moved, awkwardly, to give poor Mrs Carthew something between a hug and a shake. And that was when all hell broke loose.

GURNET

I couldn't stop him. He took me by surprise with what he went and did in the church. He let me down. Badly.

'All right,' I'd told him. 'I'll take you. But you'll have to hide under my coat, so no one sees you and goes mental. And you're not to make a noise, or let anyone know you're there. Promise? Say: "I promise." Go on, say it.'

I sounded, to my own ears, like the worst kind of instructor so can't really blame my Laurence for sealing his mouth tight shut, like he had said all he wanted to say for the moment and wasn't going to give me the satisfaction of a humble reply. I would have done the same, in his position. I did think, though, that we had an understanding. I thought he would be a good creature in the church and give me no cause for alarm.

I got that very wrong.

DILLY

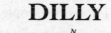

Where are you? I was thinking. *Where did you go to, spirit-wise? And Can you see me? Are you watching me grow up?*

The church on Remembrance Day is always full of daffodils. Loads and loads of them, so bright they hurt your eyes. It's coincidence, is all. Gardens and hedge-rows all across the kingdom are thick with the things, at this time of year, so what else would they have chosen as a memorial flower? Orchids? Edelweiss? And, as the clergyman always points out, the daffodil is a symbol of hope, appearing, as it does, year in year out, to announce the arrival of spring.

This year, though—around here anyway—the daffodils are late. I've seen only a few in Port Zannon and they are spindly things. The ones in church must have been brought in, from some other place—from the markets at Bodmin, perhaps, or even the Isles of Scilly. 'Spell-binder' . . . 'Bell Song' . . . 'Quince' . . . 'Early Bride' . . . each variety, I know, has its own pretty name . . . its own features and colour and style . . . its own definite place of origin.

Aurelia didn't give me a name. Or, if she did, it wasn't anywhere on the letter she left with me in the crate. Still, I like to pretend, on Remembrance Day, that the daffodils in church have a special meaning, just for me and her.

I'm sixteen now, I told Aurelia in my head. *Three more years and we'll be the same age. Then I'll overtake you, and won't that be strange?*

I never cry at Remembrance. I used to try to, but the tears never came. A lot more people than usual were crying this time though—and loudly too. Men as well as women, and people who, so far as I'm aware, didn't lose anyone close. I was surprised by so much grief, so long after the event, and so was the clergyman, I could tell.

'Your sorrow does you credit,' he said, raising his voice until his microphone crackled. 'For we must never, ever, forget what happened to our kingdom sixteen years ago today.'

'Only . . . ' He paused and cleared his throat. There was a 'but' coming. The usual 'but', I suspected, about forgiveness, and healing. About the cheery yellow of daffodils reminding us about lights at the ends of tunnels . . . beacons in stormy seas . . . the glimmer of hope that is with us, always, if we will only believe . . . only have faith in that which is kept hidden from the human gaze, like spring bulbs beneath the soil.

I kept my eyes on the daffodils and waited. But the 'but' never came. When Gurnet yelped I heard him, even through all the crying, and even though, as he admitted later, he'd stifled the sound as best he could.

'*Laur . . . !*' he yelped, almost choking as he swallowed the '*ence.*'

'Jesus *Christ!*'

That was Jenna cursing. I turned round—everyone turned—to stare at her. She was up on her chair, balancing shakily on the seat and slapping her mother's hands away.

'You imbecile!' she yelled. 'You flicking splat-brain!' She looked like she'd seen a mouse, or a rat even, for the hand that wasn't lashing out was holding her skirt flat against her legs as if she expected something to go scampering up her chair, and was getting ready to kick it away.

It wasn't a mouse, or a rat, though, running loose in our church. And it wasn't Jenna it was after.

DANZEL

I knew that creature of Gurnet's was bad news. Ever since he found the thing, and decided to take it home, I've been advising him, in all seriousness, to take it out to sea in a knotted bag and chuck it overboard.

Rabies . . . HIV . . . hepatitis . . . I've drummed home all the risks; but our Gurn was always stubborn. Even back when we were little, there was no telling the Gurn.

I thought I was seeing things, in church, this afternoon. I thought the teeny tot of cider I'd had after breakfast had been one tipple too many and had addled my perceptions. The thing was moving, fast, around and under chairs, avoiding people's feet like it had a sensor in its skull. It had grown—holy moley, how it had grown—but I recognized it all right, through a swift process of elimination (*not a cat, not a hen, not a cross between a hedgehog and a weasel, not a half-skinned rabbit with a sea urchin on its head, not a hairbrush on legs . . . that's Gurnet's creature, that is*).

Jenna was having hysterics, attracting all the attention. She'd clearly seen the beast too, but I was the only one keeping an eye on it as it lolloped and skidded along heading, not for its freedom via the open door, but for the very front of the church.

Briefly—just briefly—I looked back at Gurnet. He was sick-white and as tense as a bull that wants to charge, and rip things up, but isn't sure, yet, which direction to take. His eyes were darting up, down and all around, and Jenna's shrieks and shouts were bouncing right off him, like pins.

He caught my eye so I pointed down the aisle, mouthing '*Here, it's here!*' Only, in the seconds it took me to do all of that, the creature had moved on apace, and was at the platform, shinning up it like a monkey, with definite purpose, but no monkey-like merriment, and leaving a horrible trail, like snail slime, only wider.

The Truscotts and the Pascoes were nearest the front, their knees almost touching the platform. Old Mrs Pascoe was the first of them to spot the creature and to set up a clamour that put Jenna's performance to shame. Everyone turned, then, to see what this new commotion was all about.

The clergyman began backing away, and I for one don't blame the man. Gurnet's creature was heading right for him and, my friends, it was dribbling—salivating like a thing that hasn't eaten for several days and has just got a whiff of its dinner. I was three rows back, and I saw the drool quite clearly, hanging in strings from its whiskers.

The clergyman had nowhere to go. Nowhere to hide. He'd backed himself right up against the altar and was looking round, in vain, for an open door or window. He needed a miracle, that man, but wasn't getting one. A bit of human intervention would have done just as well, but that wasn't happening either. Everyone was too stunned—or just too old and slow—to go rushing, like good Samaritans, to his aid. Had any of us known him better, as a friend or a neighbour, someone might have risked it, but I wouldn't bet my next cup of cider on that being the case.

Then the creature stopped moving. It was scarily close to the clergyman by then—one pounce away from his kneecaps—when it froze, as if struck by an interesting thought.

Slowly, without taking his eyes off the creature's leaky snout, the clergyman reached for something behind him on the altar. He would have known what was there, he didn't need to look.

The creature was breathing, heavily. Not paralysed, I realized, or experiencing a change of heart, but psyching itself up for a serious onslaught.

The whole congregation had gone deathly quiet. We were holding our breaths . . . gripping each other's hands . . . watching the scene on the platform like it was something on the inter-telly.

Go for the candlestick, I willed the clergyman. *The big brass one. Or the Bible. Whack that mutant's brains out with both Testaments. That'll show it who's boss . . .*

Then three things happened at once:

'Don't hurt him!' Gurnet hollered (meaning *clergyman, don't harm a single hair on my creature's head*, not *creature, don't rip the nice man's innards out*).

The clergyman threw a vase full of daffodils.

The creature unfurled a pair of horrible leathery wings, flapped them once . . . twice . . . and rose into the air.

The sound of the vase, smashing to smithereens, was almost drowned by the din of people shrieking, and scraping back their chairs—determined, now, to get the merry hell out of there.

'Danzel, come on!' I felt my mother tugging at my elbow, but stayed where I was, fascinated. *He'll go for the candlestick, now*, I thought. *He'll whack that mutant clear across the platform and smack into the font.*

But the clergyman didn't budge. He didn't even raise his hands, to protect his face and eyes. He just stayed there, looked up; resigned, it seemed to me, to whatever was going to happen. It was as if hurling the vase had taken all of his strength. It was like he'd given up. And I swear on my life that, as Gurnet's creature hovered awhile, before aiming a hefty gob of spit at the clergyman's face, the sun that had been shining all morning through the stained-glass window, lighting up the four apostles in brilliant blues and golds and greens, went dim, and disappeared.

Oh well, it's a start.

But if Hopelessness is feeling triumphant, as it flaps out of the church, it needs to think again.

You don't have to be a genius, do you, to work out its game plan?

Hit those mortals where it hurts. Spit in the face of religion and let doubt spread, like a plague, through the congregation and out into the world.

Certainly, there is no hope left for the clergyman. Try though he will, to cling to his faith, it will falter, and weaken and eventually die. And everyone he meets will be affected by the apathy in him, to the extent that they, too, will begin to lose faith.

That is, if they have any faith to lose.

And here is where the game plan falters.

Hopelessness, you see, is way behind the times. Programmed, perhaps, to equate loss of hope, in its most devastating form, with the loss of religious belief, it has failed to take account of fundamental changes in the world.

It doesn't know, for a start, how close humankind came to extinction as a result of climate change, or how hard people the world over are working, now, to restore the ecological balance.

It has no inkling that, for millions and millions of mortals, hope has more to do, nowadays, with the here and now than with the great hereafter; with what they themselves can achieve, in the span of their own lifetimes, to preserve this planet for their children, their children's children, and all the children to come.

So many different faiths . . . such a hotch-potch and clash of beliefs. A catastrophic drop in oxygen levels is a great leveller, though. Everyone needs to breathe.

It is tragic, yes, and ironic, too, that it took The Attack to really galvanize the eco-movement; spurring spiritual leaders across the world to strive at last, and in the nick of time, for the common good of all.

But every cloud, they say, has a silver lining. So maybe the bigger the cloud . . .

So now hope, for most mortals, lies in the slow but steady regeneration of the world's oceans where life began, and where life-sustaining oxygen is formed.

The sea . . .

Watch Hopelessness go—out of the church and away. It almost collides with a tombstone, the big daft blob . . . then narrowly misses a tree. And the sea could be a blank blue wall for all the notice it takes of it. It doesn't even look that way, or so much as sniff the brine, as it flaps its way downhill.

Its thinking, right now, is no straighter than its flight path; its strategy too feeble to work.

Spitting on the clergyman will achieve diddly squat. He wasn't even an Eco-Christian but one of the old school.

Hopelessness needs a better plan.

GURNET

I keep telling myself it could have been worse. That Laurence could have taken a big bite out of that clergyman, or ripped him with his nails. He might even have killed the man, which would have been a worst case scenario, but he didn't. He only did a spitting, and that's not so very wicked. I've been spat at, more than once, by kids up at the school and it's not like they were beheaded for it, or even whipped.

The clergyman didn't say a word after he got spat on. He just stumbled across the platform to wash his face in the font and then back again, because there was no water in the font to do the washing with. His shoes, as he went, made a scrunching sound on bits of a vase he'd thrown at my Laurence, and he almost skidded on the daffodils that had spilled out all over the floor. I didn't like to see him stomping all over those flowers. He should have been more careful. He should never have thrown that vase in the first place.

Laurence had gone, by then. After doing the spit he flew, in an almost-straight line, down the aisle of the church, out the open door, and away. He didn't even look at me as he passed my row, and that saddened me a lot. I told myself it was because he was ashamed.

Jenna Rosdew got down from her chair, where she'd jumped, like the biggest scaredy cat, after seeing Laurence escape from under my coat. She was about to say something, I could tell, that would drop me and my Laurence right in the dung. Luckily everyone around us was making their own hubbub so no one noticed when I put my mouth right up to her hair and said: 'If you tell, they'll find out where we went on Hallowe'en. Then you'll be in trouble too, Jenna Rosdew. We all will.'

She shut her mouth after that, and made do with glaring.

Then I stared, in a meaningful way, at my Danzel, who was right near the front, and then across the aisle at my Dilly and they nodded back at me in ways that said they understood my look. My Maude wasn't in the church, so there was no need to stare at her.

Seven men went outside, telling the rest of us to stay put. Then they came back in and said it was safe for us to leave, so we did.

On the way down the hill, I heard things that made me feel very bad. Talk of guns, and dogs, and search parties. People had picked up rocks, and sticks, and were stepping along as if they were on a minefield, or expecting my Laurence to come swooping down at them any moment, the way seagulls do if you're outside the café or the tavern, eating something.

The clergyman had been taken away by the physician. And the Pascoes, who were coming down the hill behind me, were fretting, in big loud voices, because a bit of Laurence's spit had gone on old Mrs Pascoe's best coat.

I heard Jonah Pascoe call my Laurence an effing

monstrosity and I nearly turned round, then, to say scalding words to him. I wanted to tell Jonah Pascoe— to tell everyone who could hear me—that they weren't being fair. That Laurence can't help the way he looks and that, for all they knew, he had only done the spitting out of fear and surprise, because the clergyman had tried to brain him with a vase.

Spitting, I realized, might be Laurence's defence mechanism and, if this is the case, no one has the right to judge him or to blame him for something he was born to do. Even fish, which most people think of as dull creatures, can be vicious when they're threatened. A scorpion fish, for example, will stick a spine full of poison in you and a torpedo ray will stun you with a bad electric shock. Then there's the Moses sole which lives in the Red Sea and releases a venom, when it is scared, that is strong enough to freeze the jaw of a shark.

That clergyman got off lightly, if you ask me.

I went straight up to my bedroom as soon as we got home, and locked the door behind me. The sight of Laurence's empty cage made me feel like a wretched person, so I covered it up with my highwayman coat and then I lay down on my bed and stared out of the window.

All you can see from my window, when you lie upon the bed, is the sky and that is usually a good thing to look at, especially when it's dark. It wasn't dark at that moment though, so I had to close my eyes.

I heard my dad leave the house and go stomping down the alley, calling out to other men who were doing the same thing. I did not need to get up and look out of the window to know they were carrying guns. Mum did sandwiches at five. It was all she felt up to. Dad still wasn't back and Mum got very anxious in case he'd tripped over his own gun and shot himself in the foot. I couldn't eat my sandwich. I hadn't the heart.

Mum said she hoped the men would find the creature, wherever it had nested, or gone to ground, because it wouldn't do to have it at large, still, with the film people arriving soon. 'What if there's a whole flock of them out there?' she wondered. 'Or do I mean a litter? Or a swarm? What was it anyway, Gurny, could you tell? I've never clapped eyes on a hairy bird before, or one with a mouth. Never. It looked—what's the word—*prehistoric.*'

I went back to my bedroom. I thought I might try and go to sleep, to block out all the worry, but then Danzel and Dilly turned up.

'Any news?' I heard my mum ask them, as soon as she'd opened the door.

'No, Mrs Carthew,' I heard my Dilly answer. 'Not yet.'

My mum sent them upstairs and I let them into my bedroom. Danzel had cider, which he allowed me to share, thinking it would console me and make up for my loss, which it didn't.

'Gurn,' he said, 'if they find that creature, and do away with it, it will be the best thing all round. You couldn't have kept it here for ever, mate.'

'Dan's right,' Dilly added. 'We should have released it. We should have let it take its chances, like other wild things.'

'Laurence is not a wild thing,' I told her, in my sternest voice. 'He's special, and he's smart.'

Both of them doubted that very much. They didn't

say, but I could tell by their faces. 'Why did you take him to church, Gurnet?' my Dilly said. 'That was a really stupid thing to do.'

'Because he wanted to go,' I answered her. 'He asked me.'

'Oh right,' Danzel said. 'A talking mutant with a strong Christian faith. Of course. We should have known.'

They left then, to go and visit Maude.

'You should come with us,' my Dilly said, at the door. 'She's your friend too and she's going to be in big trouble, for missing Remembrance.'

'We all missed Remembrance, Dils,' Danzel said. 'Thanks to Gurnet's swamp devil, we none of us did much remembering today.'

After they had gone I lay back down on my bed and made myself look at the sky. Eventually it got dark. There were no stars, and no moon either, and I was glad about that because I thought it would give my Laurence a better chance of staying hidden, wherever he had gone.

When I heard the sound of fingers, going rappety-rap on the glass, I thought it was my Danzel, playing a joke on me. I thought he had fetched the long ladder that is kept in Fore Street, in case anyone needs rescuing from a fire in their house, and had climbed up it to give me a fright. Because he was lashed, and not thinking straight. Because sometimes he can be a total splat-brain.

Then: 'Let me in,' my Laurence called to me. 'Please, my Gary. Let me in.'

So, let's do a tally, shall we, of the damage done so far:

1. *A young mother has gone missing.*
2. *Mrs Carthew hasn't cleaned her house, or cooked a proper meal, since Christmas.*
3. *Maude Tremaine is refusing to step outside her front door.*
4. *Danzel Killick is drinking more cider than is sensible.*
5. *Jenna Rosdew has given up on Danzel, and is obsessed with the idea of a handsome young actor with sea-blue eyes and a dazzling smile.*
6. *Dilly Tonkin is pining . . . for her lost mother; for an imagined idyll at the old manor house; for something . . . anything . . . to make her feel alive.*
7. *Gurnet Carthew has grown fond—dangerously fond—of something that was never intended to be lovable.*
8. *A clergyman has been spat upon.*
9. *The demand for anti-depressants and old Mrs Tweedy's herbal tonics has risen significantly in Port Zannon over the last few months.*
10. *The daffodils are late this year. Very late.*

Teenagers, with their raging hormones and fragile self-esteems, make good targets for Hopelessness. So too, it seems, do bored housewives and exhausted mothers already at the end of their tethers.

It's not enough though, nowhere near enough, to set alarm bells ringing all around the kingdom, or send shivers down mankind's collective spine—and Hopelessness knows it. There has to be another way. Something, or someone, it can target so effectively and well that despair spreads like wildfire and hope is banished—not just from Port Zannon but all around the world.

What though? Or who?

'Talk to me, Gary,' it says. 'About the big wide world. I want knowledge, mate. I'm thirsty for it. Start NOW.'

DILLY

I was put in charge of cleaning the mermaids. With just hours to go before the ship carrying the American film crew was due to arrive and drop anchor Mum handed me a cloth, an apron, and a bucket of soapy water and told me to get on with it.

All over Port Zannon, people were busy with something or other: scrubbing their doorsteps, sweeping the cobbles, or removing tubs and hanging baskets from outside their homes, like we were told to do weeks ago because those things weren't around in olden times, when the wreckers were alive.

It was good to see so much activity, even though a lot of people were moaning about it, or looking so down in the mouth that you'd never have guessed that anyone amazing, or even all that important, was expected.

'I'll be here all day,' I grumbled to Mum. 'We should have done this last week.'

'Well, we're doing it now,' Mum said. 'And the sooner you stop moaning and start cleaning, the sooner you'll be finished.'

I put down the cloth. 'I'm fetching help,' I said. 'Otherwise I'll still be cleaning the flipping things when the ship arrives. And don't tell me we'll see it from here because it won't be the same. I want to be out there, with the others. Watching.'

'Go on then,' Mum sighed. 'But hurry . . . '

We've been caught on the hop, all of us. No one told us, exactly, when the film people were due to arrive and there's been nothing on the inter-telly until five o'clock this morning, when all our screens began bleeping at once and the announcement flashed up: *'All persons connected with the filming of Wreckers due in at Port Zannon today. Estimated time of arrival: 4p.m. GMT.'*

According to Danzel's brother's girlfriend no one living outside the port will have received that message, or any news at all, ever, about where *Wreckers* is being made. She says it's to stop crowds of gawpers descending on our beach to catch a glimpse of the Americans—Connor Blue in particular. She says it's to do with security.

I heard all this from Danzel, who stepped out of his house just as I was on my way to ask Jenna to help with the mermaids. I said news about the film was bound to have spread, though, surely? That it's up there on the international sites, for anyone to see, that Connor Blue is to star in *Wreckers* and has been looking forward, very much, to setting foot on English soil.

Dan said how did I know it was for anyone to see? How did I *know* that the authorities weren't blocking the rest of the kingdom from accessing Connor Blue's sites, and every other site to do with the making of *Wreckers*?

I told him he had more cider in his bloodstream than actual blood and was talking a load of rubbish.

'Oh Dilly, Dilly, Dilso . . . ' he replied. 'You are so . . . naive. Who do you think decides, nowadays, who sees

168

what on the inter-telly? A screen-fairy? A wise old bearded telly-god sitting on a cloud?'

And while we were on the subject, he added, it was odd—really odd, wasn't it?—that there has been nothing on the inter-telly about Laurence (only, he didn't say 'Laurence', he said 'Gurnet's pig-ugly mutant') particularly as it has yet to be captured, killed, and strung from a pole as a warning to any other mutants that might be lurking in the vicinity, or making their way inland.

'You'd think,' he said, 'that they would have posted a description, at the very least, so that folk would know what to watch out for. And a contact site for anyone who sees the thing—or gets spat on, out of the blue—to post a warning on.'

I told him that the authorities probably didn't want to start a panic, what with the Americans arriving and all. And I told him that no one outside of Port Zannon was going to see Laurence now anyway, or be spat on, because Laurence was safely back with Gurnet. I knew this, I said, because I'd been round and seen it—him— for myself. 'He was asleep,' I said. 'Laurence, I mean. He looked very well, all things considered. In fact I think he might have grown some more.'

'Oh for crying out loud . . . ' Danzel raised his eyes to the heavens. 'That is seriously bad news . . . ' And off he went, heading for a morning's work up at the farm, even though today is a Saturday and the Americans were due.

'He's coming!' Jenna said to me, grabbing both my hands and making me jump up and down with her, the way we used to do when we were little girls and looking forward to our birthday parties, or ice creams after tea. 'I can't believe he's really, really coming. That he'll be here tonight . . . right here, breathing the same air as me, seeing the same things, *maybe even drinking a milk-shot from a cup I've drunk out of . . .* '

'You need to calm down,' I said to her. 'What if he brings a sweetheart with him?'

'He won't,' she replied. 'Why would he? He's not here on vacation, Dilly. He's here to work. He won't want the distraction.'

She was wearing a new dress; low-necked and so very, very pink that, had it been a milk-shot, my mum would have added more cream, to tone it down a bit.

'But isn't that exactly what you're planning to do?' I said. 'Distract him, I mean?'

She pouted, and then she laughed. It was nice to hear her laugh. 'That's different,' she said. '*I'm* different. He'll see me as a novelty. A novelty and a challenge.'

She sounded very sure.

'Come on,' I said. 'We've got about two hundred mermaids to clean. Let's fetch Maude. She shouldn't be indoors, not today, and she's always loved the mermaids . . . '

GURNET

All this stupid fuss. All this rushing around and turning everything upside down for strangers—for *foreigners*. It's doing my head in. It's making my Laurence uneasy. He's pacing the floor of his cage—round and round in circles he's going, wringing his hands until they squeak. A minute ago he pushed his water over and I had to tell him off.

'Let. Me. Out,' he said, shaking one of his fists at me. 'Let me out, Gary.'

'No chance,' I told him. 'You've blotted your copybook, mate. You did yourself no favours, gobbing at that clergyman.'

When that ship arrives, bringing all those film people, I'm staying put. I'm staying right here with my door locked and I won't answer it for anyone. Mum says there's to be fireworks later, and a bonfire on the beach. She says she's looking forward to it, which is a miracle, of sorts. There'll be an official from the Council there, as well as all those film people, and it will be a million times worse than when the summer visitors come because the summer visitors just swim, and eat ice cream, and dig holes in the sand. They don't make us shift plants and stuff from outside our houses, or expect us to treat them like royalty.

I've checked that Connor Blue out on the inter-telly. He looks a right Pretty Nancy, with his long hair and his eye enhancers (no human being has eyes that colour without enhancers). I don't like the cut of that Connor Blue. He looks like someone I would quite like my Laurence to spit on.

DANZEL

This time, when I heard the rumble, I knew, straighta-way, what it was. And as it came at me, over the brow of the hill, I stepped out and waved both my arms.

'Afternoon all,' I said, as the van squealed to a halt, and one of the passengers opened a door. 'And welcome to Port Zannon.' I'd had a cider, during my tea break, so was feeling good and cheery. Confident, like the world really was my oyster and I was about to find a pearl.

'Hi there,' said the stranger who had opened the door. 'Can we offer you a ride?'

Can fish breathe underwater? Can a seagull eat a sandwich, crusts and all?

The stranger was an American, about the same age as my dad but with more hair and better teeth. Sitting next to him was Connor Blue—I recognized him straight off.

I opened my mouth and then closed it again, overwhelmed.

'A lift, young boy,' said the driver (one of the council-lors who came to the port a few months ago, for lunch— I recognized him as well). 'Do you want a lift, in the car, the rest of the way to the port?' He sounded cranky, like it hadn't been his idea to stop . . . like he would sooner have driven right over my boots, and make road-jam of my toes, than have me step into the big green van with its clean insides and Very Important Passengers.

I got in. Never mind the state of my boots (farms are mucky places—what can I say?). I got into that van, beside the good-looking stranger and the even better-looking movie star, and I told myself: *Young boy: you are on your way UP . . .*

'Trent, ' said the man next to me, turning, slightly, so that he could shake my hand. 'I'm Trent, the researcher for *Wreckers*. And this is Connor Blue, our leading man.'

My friends, I don't do shy. I get along like a blazing barn with everyone I meet: always a smile and a bright remark—that's me. So maybe it was being in such a confined and unfamiliar space (a space that smelt fleshy, the way our parlour does when the whole family's in it and it's too cold to open a window) that made me come over all gormless; or maybe it was being so close, all of a sudden, to living, breathing people from overseas that completely spun me out. But, whatever the reason, I had nothing, at that moment, to say. I couldn't remember my own name, for crying out loud . . .

Connor Blue filled the silence before it got too weird. He said he'd been moved to tears by the beauty of the Cornish countryside. He had made a special request, he said, to be driven from Falmouth to Port Zannon, so that he could absorb, and appreciate, all there was to see along the way. As an Eco-Christian, he said, he wouldn't normally travel in a car but since this van was powered by bio-diesel he reckoned that was all right. He told me I was blessed to have been born and raised in such an unsullied part of the world. 'Although I'm guessing you won't agree,' he said. 'I'm guessing you kids reckon it's the pits around here—dead boring, nothing going on, am I right?'

It was a direct question. It needed an answer.

'It's not all boring,' I heard myself say. 'We have our moments.'

We were driving past the church. The motion was making me feel odd: dizzy and a little bit sick, like part of me had been left behind on the road and was running to catch up. Still, I felt the need to say something—something really impressive—while I still had the chance.

'See that church?' I asked, and they turned, obediently, to look—the two Americans, and the driver, each of them interested now, if only mildly, in what I might be about to say.

'I've a friend in the port,' I continued. 'Gurnet—Gary—Carthew. He has a creature—a pet—only we don't know what it is.'

Small pause, then, for dramatic effect (oh, I can play an audience all right, just as well as Connor Blue, or any other big shot from the Hollywood hills).

'Go on,' said the driver. I caught him looking at me in the van's mirror—a sharp, quick, glance, which puzzled me. The researcher, Trent, was sitting up straighter, his right thigh tense against my left leg, like he was bracing himself for a crash.

Was I that good a storyteller, I wondered, or were these people just easily impressed? It didn't matter. I was away . . .

'Ugly isn't the word,' I said, in my own good time. 'Ugly doesn't even begin to cover it. This creature, my friends, is . . . ' I paused again, 'diabolical.'

A good word, diabolical, and not one I'd considered before, in relation to Gurnet's swamp monster.

'What do you mean, diabolical?' The researcher's voice was odd, like he was having trouble controlling it. It made me realize the seriousness of what I was saying. I was dropping friend-Gurnet in the dung, right smack in the dung and from a terrible height. But I couldn't stop. I'd gone too far.

'It got loose in the church,' I said. 'During Remembrance. It attacked the clergyman—spat in his face.'

'Yeuugh,' Connor Blue exclaimed. 'How gross is that? And during Remembrance you say? That really sucks . . . ' He had bent forward, the better to look at me—to give me his full attention. His eyes were so blue they embarrassed me.

The driver, I realized, had slowed the van right down, to give me time, I guessed, to finish my tale. He was staring straight ahead, not saying a word, but I could tell, from the set of his shoulders and from the way his hands were gripping the wheel that what I'd said had shocked him, deeply.

'What happened?' the researcher asked me. 'To the creature?'

The driver shot me a look. *Be careful,* said the look. *Be very careful indeed how you answer that question.*

Beside me, the researcher's whole body had gone rigid and it dawned on me that I, myself, might well end up in the deepest dung there is, for scaring these Americans half to death. What if they decided to turn right around, without so much as a 'hey, great little port you have here' and head back across the Atlantic? All because of me and my big mouth? What then?

No wonder the driver was giving me looks.

'It flew away,' I answered, quickly. 'Went AWOL. Disappeared. It'll be dead by now—bound to be. The nights are pretty chilly here still, and there are some seriously feral cats and things out there on the moors.'

I was gabbling. Protesting too much. Backtracking, to save my hide as well as old Gurnet's. I didn't think I'd get away with it. Gurnet 'has' a creature, I'd said. 'Has', not 'had'. Present tense, not past. *Poor continuity*, I berated myself. *Bad acting, Danzo.*

But: 'He's right,' the driver announced. 'The thing will have come to grief by now. Definitely.'

And he looked directly at me again, in the van's mirror. *That's enough, young boy,* his eyes said to mine. *That's more than enough from you.* So I kept quiet after that, and so did Trent-the-researcher, although Connor Blue was still wondering aloud, as the van pulled up outside The Crazy Mermaid, what kind of a bird or bat, native to English shores, might be our mystery spitter.

JENNA

In my mind—my imagination—it had been the perfect meeting. I'd pictured it, precisely, over and over again . . . the time, the place, the weather . . . I even knew which pants I'd have on (not that he'd be seeing them. Yet).

It would, I'd decided, be late in the evening—really late, with everyone but him and me gone to their beds. I would be walking along the beach (in moonlight, of course, and wearing my new pink dress) and he would notice me from the quay and be enchanted.

I would stop walking, then, and stand very still, just gazing at him, across the sand, while the waves crashed behind me and a breeze lifted my hair and the hem of my pink dress in a very teasing way. And I would know, by the way he looked back at me, that this was IT. Not love at first sight, because that only happens in fairy tales, but the beginning of something which, if I played all my cards right, could grow to be amazing.

I would turn, then, and walk slowly away, feeling his eyes on the back of my dress, like searchlights.

'Fools rush in where angels fear to tread.' That's what it says in *Men: How to Catch and Keep One*. And I am nobody's fool. I must have imagined my first encounter with Connor Blue more than a hundred times and every time it's seemed so real, and given me such a tingle, that it had come to seem inevitable that this is how it would actually be.

Never once, let me tell you, did my fantasy involve standing on a wobbly stool at The Crazy Mermaid, with an apron over my new dress, a fishy-smelling cloth in my hands, and a tin mermaid, as thin as a wafer, bouncing around on its string and avoiding all my attempts to catch and clean it like it was properly alive and deliberately doing my head in.

'Dilly Tonkin,' I was yelling, 'if we're not done cleaning these flicking things in half an hour I'm off. I haven't oatmealed my face yet today, or shaved my legs, and if that flicking ship comes in before . . . '

'Oh.'

It was Maude who'd said that. I'm surprised I heard her—that 'oh' was like a little drop of rain falling compared to my torrent of total IDIOCY. But thank the stars I did hear her before finishing my sentence, because it had been on the tip of my stupid tongue to say ' . . . before I've finished beautifying myself for that sex-god Connor Blue', and there would have been no recovering from that. Ever.

For THERE HE WAS. Connor Blue. Right there on the threshold of The Crazy Mermaid, framed against the sea and the sky, and so meltingly gorgeous—so beautifully REAL—that I went as wobbly as my stool and almost fainted dead away.

There were two other men with him—that pervy councillor for one—but I paid them no mind. I just gazed and gazed at Connor Blue, clutching my fishy-smelling cloth to my heart and thinking: *Oh. My. Stars . . . This isn't at all how I wanted it to be. But notice me anyway, Connor, go on, go on. Not just to say hello to, but really, really, really . . .*

'Hi,' Connor Blue said as he stepped into our café . . . our space . . . our lives.

Dilly was staring just as hard as I was, her mouth a googly 'O' of surprise and the mermaid she'd been washing clenched so tight in one hand it looked like she was killing it. Maude, the sap, was clearly wishing, with all her might and main, that, on this day of all days, she had stayed in her parlour, with the curtains drawn. Her hair was like a waterfall, all over the flicking place, and she looked more than usually terrified.

Look at me, I willed Connor Blue. *I've been waiting for you for ever. Just look and you'll understand. That I'm yours for life . . . for all eternity . . . for just one night, if you want. Only look. Look at me before I explode, or cry, or go rushing in where angels fear to tread.*

But he was looking straight at Maude.

'Neat apron,' he said, with a scamp's wink.

Maude glanced down at herself, like she'd forgotten what she had on. Then she looked up again, blushing like a rose. She was standing very still, on her rickety stool, and her hands were clasped around her cloth like she was about to perform some holy ritual with the thing.

The apron she was wearing belongs to Dilly's dad. Dilly had offered it to me—'It's extra large,' she'd said, 'it'll protect more of your dress,' and I'd told her to get lost. I'd told her I'd sooner cover my dress with a pinny made of lavvy paper than sport a stupid slogan on my chest, for any old passer by to have a snigger at.

'Catch of the Day' . . . Since when was that even funny?

The irony is, it was funny on Maude but for all the wrong reasons. It had made Dilly and me laugh, anyway, when she put that apron on because a) it swamped her and b) you don't think of Maude in a raunchy way, like she'd be a 'good catch' one day for some boy or other. She's too timid for all of that; too far back in her own shell.

Don't look at her. Look at ME . . . I wanted to screech like a she-witch, but I didn't. I wanted to tear off my own apron, leap from my stool, and shout: 'Hey, Connor! Never mind what's written on mopey-Maude's chest, feast your eyes on MY thingies,' but I didn't do that either.

I just watched the way Connor Blue's face went, as he continued to gaze at Maude. How his eyes softened (Oh. My. Stars. How blue are those eyes . . . ?) and his whole expression became gentle and fond.

He opened his mouth to say something, only Dilly's mum came rushing out from the kitchen then, offering welcomes, and milk-shots, and apologies for the chaos; for not being better organized.

'Hey, don't worry,' Connor Blue told her in his gorgeous, gorgeous voice. 'I'm early—ahead of the game.' He was shaking her hand, all very polite, but his whole body, his whole *being*, was slanted, still, towards Maude (off the stool now, the mope, and shedding the stupid apron) and he had an air of delight and surprise about him like he'd stumbled into a cave and found treasure.

And I knew, then—with a sad, sick, spiralling in the pit of my stomach—that my moment hadn't just passed, it had been blown clean out of the water.

DANZEL

I was kicking myself. Having regrets. I was feeling so bad about mouthing off in the van that by the time the bonfire had been lit, down on the beach, and the councillor had finished his Big Speech of Welcome, I was four sheets to the wind, on as many cups of cider, and having a quiet sit down (it would have been a lie-down, but what can I say? I was in company; there were appearances to keep up).

Little Sheila came over, wanting to perch on my knee. I held out my arms, glad to see her; full of pity for the little scrap because there's still no news of Nance.

'You smell funny,' she accused, before spinning on her heels and running off, back to her dad.

The whole of Port Zannon had turned out to party—at least that's what it looked like to me, until Jenna and Dilly came and plonked down either side of me, on the bit of old blanket I'd spread out on the sand, and I realized we were two people short of a gang.

Maude had gone home. Gurnet hadn't been seen all day.

'I'll talk to Maudie,' I said, attempting to get up. 'She shouldn't miss the fireworks. I'll talk her round.' I said nothing about Gurn, and hoped Dilly wouldn't either.

'Forget it.' Jenna tugged my arm, hard. 'Maude doesn't care about the fireworks. It was her choice not to come. Leave her alone.'

She tugged at me again, even harder this time, so that I stumbled and fell, all of a sprawl, right on top of her.

'Jen-Jen,' I said, removing my nose from her cleavage, 'I didn't think you cared.'

'I don't, splat-brain,' she answered, pushing me away, quicker than I could move. 'And you stink of cider. You want to watch out.'

'I'm a bad boy,' I agreed, mournfully. 'A bad boy and a rotten friend.'

I was maudlin, I'll admit it. The cider does that to you sometimes and, to be honest, I wasn't coping well with having the Hollywood contingent on our little bit of shore.

Adorable. That's the word I kept hearing as they milled around my blanket and away towards the fire. Everything about Port Zannon was utterly adorable. Except the cold. They were having trouble adoring that; huddling as close as they could to the bonfire as darkness fell and sending their man with a dinghy out to their ship for warmer things to wear.

'Fetch my muffler, will you?' I heard one of the women call out. Muffler. It sounded like something you'd use to smother an enemy.

'Where's Trent?' someone else shouted.

'Exploring,' came the reply. 'He took the cliff path out of the harbour, about two hours ago.'

'Is he crazy? When's he coming back? There are no lights up there. And it's so *cold*.'

'Oh, he'll be OK. He took his torch, and even a sleep bag. He wants to watch for badgers. You know old Trent . . .'

Their voices, my friends, are weird. Not just twangy, like in the movies, but . . . I don't know . . . happy and loud and so self-assured that I couldn't help thinking what a cartload of mopes we English must seem to them.

It was like they—the Americans—had come down from another planet, to colonize our port, because we're all too uptight and miserable to deserve such a pretty piece of the planet. Even their ship was looking out of this world; as big as a town house (too big, anyway, to come all the way into the harbour) and ablaze with coloured lights.

Connor Blue had been given a chair on the sand. They all had, but his was the biggest and, like a king, he was holding court: chatting to the locals as they approached him, one by one, and accepting bits of barbecued mackerel like they were the best thing he'd ever tasted, which you can bet your life they weren't.

'Do you think one of those might be his sweetheart?' Dilly wondered, peering at some youngish women who were sticking close by Connor's chair.

'No,' said Jenna, quickly. 'Two of them are actresses, that one in blue looks like a make-up artist to me and the others are just gofers, I reckon.'

'Just whats?'

'Gofers. They go for things, to keep the star happy.'

'What kinds of things?'

'Well, I don't know, Dilly. Cold beers, I suppose. Or hot women. Whatever the star wants.'

'That doesn't sound like a very nice . . . Eek, Jen. He's *looking* at us.' Dilly giggled—a rare thing for her and unsettling to hear. 'Should we wave to him or what?'

'No, ignore the arrogant flick-face. Don't give him the satisfaction.'

'*What?*' Again the silly giggle. 'He's not arrogant, Jen. He was lovely in the café, and ever so sweet to Maude.'

'Hah!'

I rose to my feet then, a touch unsteadily, and looked around for somewhere else to be. I wasn't keen on moving, didn't want anything to eat, and had no intention of dazzling any of those American women with my knock-out charm and biting wit until I was no longer quite so lashed. But Dilly's giggles were grating on my brain. I needed to get away. I made up my mind to head home.

It's typical, if a little quick, for Jenna to have changed her mind about the wonderful Connor Blue. He must have snubbed her, I decided, as I set off up the beach. That would have done it. But what was Dilly's nonsense all about? I couldn't help hoping that she, of all people, wasn't falling for old Blue Eyes. To my surprise, as I staggered a bit over a dip in the sand, I realized I might be just a tiny bit jealous.

'Hey, Danzel?' It was my brother, Michael, shouting after me, for the whole beach to hear. 'Where are you going?'

I cringed. The Americans would think I was a light-weight, leaving the party so early.

'Home,' I yelled back. 'To fetch a muffler.'

There were candles burning in jars, all along the quay, and a little bit of a moon to light my way along Fore

Street. It felt odd being the only person around—the only local not whooping it up on the beach, or worshipping at the feet of King Connor. Turning into Squeeze Belly Alley I stopped pretending to be able to walk straight. I even hummed a cidery tune as I lurched from left to right, playing pat-a-cake with the walls.

Gurnet's bedroom was in darkness, as usual, but his window was open—to let a bit of creature-stink out, I expect. I'd spotted his mum down on the beach and his dad, I knew, was out at sea, hoping for a bumper catch to impress, and feed, the Americans.

I was feeling bad, still, about old Gurn. I thought about calling up to him, or going round to his front door. Then I thought, *No. Waste of time. He'll be out with his old man—bound to be.*

My friends, I have never known violence, except through the media of film. A gang of inlanders tried it on, once, up at the school, but I talked them round. We are friends now. I am everybody's friend. Never in my life have I had to ward off a kick or a punch, and I have yet to feel the sting of a whip, despite the fact that, when it comes to the laws on drinking, I'm sailing pretty close to the wind.

Here in Port Zannon, the violent crime rate is a big round zero. Of course it is. Why would you attack a neighbour? It would be like hurting family. Unthinkable. Even summer visitors treat us, and each other, with respect. Not, I suspect, because they genuinely love all humanity but because troublemakers lose their right to a holiday, and never get it back.

So I had no fear of anything, or anyone, as I continued

along Squeeze Belly Alley, bouncing myself from wall to wall, like a little kid. Nor did I hear footsteps until they were right up behind me, hard on my heels in the dark.

I half turned, then, expecting . . . I don't know . . . My brother? My father? Family, anyway, or a friend. Someone who would say, 'Hey, Dan, I'm heading home too,' or 'Aw, come on, Dan, come back to the beach. The fireworks are about to start.'

I was relaxed, anyhow; a big smile on my face, a greeting on the tip of my tongue, when my shoulder collided with the other person's chest so that I staggered, and almost fell. *Hey*, I thought, staring dizzily at the ground, expecting, any second, to make contact with it. *Michael? Dad? What are you—?*

Even while being hauled upright, and spun back round, I assumed that this person was merely setting me on my feet. I reckoned that, if it wasn't my own dad, or my own brother, handling me more roughly than I appreciated (but knew I deserved) it would be Dilly's dad, or Maude's dad, or even Gurnet's dad, returned early from fishing and giving the party a miss. I thought that, at worst, I was going to get an ear-bashing for being so obviously lashed: a lecture, with no holds barred, from a man who has known me since cradlehood and has my best interests at heart.

Only when a man's arm slammed up against my windpipe, and a man's hand clamped over my mouth, gagging me . . . hurting me . . . forcing my own teeth to bite my own tongue . . . only then did I realize, with no small shock, that this wasn't anyone who knew me, or cared. That this was what violence felt like. The real deal.

DILLY

The fireworks took my breath away. I'd never seen anything so lovely. When my eyes filled with tears I didn't bother hiding them and before long I was sniffing and snuffling like a baby with a cold.

'What are you blubbing for?' Jenna gave me a shove. 'What's got into you?' I couldn't explain. Not then. Not to her. I couldn't find the words to say how I was feeling: about the day, about Danzel being an idiot, about the excitement of the party that was tinged all through with sadness because I didn't feel a part of it. Not completely, the way I thought I should.

Maybe I'm just not used to crowds. Or maybe it's like my grandpa Tonkin says: I'm not a shaker, or a stirrer, or a crazy party animal. I'm one of life's observers. A girl who sits quietly, watching the world go by. Daffodil among the lemons.

Jenna (the biggest shaker and stirrer I know, usually, and unquestionably a party animal) was sitting quietly too, and scowling at her own feet. She didn't even 'ooh' and 'ahh' when the American flag lit up the night sky and then rained down on the sea, red, white, and blue. She was still smarting, I could tell, over the way Connor Blue had as good as ignored her, earlier. He had ignored

188

me too—apart from saying hello—but, then, I haven't spent the past three months wondering which pants to wear in honour of his arrival.

'Don't take it out on Maude,' I said, as the sky bloomed with daisies; silver-white petals exploding out of golden centres; new ones unfurling as the old ones trailed away. 'Don't be nasty, next time you see her, just because Connor Blue paid more attention to her than he did to you.'

'Shut up, Dilly,' Jen snapped back. 'You don't know what you're talking about. And, anyway, you're hooked on him too. You were giggling like an idiot earlier, when you thought he was eyeing us up.'

It's true. I was. But I'm not hooked on Connor Blue. He's certainly handsome (even more, in real life, than on the inter-telly) but too awesome . . . too *separate*, some-how . . . for me to want to do more than look at him. Safely. From a distance. I don't know why I went all giggly when he happened to glance our way. Maybe I did it to seem normal—an ordinary girl having a wonderful time. Or maybe . . . it's possible . . . I was trying to irritate Dan.

'Sounds like someone over there wants him the most,' I said, distracted by a woman's squeal.

'Who?' Jenna turned, sharply, her gaze following mine as I peered towards the place where Connor Blue was sitting surrounded by other film people who, up until that moment, had all been watching the sky, but were watching something else now—an even bigger spectacle.

'Oh my God. Tell me I'm dreaming.'

Above us, the one word 'WELCOME' wrote itself in

gigantic spurts and sparkles, illuminating the beach and everyone on it.

'Afraid not,' I said, a shudder of sympathy going all the way through me. 'I'm afraid this is really happening!' And the two of us watched, appalled, as Jenna's mum, dressed in a silver sequinned tail and not much else, hopped and flopped the last couple of feet to Connor Blue's chair, and launched herself onto his lap.

He knows something. The man with his arm around Danzel Killick's throat knows a very great deal about the creature that spat in the clergyman's face. Not just that it is ugly, with at least one disgusting habit, but that it is truly dangerous.

How does he know this? How can he know who or what this creature is when there is no known record of its existence and no one living who could possibly be aware that Pandora's box has been hidden, for centuries, in a house above Port Zannon, with the worst of all evils inside it, escaping bit by bit?

It is impossible. Unimaginable.

Surely?

'Tell me again,' the man murmurs in Danzel's ear. 'The name of the boy with the odd-looking pet. And then show me where he lives.'

Young Danzel is stricken, his eyes huge above the hand that covers his mouth.

He makes a muffled sound. 'Mneeuuur,' he goes, meaning: 'Move your hand, sir. How can I answer if you don't move your hand?'

'No screaming,' the man tells him. 'You're not a sissy are you? No, of course not. Just a hopeless little drunk . . . ' And he takes his hand from the boy's mouth, wipes his palm against the seat of his own trousers, and then pats the boy's backside.

That pat—the casual intimacy of it—disturbs young Danzel more than anything. He slumps backwards against the alley wall, partly for support as he waits for his legs to stop trembling, but mostly to cover his rear.

'It's you,' he breathes, as the man leans over him.

'Yes, young boy,' the councillor replies. 'It's me. And I'm waiting for some answers.'

Danzel nods, and takes a deep breath. 'Gary Carthew,' he says, his voice breaking. 'It's Gary Carthew's pet. At least it was. You said yourself, sir . . . in the van . . . it'll be dead by now. Bound to be. And Gurnet—Gary—won't be home. There'll be nobody there. No one . . . ' He glances, automatically and without thinking, up at Gurnet's open window.

The councillor notices. He doesn't miss a trick, this man. 'And that's Gary's house, is it?' he says, after a quick look for himself. 'And is that his bedroom? Is that where he keeps his "pet"? It is, isn't it? And it didn't go AWOL did it, after escaping from the church? It's up there now. Am I right?'

'No,' Danzel says. 'I mean . . . '

The councillor has raised one hand; raised it and paused, as if wondering whether to strike Danzel Killick or stroke his cheek. There is no one around, no one to bear witness. He could do anything he wants to this young boy—anything at all—and he'll do whatever it takes to get to the creature that spat in the eyes of the clergyman. He stands to gain, you see, financially and for life. Not from the authorities, or even from the king, but from enemies abroad—big fish who have found out about the existence of Hopelessness and are desperate to get hold of it.

For what a powerful weapon Hopelessness would be in the right—or, rather, the wrong—hands. Imagine it cloned! Imagine it unleashed, under the strictest of controls, to subdue whole communities . . . whole continents, even.

'Well?' the councillor snaps. 'Is it up there or not?'

'Yes,' Danzel admits, mesmerized by the raised hand. 'It is.'

GURNET

I heard the knocking at my front door but didn't answer it. I thought it would be Danzel, or Dilly, or both of them together, come to winkle me out of my room for the party on the beach. It made me scowl, that knocking. Those two, I told my Laurence, should know by now that when I say I'm having none of something I mean it.

As well as the knocking, which went on for a very long time, I could hear fireworks ripping up the sky. They weren't happening where I could watch them properly (which was fine, I didn't care) but from where I lay, I could see a big reflected glow, interfering with the night.

I'd covered Laurence's cage with my highwayman coat. It's called sensory deprivation and I thought it would calm him down. I also needed a break, for a while, from having to watch him cry. It wasn't proper crying, I can tell you that for certain. He'd been acting up all afternoon; turning on the waterworks so I would have compassion and let him out. I had no intention of doing that thing but even sham tears, if they carry on for long enough, are hard to ignore. They would have got to me, eventually, and then I would have been sunk.

'Take me!' he'd hollered, as I threw the coat over him.

'To the party on the beach. Take me!'

'On your bike,' I'd told him. 'You've broken my trust.'

To make up for doing what I did with the coat, and to show that I still cared, I'd been teaching Laurence some more about the ways of the world. It's something I started doing after he spat in the clergyman's face, so that he will understand about places, and people, and about the importance of behaving properly (by which I mean, in a civilized way) even when you're frightened, or feeling peculiar, or people are doing your head in. Not that I'm planning any more outings for that pet of mine. I've learned my lesson there. But it doesn't hurt to educate him, and I like it that he listens to me and really seems to understand.

Laurence enjoys it best when I talk about the sea, which I do a lot because it is the thing I know most about.

'More,' he says. 'More about the sea please, Gary.'

I like it, very much, that my Laurence calls me Gary.

When the fireworks started, and the knocking came at the door, I was talking about how everyone on this planet would be dead or dying by now if we hadn't stopped pouring filth into the atmosphere and mucking up the oceans like it didn't matter, and would make no difference to anyone in the long run (or the short run as it turned out). I was trying to explain things the way my dad explained things to me when I was about nine.

'Laurence,' I was saying, 'it's like this, mate: when we say "planet Earth" it gives a false impression. We ought to be saying "planet sea" because there's more sea than there is dry land and more important forms of life in the ocean than ever grew feet and walked. Things like

194

plankton which are smaller than dots but do important jobs, like producing oxygen, which is the stuff we all breathe.'

I kept right on talking, all through the annoyance of the knocking, and carried on after it stopped:

'The plankton were dying,' I told Laurence. 'The seas were too warm and too gunky for them, because humans were treating the world like a dustbin and a lav. The corals were dying too and so were all the fish. The sea is still warmer than it ought to be, and some things are still pretty sick, but it hasn't got any worse because everyone in the whole world is working hard to make things better.'

The fireworks grew louder. They were so loud, those things, that I didn't hear the fire ladder go clunk against our house, or the clump of someone's feet coming up the rungs.

'You may think,' I told Laurence, 'that The Attack was the worst thing that could ever happen to people, but it wasn't. It would be worse, wouldn't it—a lot worse— if no oxygen came out of the sea and we all stopped breathing. But you're not to worry, mate, because Marine Biologists—that's what the important specialists are called—are doing a good job, nowadays, at keeping the oxygen coming. They are clever people those Marine Biologists—almost as clever as plankton—and they are bringing more hope to the world with every month that—'

I stopped. I stared. I rubbed my eyes. A shape—a man's shape—was at my window, about to come right in. The window was open, because Laurence prefers it that way now that spring is here. He says the sea air does him good. I would have closed that window when the fireworks started but, because of feeling mean about the coat, I hadn't. Seeing the man-shape there made me wish I had followed my own inclination instead of doing my pet a little kindness.

It is a human response, as well as the instinct of a lot of sea creatures, to scrunch up small whenever danger threatens. So that is what I did when I saw the looming man. I drew my legs up, close to my chest, hugged my knees, and put my head down low. Peering over my kneecaps felt odd. They were like two knobbly hills, and my eyes felt like creatures coming out over the top.

The walls of my room are black, and I had no candles burning so the man did not see me as he let himself in. He didn't even turn towards the headboard of my bed, which is where I was huddled, right up in the corner. My eyes saw him though, in the firework-glow from the sky, as he stepped onto the end of my bed like it wasn't someone's private sleeping place at all but a public right of way.

The first thing I noticed was he was wearing sunglasses, even though it was night. Then I saw he had big thick gloves on as well, even though it wasn't cold. These two facts gave me so much food for thought that I didn't notice other more important things about him, like the fact that he had a net slung over one arm, along with some sacking and a rope.

'More,' I heard my Laurence say, his voice muffled by my coat. 'More about the people bringing hope to the world. More please.'

I heard the man let out his breath. Then I heard a click as he switched on a torch and directed the beam at Laurence's cage.

'Hey,' said Laurence, from under my coat. 'I can feel that, mate. Switch it off.'

My bed creaked as the man stepped off it. Outside, more fireworks ripped up the sky and, in the light they made I saw the man move forward, with definite purpose and intent. That he was a predator, with my Laurence as his prey, was immediately clear to me.

My fishing knife was on my bedside table, beside my candlestick and my drink of water. I'd taken it from the pocket of my highwayman coat, before throwing the coat over Laurence's cage. If I hadn't, it might have fallen through the chicken wire and bashed my Laurence on the head. Or Laurence might have opened it up and done cuts to his hands. I felt proud as I reached for my knife, that I had been so careful about health and safety where my pet was concerned. It made up for not closing the window.

A Moses sole releases venom. A torpedo ray will do a nasty electric shock. I am neither of those things, but I know how to use a knife. Gutting is what I do best, and my slicing is always clean.

DANZEL

I went home. I had no choice. That councillor had me over a barrel. *Go home, young boy,* he told me. *Go home and forget you ever saw or spoke to me tonight. Because should you happen to forget, and mention it to someone . . .*

I didn't need it spelling out. I know a veiled threat when I hear one. But he spelt it out anyway, just to make me squirm.

'Such harsh penalties we have now,' he said, managing to make 'harsh penalties' sound like 'lovely treats' although they're clearly anything but. *'For under-age drinkers, I mean. I would hate to have to inflict them on one such as your-self . . . a boy with so much promise . . . a boy who could have any job he wanted—a career at the Council Office in Bodmin, even—once he leaves the school . . .'*

I was feeling sick by the time I got home, and dirty too, inside and out. I took a shower, swallowing water as it needled me in the face—gulping the stuff, before it got too hot, like it could cleanse me through and through. Then I put fresh clothes on and sat for a while, collecting my thoughts.

He scared me . . . he hurt me . . . he might hurt me some more . . . I betrayed my best friend . . . he hurt me . . . he scared me . . .

They were like cinders, or sand flies, those thoughts; so troublesome it was hard to keep still while they settled. And the worst thought of all—the one that bothered me the most—was this: *Did Gurnet go fishing or not?* That thought, my friends, simply would not go away. I could have tried to block it out. I could have helped myself to more cider and kept on quaffing until it left me alone.

Instead, I stood up, found my boots, and followed that thought out the door. All along my street I followed it, round the corner, back down Squeeze Belly Alley—and smack into the fire ladder where it rested, in the dark, against the side of Gurnet's house.

'Gurn!' I called up (although it came out more croak than yell). 'Hey, Gurn, are you there?'

I could feel my heart pumping. I could feel all the water I'd drunk swilling around in my gut. Gurnet's bedroom window was wide open still. Should the councillor poke his head out it would, I knew, be all up for me.

I checked my watch. 8.43. The fireworks had finished but the music and dancing were in full swing. Someone—Dilly's grandpa, probably—was sawing away on a fiddle and I could hear people whooping and laughing down on the beach like this was the best fun they'd had in ages which, for the locals anyway, it was.

It would all stop, I knew, at nine on the dot. In just over ten minutes everyone would be heading home, or back to the ship.

I gripped the sides of the ladder, steadying myself. Then I called up, again, louder this time: 'Gurn! Answer me! Are you home? Are you all right?'

To be honest I was hoping, above all things, for

continuing silence. I was willing Gurnet to be far out at sea, trawling for mackerel with his old man, and the councillor long gone. I wasn't worried about the creature. The creature could have been throttled, or dubbed a rare breed and promised the run of its own meadow, for all I cared. It was knowing how Gurnet was going to feel—and act—with his swamp mutant gone that kept me fused to the ladder, blinking up at the window.

I'll count ten seconds, I was thinking. *Then I'll go. At least no one can say I didn't try.* When that big old Gurny-head with its shock of greasy hair came suddenly into view I did a double take: part dismay that he was home after all, part relief that he was all right.

'What's occurring?' I called, managing to sound truly puzzled, and one hundred per cent innocent. 'Why the ladder? Did you start a fire? Bad timing, Gurn, with the whole port down on the—'

'You have to help me,' he cut in. 'It's serious, Danzel. And Maude . . . I need my Maude to come. Fetch her. Fetch Maude and meet me back here. No . . . not back here, behind the fish shed, where the cliff path starts. Put the ladder back first, Danzel, and then fetch Maude. Tell her to bring a torch. And if anyone sees, don't say a word . . . don't drop me in it.'

He shut the window then, before I could throw any spanners in his works, or ask *why, Gurnet?* Why Maude? Why the fish shed? Why, oh, why the terrible urgency? (As if I hadn't already guessed, with a sinking of my treacherous heart.)

Don't drop me in it.

But I'd already done that, hadn't I. The least I could

do now, I told myself, was return the ladder to its rightful place, call for Maude and then listen to my old friend mourn the loss of his creature. We would hold his hands, Maude and I, while he ranted a while, and I would promise to take him hurling.

'First thing tomorrow, Gurn,' I would say. 'We'll go up on the cliff and chuck some stones. We'll choose the biggest rock and hurl stones at it until the tide comes in, or your arms have had enough.'

I was hoping—how I was hoping—that Gurnet hadn't seen his creature taken; but had come home to an empty cage and an open window. That he had no idea who in the world might have taken his Laurence and would never, ever, know that I, Danzel Killick, one of his closest friends, had spilled so many beans.

'No problem, Gurn,' I called up, even though the window was shut, by then, against me. 'I'll look after things. It'll be all right—everything will be sing-song, mate, don't worry.'

It was as I adjusted my grip on the ladder, preparing to lift it away from the wall, that my fingers touched something wet. Seagull poop, I thought. It'll wash off.

But, as I swung the ladder sideways, the wetness trickled, stickily, over my knuckles and in between my fingers. It didn't feel like anything a seagull would excrete, unless it had been dining all day on treacle. My palms were slick with the stuff. It was all over the ladder's rungs. And I knew, even before I looked, what colour my fingers would be.

You bastard, I thought, wishing hellfire and brimstone on the head of that councillor. *What did you do to that creature? Rip its guts out? You could have wrung its neck, surely? Or smothered it with a pillow?*

For as long as it took to turn into Fore Street and dump the fire ladder back on its hooks I actually felt some pity for Gurnet's pig-ugly swamp monster. As for having its blood on my hands . . . my friends, the irony of that wasn't lost on me.

See them hurry. Danzel Killick and the girl, Maude. Hand in hand they go, running through the alleyways of Port Zannon, intent on reaching the fish shed before friends and family come up from the beach and catch them on their mission.

'He'll need kid glove . . . handling,' Danzel pants. 'Seriously, Maudie, expect to find him . . . in bits . . . '

But Gurnet, when they reach him, seems extraordinarily calm. He is wearing his highwayman coat and has a rucksack on his back, with his sleep bag rolled on top. At his feet is an extra piece of luggage: the cat carrier he took from the old manor house. Inside, bawling its eyes out, and kicking its stubby feet, is Hopelessness.

'What the—?' It takes a moment or two for Danzel to understand—for the implications of the creature's living, bawling, kicking presence to sink in. When they finally do, he feels dizzy.

'Gurnet,' he says, leaning against the fish shed's wall. 'I thought . . . ' He catches himself, on the verge of giving away more than he is supposed to know. Then: 'There was blood on the ladder,' he says, managing, somehow, to keep a steady voice. 'Whose is it, Gurnet? What happened?'

So Gurnet explains, quite matter-of-factly, about how a man-shape appeared at his window and came into his room to steal Laurence.

'I didn't kill him, Danzel,' he says. 'I just sliced him a bit. There were no guts, and I didn't do a stabbing. I didn't stick his lungs or go into his heart.'

'Oh good,' Danzel answers. 'Terrific. Just a bit of grievous bodily harm was it, Gurn? Fabulous. Nothing to worry about at all then . . .'

The Council's van, Danzel knows, is no longer parked outside The Crazy Mermaid. He knows because he checked. The fact that the councillor's wounds didn't stop him driving away means he'll probably live to tell the tale. But it's the telling of the tale, Danzel knows, that will bring the worst kind of trouble crashing down.

Maude has taken Gurnet's hand. Who was it, she asks quietly, who climbed into his room? Who was it who wanted the creature?

Gurnet tells her he doesn't know. 'He was wearing sunglasses,' he says. 'And gloves. Why would he have sunglasses on, Maudie, when the sun wasn't shining and it wasn't even day?'

To protect his eyes, Maude guesses, from Laurence's spit. Yes . . . to protect his eyes, that's why. That's it.

'For crying out loud . . .' Danzel has slumped to the ground. He is sitting on the turf with his back against the boards of the fish shed and his head in his hands. And he is shivering.

'The man's suit was green,' Gurnet adds. 'When he dropped his torch . . . before he got himself back to the window . . . I saw, by the light from the torch, that his suit was green. A special green. Like the ones the councillors wear.'

'You've really done it this time, Gurn,' groans Danzel. 'You've really, really, gone and done it . . .'

Maude sighs and asks Gurnet what he intends to do now.

'I'm taking Laurence back to the manor house,' Gurnet tells

her. 'To the place where we found him. He'll be safe there. You
need to help me, Maude. I don't know how the wall opens. You
did that bit. How does it open, Maude? Tell me what to do?'

Maude looks down at Danzel and he looks up at her.

'Well?' says Danzel. 'Tell him, then.'

Maude says she can't remember. That it's all a total blur. But
if she goes back, she says, to where the mural is, she might be
able to work it out. She says she feels bad, really bad, about
releasing the creature in the first place.

It doesn't belong here, she says. It's dangerous. It attacked a
clergyman. It needs to go back behind the wall.

Gurnet opens his mouth to say something.

But: 'All right!' Danzel jumps to his feet, a decision made.
'Enough talking. Let's go. Leave the rucksack though, Gurn, and
the sleep bag. We'll be back before dawn. And we'll have worked
out, by then, what to say to people—how to get you off the hook.'

'Oh, I'm not coming home,' Gurnet informs him, blithely. 'I'm
staying with my Laurence. And you're to keep it a secret, Danzel.
You too, Maude. You're not to tell anyone, not even Dilly and
Jenna. Do you promise? Say to me "I promise", Danzel. Say "I
promise I won't drop you in it." '

Danzel is already walking. Away from the fish shed towards
the cliff steps. He can hear people leaving the beach. They are
heading for home and will not come this way. From the top of
the cliff he will have a clear view of the Americans' ship, lit up
like Christmas at the harbour mouth. And the pain he will feel
at not being on it . . . at being barred, by fate and circumstance,
from the razzle and the dazzle of a life like Connor Blue's . . .
will be almost more than he can bear.

'I promise, Gurn,' he says into the dark. 'I promise I won't
drop you in it.'

JENNA

'Don't talk to me,' I told my mum. 'Don't talk to me ever again. You're a disgrace. A hideous embarrassment. I'll never forgive you.'

'I'm sorry,' she pleaded. 'It was a dare. Ellie Tonkin dared me to "do a crazy mermaid" and I just thought, what the heck? I'd had a couple of ciders, darling and . . . well . . . it's not like I showed everything is it? My bottom half was decent.'

'I *said*,' I yelled, 'don't talk to me.'

I went to find Dilly. I wore my pink dress again and a little bit of lipstick, just in case Connor Blue was having breakfast in the café, or taking a stroll around the port. I meant to apologize to him, the first chance I got. You won't find 'I'm so terribly sorry my mother flashed her thingies at you' in *Men: How to Catch and Keep One*'s top ten conversation-starters but hey . . . it's original.

'Oh, Jenna,' Mrs Tonkin said, as I stepped into The Crazy Mermaid. 'Sit down. I'll bring you a milk-shot. On the house.'

She looked sheepish, and rightly so. She should have known my mother would rise to that dare.

The café was crowded. It was like visitor-season, only without all the children and the strong sense of holiday.

I recognized most of the people from last night: the two actresses, the woman who looked like a make-up artist and some men who, I guessed, worked the cameras, or the lights, or whatever. When they looked up and said 'Good *morning*' I went the colour of my flicking dress, convinced they could tell, just from the shape of my face and the size of my thingies that I am THAT woman's daughter.

There was only one free chair, at a table for two set apart from the others, for privacy.

'Do you mind?' I said to the man sitting there—a man I didn't remember seeing at the party, which allowed me to hope that he would avoid my mother's antics as a topic of conversation.

'Not at all—go right ahead.'

He had some papers spread out on the table, next to his cup of tea. He looked OK, in an older-man sort of way, but he wasn't Connor Blue. Connor Blue wasn't there.

'Trent,' the man said, rising to his feet and holding out his hand for me to shake. 'I'm the researcher for *Wreckers*.'

'Right,' I said, not the slightest bit interested. 'I'm Jenna.' I shook his hand and sat down. I thought he would carry on reading, but he didn't. He just smiled, in a vague sort of way, and took a drink of his tea. 'Is that the script then?' I asked, looking sideways at his papers. I was no more interested in them than I was in him; I was being civil is all—and buttering him up, of course, because he works with Connor Blue.

He sighed and put his teacup down.

'It's all right,' I said, quickly. 'I'm not really . . . '

'No, no . . . I'm sorry. I don't mean to be abrupt. I've been doing some research of my own. A wildlife study of sorts and . . . well, I'm kind of stumped by something.'

'By what?' I asked, politely.

He shuffled his papers into an untidy pile and sighed again.

'Something I was looking for,' he said. 'Something pretty rare. It isn't where I hoped—where I reckoned—it would be.'

Mrs Tonkin came over just then with my milk-shot.

'Ten minutes,' she said to me. 'I can let her go in ten minutes.' She meant Dilly. 'More tea, sir?' she added, turning to the American. 'Is there anything else I can get for you? Something to eat perhaps? I can do you a crab omelette, or something nice on toast.'

The man, Trent, said no, thank you, he never ate before noon.

I took a sip of my milk-shot. Trent waited for Mrs Tonkin to go back to the kitchen, then opened his mouth to go blithering on some more about whatever boring animal had managed to keep out of his way.

'Are you friends with Connor Blue?' I asked, before he could get a word out. 'He must be amazing to work with.'

'Yes,' he said, surprised. 'Connor's a neighbour of mine, back in LA. He's a great kid.'

'I'd do anything to work with him,' I said, lowering my voice and willing my eyes to glow. 'It's what I want to do properly one day. Acting, I mean. It's my dream.'

I held my breath in case this splat-brain laughed at me. He didn't, so I carried on:

'I'd make a good extra on *Wreckers*. And if there's a speaking part going . . . well, I've got the right accent for it, haven't I? Who better to play a Port Zannon maid than a Port Zannon maid? Don't you agree?'

He didn't answer but the look on his face was respectful enough. *Go on, then,* it said. *I'm listening.*

I wasn't sure what else to say. I hadn't planned any of this—didn't know, quite, how to sell myself as a girl the American film industry (or, rather, Connor Blue) couldn't afford to ignore.

'And I'd have no objections to going topless,' I heard myself say. 'Not if the role demanded it.'

He looked so taken aback, then, that I could have bitten the tip of my tongue off. 'Oh well,' I added, quickly. 'If you could just bear me in mind . . . So . . . um . . . what was it you were saying just now, about the wildlife?'

He needed no more prompting, the sap. Wherever he is in the world, he said (meaning wherever he's sent on location) he likes to go off on his own, to observe and make notes on native birds and animals. 'It's my hobby,' he said. 'I'm interested in how populations and demographic patterns are altering in these more eco-friendly times. It's a fascinating subject, Jenna.'

I said it sounded it. But I had my eye on the door, willing Connor Blue to come in. I was wondering whether to ask Mrs Tonkin to bring a third chair to our table, just in case.

'Badgers,' Trent added. 'They're my biggest thing. I'm especially fond of badgers.'

'Hmm,' I said, thinking, *bore me some more, why don't you . . .*

'In fact,' he said, leaning closer over the table, 'I hear that a badger got loose in your church recently, and caused quite a rumpus.'

I took my eyes off the door.

'That wasn't a badger,' I said.

'Really?' He took another sip of his tea, although it must have been stone cold, it had been sitting there so long. 'What was it then?'

'I don't know.'

'Well, what did it look like? A weasel? A cat? A bird?'

'Yes.'

'Sorry—which?'

'All of them. It looked a bit like all of them.'

I drank the last of my milk-shot and looked around for Mrs Tonkin. I wouldn't wait for Dilly, I decided. This man—this Trent—was getting on my nerves.

'If it *was* part badger,' he said, 'I'd be interested to know.'

'But it flew,' I told him, trying not to laugh. 'Badgers don't fly.' *Bonkers*, I thought. *This man is as mad as a broom. Or maybe all Americans are like this. How would I know?*

'Well, no,' he answered, quickly. 'Of course badgers don't fly. Which is what . . . which is why . . . this one needs to be found. In certain circles . . . among people who study these things . . . it could cause a real sensation. Those people would pay good money, Jenna—*I* would pay good money—to find the animal that went for your preacher.'

I looked at him properly. I wasn't sure I'd understood.

'Are you saying,' I said, slowly, 'that whoever found that creature for you would get a reward?'

'That's exactly what I'm saying,' he answered, looking

me straight in the eye. 'Only she—or he—would have to keep the whole business quiet—strictly between our-selves. There are regulations, after all, against taking an animal from one country to another, even in the inter-ests of mammalian research.'

'Right,' I said. 'And what if she—or he—wasn't both-ered about money—as a reward, I mean—but would like something else instead. Like the chance to be in *Wreckers*; to act with Connor Blue.'

Trent turned a chuckle into a cough. 'Ahem—I guess that could be arranged,' he said. 'Yes . . . I'm pretty sure it could.'

I felt my spirits lift. I felt them soar right through the roof of The Crazy Mermaid and away to Cloud Nine.

'Could I kiss him?' I said. 'As part of the film. Could I kiss Connor Blue?'

Trent shook his head, but it wasn't a no because he was trying very hard not to smile. 'Jenna,' he said, 'you are one ambitious and determined young lady. Let's see how we go on, shall we? Now that we have a deal. We do have a deal now, don't we?'

Fair enough, I thought and nodded.

'The creature flew off,' I reminded him, 'No one knows where it went to.'

'So I understand,' he replied. 'But if it's the kind of creature I think it is, it won't have gone far. It'll be lying low somewhere, regaining its strength. Am I right in thinking it was somebody's pet for a while? A local boy—Gary Carthew. Do you know him?'

'I know everyone,' I said. 'I was born here. I've never left.'

'So will you talk to Gary for me? Just as soon as you can? See if he has any idea where the animal might have gone to. I'd ask him myself, but I don't know how he'd respond. To being quizzed by a stranger, I mean.'

'Badly,' I replied. 'He would respond very badly to that.'

I was about to ask who had snitched, about Gurnet having the creature, but Dilly appeared then, her hair all frizzy from the steam in the kitchen, and a look on her face that said she pitied me, still, over what my mother had done. She would go along with anything I wanted to do, I knew, for as long as her sympathy lasted. And I wanted to find Connor Blue.

'I have to go,' I told Trent. 'But I'll see you in here later shall I? This evening perhaps.'

He nodded.

'Mum's the word, right?'

'Right,' I said, standing up. 'Just don't *ever* mention mine . . . no, I'm joking . . . I know what you mean.'

As I moved around the table I sneaked a proper look at the pile of papers next to Trent's teacup. They looked like something he had printed off the inter-telly and the title, on the top page, was easy enough to make out. *Graeco-Roman Myths*, it said. *How The Original Tales were Altered or Suppressed.*

It seemed an odd choice of reading, for a badger fanatic.

DILLY

'Haven't you heard?' I said to Jenna. 'Gurnet's run away. He left a note saying that all the fuss and bother over the Americans was doing his head in. Mrs Carthew's going frantic.'

'No! You're kidding me. He can't have. Where's he gone?'

'No one knows.'

'To search for that disgusting creature, I suppose. We have to find him, Dilly. He could be scrambling down cliffs for all we know, or sticking his stupid head down fox holes. What if he hurts himself? What if he falls down an old mine shaft, or goes looking in caves and gets cut off by the tide?'

I'd never heard Jenna so worried. About anyone. And it was good to realize that, for all her sniping, she cares about Gurnet every bit as much as Danzel, Maude, and I do.

And so I told her not to fret. That Gurnet would be fine. He had taken his tent, I said, and his sleep bag, and enough food and water to last a while. He had also taken Laurence.

'*What?*'

She stopped dead in her tracks (we were pacing the beach for about the fiftieth time, on the lookout for

213

Connor Blue) and grabbed hold of one of my arms.

'What do you mean he's taken Laurence? I thought the thing had vanished. Disappeared. Gone AWOL.'

'Well it didn't,' I told her, tugging my arm free. 'It went straight back to Gurnet, like a homing pigeon.'

'Oh. My. Stars . . . '

I had sand in my shoes. My legs were aching from all the walking up and down and I was due back at The Crazy Mermaid to serve lunches. Connor Blue had ordered lobster. He had gone to church, for the morning service, but would be in the café by one.

I hadn't told Jenna, about the church or the lunch. It was mean of me, I know, but she would only have gatecrashed the service, inappropriately dressed, or followed me back to the café and hung around to drool. It's only a matter of time, I fear, before she flaunts herself at Connor Blue in something so revealing that she might as well be naked.

'I'd better get back,' I said. 'To help Mum. Are you going home for your lunch?'

Jenna pulled a face. 'Yes,' she said. 'Worst luck.'

She was looking away towards the clifftop, shading her eyes against the brightness. She wasn't thinking about home, or lunch, or even about Connor Blue. Nor had she spotted anyone up on the cliff for there was no one to see even though it was a fine day—perfect for walking.

'I think I know,' she said slowly, 'where Gurnet might have gone. I *think* I'm right but it would be a weight off our minds, wouldn't it, to find out for sure?'

I tracked her gaze along the sweep of the cliff, to the

point at which, although you can't tell from the beach, the path curves sharply inland with no clues any more—no sign—about precisely where it goes.

'The old manor house,' I said, pleasure blooming in me, just from saying the words. 'He's gone back to the manor house, hasn't he?'

Jenna shivered, and then hugged herself with her own arms.

'You'll come with me, won't you?' she pleaded, grabbing me again. 'This afternoon, as soon as you're free. We needn't tell the others, need we? It can just be you and me. I'd go by myself but you know how that place spooks me out. You will come, won't you? To look for Gurnet? To make sure he's safe?'

'Of course,' I said, giving her a hug. 'Of course I'll come with you.'

DANZEL

When we got to the manor and found the wall already opened, Gurnet went bananas.

'We left it shut,' he hollered. 'Didn't we, Maude? That wall was shut tight when we left after Hallowe'en. It was, Maudie, wasn't it? Didn't we shut the wall?'

I told him to calm down. I told him that maybe the mechanism hadn't fastened properly after he and Maude tampered with it. I advised him to stick the creature right back where he'd found it, anyway, and wedge the door shut with a chair or something. 'We can come and visit it,' I said. 'It's school holidays now, Gurn. We could come every day, if you want.'

Secretly I was thinking: *Die, creature, die.* It had caused enough trouble.

Then Maude announced that something else was wrong. There had been a box, she said—an old wooden box—in the space where the creature had been. But it wasn't there any more. It had gone.

I was about to say fat limpets to any box; that we had more important things to worry about than a box, like what was going to happen to us—to all of us—once the councillor recovered from Gurnet's delicate bit of knife work and came after our sorry hides.

I was about to wrench the cat carrier from Gurnet's arms and shove it behind the wall myself, if he didn't hurry up.

And then the creature spoke:

'Don't put me back there, Gary,' it said. 'Please, my Gary, don't.'

I swear, I thought my mind had gone to wisps and shards. Either that or my friend Gurnet had perfected the art of ventriloquism in that pit he calls a bedroom, and was trying it out, as a joke.

I shone my torch at the cat carrier. The creature, I told myself, would be asleep, or licking its filthy toes, or sniffing around for food . . . doing something reassuringly creature-like anyway.

'Oi!' it snapped, shaking the bars of the carrier with its disturbingly human hands. *Piano playing fingers,* I thought. *It has piano playing fingers, like some foul little Mozart-monster.* 'You're blinding me, mate. Let me out. Let. Me. Out.'

'See,' Gurnet declared. 'I told you Laurence is smart. I told you over and over, Danzel, and now you know.'

'Yes,' I answered, faintly. 'Now I know.'

Maude had gone right up close to the wall, and was shining her torch on the mural. She didn't seem shocked, or even surprised, that the creature could speak. I got the feeling she hadn't even noticed. She said it was all coming back to her; that she remembered what to do, to make the door in the wall swing open and shut.

'Show me,' Gurnet demanded. 'Then, if I need to, if I hear that man-shape sneaking around, I can hide Laurence there all by myself.' ('Just for a while, mate,' he added, before the mutant could raise any objections. 'Just until it's safe for you to come out again.')

I had to ask: 'How long do you reckon you can camp out here, Gurny? Without food and fresh water, I mean?'

'We've got food,' he said. 'And water. And when it runs out you can bring us some more. Or we'll drink the rain. It's bound to rain. And I'll go fishing—there's fishing stuff upstairs, in one of the crates. Or I'll trap a seagull, and knife it, and cook it on a spit.'

'For crying out loud . . . ' I muttered. *'For crying out loud, Gurn . . . '*

But there was no telling him. No talking him round. He would go to the attic, he said. It would be nice and dark up there, even in broad daylight, and there were lots of big boxes to hide Laurence behind. He would form a barricade of boxes he said, up there in the dark, and then they would both be safe. And off he stomped, heading for the staircase as if he owned the place. I shone my torch after him—to help light the way . . . to keep track of him, while I could, *I* don't know. And I swear the creature stuck two fingers up at me as it was carried from the room.

Maude looked close to tears. It was all such a mess, she said. And all because she had opened the wall and let the creature out. And there *had* been a box, there really had. A box with a pile of chains beside it. And now there were only the chains, so who could have come in and taken the box? Who else knew how to open the wall?

'Hang on,' I said. 'Hang on a minute, Maude . . . that creature *spoke*, just now. Didn't you hear it? Didn't it spook you out?'

No, she answered, vaguely.

'What—you didn't hear it or it didn't spook you out?'

Both, she said.

I gave up.

'Come on,' I said to her. 'Don't worry about the box. I'll come back tomorrow. Gurn will have had enough, by then, of playing fugitives-in-the-attic.'

This wasn't a game though, I knew that much. What I didn't have a clue about—and still don't—is how to sort things so that the creature disappears, the Gurny-one comes home, and I . . . I can get on with the rest of my life without dreading the sting of a whip, or worse.

I needed a drink. Badly. After hearing that mutant string words—whole sentences—together, as clearly as any human, I needed a drink like a herring needs water. But I didn't give in and have one, not when I got home, at some late and lunatic hour, and not since. You could say that's the one good thing, so far, to have come out of all of this. Or you could say: *Hah! A week at the outside and he'll be tapping that barrel again, the hopeless little drunk.*

Well, you can think what you like. A boy can only do his best.

I promised Maude I'd go back to the manor today, but I can't. I'm wiped. I've got the trembles. And Mum's doing a big Sunday dinner which I need to be at because Ned and his girlfriend are coming over from Bodmin and we haven't seen them in months.

I need to eat. I need to think. I need time to work out what to do. Gurnet will be OK without me for a day or two. He has food and he has water and it's not like he's

219

stuck for company. Or conversation.

Let me out. Let. Me. Out.

They're banging around in my head, those words. They're haunting me. Time . . . that's all I need. I'll feel better after my dinner and a decent night's sleep.

DILLY

I nearly dropped a plate when one of the American's pockets started singing. I nearly jumped right out of my skin.

'Sorry,' he said. 'Excuse me.' And he put a hand in his pocket and took out a tiny little inter-phone. I felt daft, then, for imagining he had an elf about his person, or something equally strange. I was also intrigued. You have to be pretty important—in this country at least—to be able to communicate, just like that, with anyone, at any time.

I wished Danzel had been there. He would give anything, Danzel would, for an inter-phone of his own, or at least a go on one.

'So I was right,' the man said, to whoever he was speaking to, wherever in the world. 'Have we fresh information? What else can you tell me?'

I set down his lunch plate and moved away. There was no one else to wait on, but it's rude to hover. Then Connor Blue walked in.

'Hi,' he said to me. 'Dilly, right?'

'Yes,' I said, blushing like a sunset as I remembered how, in my dream, he'd called me Daffy and brushed my hair.

He beamed at me, happily and easily.

'The director and some of the others are on their way over,' he said. 'A table for eight should do it, if it's not too much trouble.'

I led him to the longest table, the one with the mermaid painted all down its length, heavily varnished so that she'll never fade away or get rubbed out by the picking up and putting down of knives and forks and spoons.

'You know what has to be done,' I heard the man on the inter-phone say. 'So do it. I'll handle things here.' And he stood up and ran for the door, head-butting mermaids left right and centre in his hurry to be gone.

'Hey, Trent!' Connor called after him. 'What's the problem? Are they messing with the script again? Do we start shooting tomorrow or what?'

'I'm dealing with it,' the man replied over his shoulder. 'And it's still a five a.m. start, so far as I know.' And then he was gone.

I blinked, astonished by his hurry.

'Stress,' Connor said, sitting himself down above the mermaid's swimmy face. 'There is still *way* too much stress in this world—in my part of it, anyway. He should have come with me to church this morning. It was beautiful in there; peaceful too—just practically empty which is sad. Just me, the clergyman and three little old ladies.'

I didn't know how to reply. I felt embarrassed: Godless and sort of grubby even though I'd showered earlier, and sanitized my hands after coming off the beach.

Connor picked up one of our scallop-shaped table mats, smiled at it and put it down. 'Eco-Christianity isn't that big a deal over here yet is it?' he said. 'Although I've heard it's gathering speed.'

I cleared my throat and found my voice.

'We do it at the school,' I told him. 'Study it, I mean. My instructor says it's the best and most hopeful direction the Church has taken in centuries and we ought to be glad that so many believers are as concerned, now, with saving this world as they are with reaching the next. He says if countries which were big polluters hadn't seen the light we would all be living on borrowed time. We're not big polluters in this kingdom, which is why Eco-Christianity hasn't really caught on, I suppose.'

I stopped for breath, amazed at myself—not just for remembering the lesson, but because talking to a famous movie star wasn't so hard after all. If anything, it was a whole lot easier than racking my brain for something fresh to say to a local.

Had I gone babbling on for too long though? What if I'd struck him as rude, or too much of a know-it-all? Making conversation can be such a stressful thing . . .

But Connor Blue was looking at me kindly. And he was listening too. Really listening.

'But it's still about God,' he said. 'It's still about believing in Jesus, right? And in what the Bible says. It's still about going to church.'

'I know,' I answered. 'I just think that, since the Attack . . . '

'Dilly? Why is that fish pie still sitting there? Didn't he like it? Where's he gone?'

I turned away from Connor Blue, sorry that the rest of our debate looked like being lost to a wodge of herring and mash.

'He had to go,' I told my mum. 'He has an inter-phone, Mum. It went off, he spoke to it, and then he left. It sounded serious—he was in a real rush.'

'Well,' Mum said, doing her best to sound concerned instead of cross about the pie. 'I hope it wasn't bad news from home—from America.'

Connor Blue touched my arm. It wasn't *that* kind of a touch, although if Jenna had seen, she would have wanted me dead.

'Pass the pie, Dilly,' he said. 'I hate to see anything go to waste.'

He winked at me then, as if he knew, as well as I did, what my mum was really thinking. (That her lost customer should have stayed long enough to eat his lovely lunch—every bite and crumb of it. That even if the whole of his family had caught some kind of plague, or his dog had been run over by a tram, he should still have sat tight and finished off his pie.)

The wink thrilled me. But it wasn't *that* kind of a thrill. *This is what it's like,* I thought, *when you meet someone new—a stranger—and it's as if you've known them all your life. We're on the same wavelength, me and Connor Blue, even though he's world-famous, and an Eco-Christian, and as beautiful as the day, and I, Dilly Tonkin, am none of those things.*

'But it's gone cold,' Mum protested, as I fetched the plate of pie and set it down on the mermaid's face.

'Perfect,' Connor replied, waving his fork in the air, and sharing another knowing look with me. 'It'll be perfect as it is. Just the thing before lobster.'

'Oh, heavens,' Mum gasped. 'The lobster . . . ' And off she hurried, back into the kitchen.

I watched Connor Blue eat the pie. Even his fingers, holding the fork, were beautiful. I could imagine him, very easily, kneeling in the church, spotlit by sunbeams and saying his prayers.

'This is delicious,' he declared. 'As I said, I hate waste. And this is a great little place, Dilly. Although . . . ' He moved his plate, and the mat underneath it, away to the side of the table before continuing to eat. It put him at an awkward angle, until he thought to move his chair along as well, and it looked, to me, like an odd thing to do until he said, with a rueful little smile, that he'd felt sorry for the painted mermaid.

'I know she's not real,' he confided. 'But I felt like my plate was squashing her nose!'

No customer, so far as I knew, had ever thought like that before. Not enough to want to move along the table, anyway.

'She's lovely,' Connor Blue said, twisting his head for a sideways view of the mermaid's face. 'She looks like your friend. The one who was in here yesterday, wearing that nutty apron.'

'Maude,' I said. 'That was Maude.'

He repeated her name, like it was the most beautiful word in the whole of the English language; as if it was melting, like sugar, on his tongue.

'Maude's sad,' I told him. 'She's always been the quiet one but now she's sad as well, although there's no reason for her to be, that any of us can see. It's . . . it's like she's going to waste, and it's a shame. '

I felt old, as I said all of this, like a matchmaker, or someone's maiden aunt.

'Really?' Connor Blue put down his knife and fork. 'I hate to think of her—of anyone—being sad.'

I was about to say more, about how Maudie loves the sea, and about her beautiful singing voice which she's always been too shy to make the most of. But the door opened then and the café was crowded, suddenly, with more people from the ship; all chattering like gulls, and heading for Connor's table.

I took orders. I fetched jugs of water and a basket of bread. I told those who asked that my name was Dilly, short for Daffodil. And the dream in which Connor Blue called me Daffy and held me in his arms no longer struck me as *that* kind of dream. I don't have to worship him, I realized, or want him like Jenna does. We had spoken the way good friends do, and shared an understanding. In that short space of time, whether he realized it or not, Connor Blue had made me feel special. In return, if I can, I will help him do the same for my friend Maude.

There is more light, in the attic, than Gurnet had expected—
long rays of it coming in through gaps in the rafters, where tiles
have slipped and roof-stuff fallen in.

Gurnet tells Hopelessness that it doesn't matter; that every
cloud has a silver lining. Then he ferrets around in the kitchen,
finding two rusty buckets, several pans and a chipped pudding basin, which he positions just so, on the attic floor, to
catch any rain that might fall. We will drink the rain, he tells
Hopelessness, and wash our faces in it. He moves some of the
trunks and crates around, forming a barricade in front of his
pet's carrier.

Then he sleeps, without stirring, until the sun rises high
above the house and touches his face, through the rafters.

'Let me out, my Gary,' Hopelessness calls, from behind two
crates marked 'Christmas decs' and 'baby things'. 'Just for a
minute, to waggle my feet. It's safe now, mate; go on.'

But Gurnet isn't as daft as he's painted. His creature is as big
as a piglet, now, and hasn't flown in weeks; all the same it could
still disappear through a hole in the roof, and Gurnet is taking
no chances.

'I'm going out,' he says. 'To get the lie of the land. There might
be a well out there with fresh water in it, or a shed with traps
stored away. Rabbit traps. Would you eat a bit of rabbit, mate,

227

if I caught one and cooked it up?'

Hopelessness doesn't reply.

'Don't sulk, Laurence,' Gurnet tells it. 'I hate it when you sulk. Here—have this biscuit. It's salt dough—your favourite. I'll bring you something back shall I? A surprise. And then I'll tell you more sea stories. OK?'

Just go, if you're going, thinks Hopelessness. Get out of my face.

Gurnet hums as he bounds down the stairs. Despite everything, he is happy to be here; away from all the fuss and bother in the port. He doesn't want to think about the man he sliced. When those thoughts come he hums louder, drowning them out.

Through the kitchen he goes, and out into the sun. It is a lovely afternoon and he wonders about taking his Laurence for a walk (if, that is, he can find a length of rope to use as a lead and something to turn into a collar—a scarf, perhaps, or even a length of tinsel from the box marked 'Christmas decs').

The sun is hot on his head. He can see bluebells spreading like floodwater beneath dense shrubbery and he can hear—yes he can—the sea.

He can't recall any sea-noise from the last time he was here. But it had been October, then, with the wind wuthering and branches tossing and Jenna Rosdew going on and on, jangling his nerves. Even while digging for worms, for his creature's first meal, he had been oblivious to the sound of waves. But he hears them now—the familiar smash and suck of them—and knows that they are near.

He had assumed—they all had—that the manor grounds stretched a long way off on all sides, with the house in the centre like the pit of a plum. It dawns on him now that the back of the house is a lot closer than he'd realized to the edge of the cliff.

Following the path that circles the building, Gurnet sends little thoughts winging up towards the attic. 'If I'm right,' he tells Hopelessness in his head. 'If this place is where I think it is, there'll be steps going down the cliff into a little cove. Just a tiny cove, mate, not one a person would normally go to but one I've seen about a million times from my dad's boat. If I can get to it, if the steps are safe, we'll go fishing off the rocks. I'll bring you down, if you promise to behave. I'll let you see the ocean, and maybe even have a paddle.'

There are outbuildings behind the house, tumbled to rack and ruin. For a moment Gurnet thinks he might have to risk his neck in one, to look for a machete, or an axe. He reckons it will take several days, at least, to hack a way through the shrubbery to where it ends, he is certain, in a sheer drop down to the cove. It is odd, he thinks, to be able to hear the waves but not see them. The rhododendron bushes, back here, are almost as tall as the house, their blooms as big as jellyfish, deep red against the green, and the mass of them impenetrable, or at least that's how it seems.

When he spots a way in he punches the air. 'Yay!' The contractor responsible for maintaining a path has been doing an excellent job, back as well as front. Gurnet hopes he is well paid.

The path is clear. Branches meet high above it, thick with leaves and clotted here and there with the big red flowers. It takes Gurnet less than half a minute to sprint its entire length and then he is out, his breath catching in his throat as he takes in the view.

Every day of his life, Gurnet has looked at the sea. It is as familiar to him as his bedroom ceiling and as dear as any friend. Should he ever be forced to go inland he would find it hard to breathe. This, though, is a new perspective, and for a moment *he feels like a summer visitor, entranced.*

The steps leading down to the cove are rickety and old, with nothing to catch hold of should you slip. Gurnet minds his feet as he goes, risking occasional glances out to sea just in case a fishing boat slides by. If it does he will have to duck, because heaven forbid that his father should see him, picking his way down the face of the cliff like a boy with no worries and nothing better to do.

The Americans' ship is moored around the headland. No one will spot him from there, And no one ever swims this far round, not even in high summer. The currents are too strong and the rocks would rip your flesh to ribbons.

When he reaches the cove, jumping with a thud onto untrodden sand, Gurnet does a little dance. And why not? He is having an adventure. This tiny beach may only be a spit away from home but it is foreign territory to him and he is thrilled—over the moon—to have reached it on foot, and all by himself.

It isn't long before he spots the cave. It's dark mouth is obvious, when you're practically on top of it, but Gurnet has never noticed it from his father's boat, not once in all these years. And if its position was ever inked on a map, or etched in a smuggler's memory, nobody knows or cares any more. There could be anything in there, Gurnet marvels. Skeletons, emeralds . . . anything.

'Yeeoooow!' he howls, leaning down and peering in. 'Yeeow, yeeow, yeeoooow!' He ducks lower. It is pitch black in there. Nice, he thinks. Perfect for the Gurn.

He must be careful not to bang his head, as he crawls right in.

'Yeeoooow!' he howls again. The echo is slight. There is no great width or height, after all, to the inside of this cave; instead, it tunnels inwards, narrower, even, than Squeeze Belly

Alley, and so very low that only a child or a carnival-boy could stride along in comfort.

Undeterred, Gurnet shuffles forward on his hands and knees. The sand beneath his palms is damp but not sodden. High tide, he is sure, doesn't come this far. He can see something—the outline of something—a yard or so ahead. He hopes it's what he thinks it is; what it looks like, from his angle.

This is Gurnet's lucky day.

'Yay!' he thinks. 'Yay! Yay! Yay!' And he grabs, with both hands, the prow of a boat: a fibreglass rowing boat, still launchable under its ancient tarpaulin; still seaworthy and fit to go, even though the last person to touch the oars has been dead for sixteen years.

JENNA

Dilly dawdled. She drove me mad. I thought she'd be along that cliff path in a streak, she's been whining on that long about going back to the old manor.

But 'Slow down,' she called after me. 'It's too lovely a day to hurry. And look at the gorse! And the primroses! How come things are flowering up here when everything's so late, or so droopy, down in the port?'

It was like having old Mrs Tweedy in tow, or the flicking badger man.

'Will you keep up, for crying out loud,' I snapped, stopping just long enough to give her what for. 'Aren't you worried? Don't you care that Gurnet might be eating poisonous berries somewhere, or losing what's left of his mind?'

'Gurnet can look after himself,' she replied, bending to pick a stupid daisy or something. 'But it's nice that you're so bothered. It makes me feel like we're a proper gang again—you, me, Gurnet, Danzel, and Maude. Like when we were little; us against the world. You and I ought to do a good turn for Maude, next, don't you think, Jen? Something kind, to give her more confidence in herself. We ought to fix it so she meets Connor Blue. Properly, I mean. I think he really likes her. '

I didn't want to hear any of that. I turned, abruptly, and stomped on. Then: 'If Gurnet's at the house,' I said, not looking round, only raising my voice. 'We'll say a quick hello and then leave him to it. No point trying to get him to come back to the port, he'll only have one of his turns. We'll make sure he and that badg—that creature-thing—are OK and then we'll go. All right?'

'All right,' Dilly replied, in that maddeningly dreamy way of hers.

'I mean it, Dilly. I'm not hanging around.'

'Fine,' she said, and I heard her panting as she ran to catch me up. 'That's fine, Jen.'

She still sounded only half there, but at least she was matching my pace, at last, and had stopped twitter-ing about the gorse, and the primroses, and all things bright and flicking beautiful. *Good,* I thought. But then we reached the manor gates . . . found the broken bit of wall, and stepped through into . . . well . . . heaven on earth, I suppose. And it was my turn to stand as still as a pole, marvelling over the things mother nature can do.

'Wow,' I said.

'I knew it,' Dilly whispered, clutching at my sleeve. 'I knew it would be like this.' Her voice had gone all trembly.

'Well don't *cry*,' I said. 'There's no need to *cry*, is there?'

We stepped forward. No we didn't—we tiptoed, the way we did when we were six and she was Pease Blossom and I was Mustard Seed in some stupid ballet thing we did at the school.

'Remember when Michael and Nance got married?' Dilly said, still in her hushed and holy voice. 'And they had that tunnel made out of willow and red roses, for all the guests to walk through?'

I remembered.

'This is like that,' she sighed. 'Don't you think? Only greener. And longer. And the rhododendrons are bigger than any roses. Wouldn't it be wonderful, Jen, to get married up here? To walk down this path, with the love of your life, and have the ceremony in the house?'

'Dilly,' I said, 'put a brick in it.' But, even before she'd spoken I'd been imagining a similar thing . . . my dress, changed from pink to pure white, with at least six yards of it trailing behind, and a wedding veil as fine as spider threads drifting around my face, and Connor Blue beside me, hip to hip in the narrow space, his hand resting lightly on the small of my back: *You're mine . . . you're mine . . .*

By the time we reached the house I was in a lather of wanting. I could have laid myself down, right there on the bumps of the gravel and lost myself in more imaginings . . . romantic ones . . . naughty ones . . .

'*I'm yours . . . yes . . . all yours . . .*'

'Come on,' said Dilly. 'Let's go in, and call him.'

'Who?' I said, all vagueness myself now.

'Well, Gurnet, of course, who do you think? We can't just creep up on him—not Gurnet.'

And so we went into the house, through the kitchen with its big old broken down stove and floor tiles the colour of dried blood, and we called that splat-brain's name until the whole of the downstairs rang with it. Up the wide wooden staircase we went and I didn't feel anywhere near as scared as before. For one thing, it wasn't Hallowe'en. For another, it was light enough to see where we were going. Also, Dilly knew her way around—or thought she did.

'That's locked,' she said, as I moved towards the first door we came to, up on the first floor landing.

'No it isn't,' I told her, pushing the door wide open. 'See?'

And Oh. My. Stars . . .

I stepped in—just one step—and gawped like an idiot girl. The bed alone was straight out of a Hollywood movie—high and wide, with carved posts, as thick as legs, and heavy golden curtains. And the windows had deep stone seats set into them where you could sit in the moonlight, or candle light, or any light you wanted, having your face kissed off by the love of your life.

'Gurnet!' I yelled. 'Are you in here?'

I ran to the wardrobe and wrenched open the door. Moths flew out, or maybe they were midges, but they didn't bother me.

'Oh. My. Stars!' I breathed. 'Dilly—come and look.'

There were gowns in there. Beautiful old-fashioned gowns in all my favourite colours: hot pink and violet, deep red and softest mauve. Rhododendron colours. Perfect. I pulled one out by its hanger and held it against my front: raspberry silk; so beautifully made, so cunningly cut and stitched, that it would cling, I could tell, in the sexiest way imaginable.

I swung round to show Dilly. 'What do you—?' I began and then stopped.

'I'm . . . I'm just cleaning the mirror,' she faltered. 'It was thick with dust. Filthy.'

She was using her own pocket handkerchief, rubbing away like a char. And from the jittery sound of her you'd think the dust would have choked us both to death if she hadn't gone straight into spring-cleaning mode.

'For crying out loud, Dilly,' I said. 'Do you have to behave like you're sixty? Come and look at the dresses. Try one on.'

But no, she said. It wasn't respectful. We had no right to be rummaging through a dead woman's things. We'd come looking for Gurnet and if he wasn't hiding in the wardrobe, or anywhere else in this room, then we ought to keep searching.

'The attic,' she said. 'I'll bet you anything you like he's up there.'

I moved towards the bed, still holding on to the gown.

'You go and check,' I said. 'I'll wait for you here.'

'But . . .'

'It'll be better if you go by yourself. Gurn and I . . . well . . . we strike sparks off each other, don't we? It's always been that way. He's less likely to have one of his turns if I'm not there to rattle him. Go and look, Dils, then come back here and tell me.'

She hesitated. I pressed the mattress with one hand. It was soft, like dough or the breast of a swan.

'What?' I said. 'You're not scared are you? I thought you liked this house. I thought you felt "connected" to it, like a flicking spirit-girl or something.'

She went then. I waited until I couldn't hear her footsteps any more, and then I took my clothes off. The raspberry-silk went over me like a second skin. I loved it. I loved myself in it. My thingies, in the mirror, looked amazing—on show, but in a classy way.

I did a twirl, loving how the skirt billowed out from the tightly boned bodice.

Connor Blue, I thought, *you don't know what you're missing. This room . . . this bed . . . this dress, with me in it . . . we'd take your breath away.*

I danced across the floorboards, feeling every inch a star. Getting up on the bed was like scaling a monument but I managed to do it without tearing the dress. Lying back I thought how funny it was (and how very, very sexy) to be on a bed big enough to turn somersaults on—a bed designed for so much more than eight hours sleep, for one.

I closed my eyes. I ran my fingers over my hip. It was easy enough, in the mood I was in, to pretend that my hand was Connor's . . . to imagine him right there next to me, unable to resist . . .

How to get him here . . . how?

By the time Dilly came clattering back from the attic, saying no trace of Gurnet, so we might as well go home, I had the beginnings of a plan.

DANZEL

My brother Ned's girlfriend is called Carlyn. Not Carolyn or Carly Ann or any of those other things she gets called by mistake, but Car, as in automobile, and lyn.

Remember that name, my friends, and that you heard it here first, because that girl is on her way UP.

She and Ned were late. They're always late when they come to us although it's not as if their horses aren't up to the journey. It's not like they have to keep stopping.

Mum had catered for lateness—so much so that lunch still wasn't ready when they finally breezed in, their faces pink from the ride. 'Go and get some fresh air,' Mum said, like they hadn't already had plenty of that. 'Go and look at the Americans' ship—go on, I know you want to. Dan, you go too. Just be back here by four.'

Ned said not being funny but he didn't give a rat's claw about the Americans or their ship. He said he'd rather pop round to Michael's, to find out how he's coping on his own with little Sheila.

'But you'll see Michael later,' Carlyn complained. 'At lunch.'

'You don't have to stick with me,' Ned told her. 'Go to The Crazy Mermaid with Dan, for a milk-shot. Connor Blue might be there, you never know.'

Carlyn pulled a face, like she was way above swooning over movie stars like some daft kid. But she took my arm anyway and said 'Come on, Dan. Let's give your big brothers some time and space.'

She didn't mention Sheila, nor did she need to. I knew for a fact, and so did Ned, that she would sooner have gone to hell for a roasting than spend more time than she had to with our niece.

Carlyn likes everything perfect, and Sheila is far from that.

The Crazy Mermaid was empty and Mrs Tonkin pleased to see us. It had been frantic earlier, she said, with almost all the Americans in for lunch. But they were back on the ship now, having naps, or rehearsing their lines, or whatever.

'Is Dilly around?' I asked.

Mrs Tonkin pulled up a chair, sighing as she took the weight off her feet. 'She went for a cliff walk with Jenna,' she told me. 'Although I'm guessing it led no further than the top of the steps. They'll be watching the ship, the minxes, hoping to spot Connor Blue.'

Damn that Connor Blue, I thought. I wish he'd never come.

Connor Blue, Mrs Tonkin said to Carlyn, has to be one of the nicest young men alive. 'No airs and graces and *so* handsome, you wouldn't believe. And an Eco-Christian too, really committed.'

'Oh, I know,' Carlyn said. 'I met him last week, in Falmouth.'

We stared at her, like . . . *what?*

'I went down with my boss, to meet the ship,' she went

239

on, enjoying our faces. 'My boss was going anyway, to do the Official Welcome thing and to drive Con here. He—Con, that is—didn't want to sail from Falmouth with the others. He wanted to see the land.'

She paused to sip her milk-shot. I hadn't touched mine. I was waiting, heart in mouth, for whatever else she had to tell us. Not about Con-the-Irresistible but about the other one. Her boss.

That weasel . . . I thought, aware that I might be turning pale. *The councillor Gurnet sliced . . . the one who got me in the alley . . . he's Carlyn's BOSS?*

'I sat next to Con in the car,' Carlyn added, smugly. 'And at lunch too. We had a pie and potato lunch at The Jamaica Inn and . . . ' She leaned forward, for dramatic effect . . . 'when they dropped me home, before driving on here, *he came in for a cup of fennel tea.*'

'Ooo, Carlyn,' gushed Mrs Tonkin. 'A cup of fennel tea. You'll be the envy of every maid in the port . . . '

Carlyn smirked and set down her glass. 'That's what my boss said,' she answered. 'The exact same words. I'm going to ask my boss at work tomorrow if I can do the Official Goodbye thing as well, after filming's finished.'

I swallowed, hard.

She doesn't know, I realized. *She has no idea what happened in Gurnet's room last night . . . that her boss's blood is all over the fire ladder . . . that he'll be after Gurn, and me too, with a vengeance.*

'Any news of Gurnet?' I aimed the question at Mrs Tonkin, but kept my eyes on Carlyn. One flicker . . . one blink . . . and I'd have known she knew only too well what had happened to her boss but had been told to

240

keep quiet . . . to do Sunday lunch as normal . . . to say nothing at all that might put the wind up her boyfriend's pathetic little drunk of a brother, or the knife-wielding lunatic from Squeeze Belly Alley, until the full weight of the law could be swung into action and brought down on their miserable heads.

'Oh the silly boy,' Mrs Tonkin said. 'The Carthews are worried sick.'

'What's he done?' Carlyn asked in what certainly sounded like her usual tone of barely concealed boredom.

'Run away,' Mrs Tonkin told her. 'Honestly . . . first Nancy, now Gurnet. There must be something in the air.'

Carlyn wrinkled her nose, like whatever was in the air smelt of old pants. 'Hmm,' she said. 'He's the simple one, isn't he? The one only a mother could love.' Then she checked her watch as if being on time for dinner was way more important than any missing halfwit. *No loss there then*, I could imagine her thinking. *Better he dies now, of exposure or whatever, than ends up a drain on the Council's resources when his parents can't look after him any more.*

She is such an ice queen, that one. You have to admire it, just a weeny bit. Clueless, though, about the stabbing— I was certain, by then, of that.

'Look what I've got,' she said, shifting all the attention back her way. 'They gave it to me. For work.' And I couldn't hold back a gasp—all right then, a squeak— of pure envy when she took an inter-phone out of her pocket and set it on the table. It wasn't the latest model, nor was it all that new. At least ten people at the Council had probably used it before my almost-sister-in-law but all the same . . .

'Give us a go, Carlyn,' I begged. 'Go on, be a diamond.'

'Sorry,' she said, snatching the thing up before I could pounce. 'And anyway, who would you call?'

She had a point, the she-witch.

'I know people,' I blagged. 'You'd be surprised.'

'Horse dung,' she laughed. 'Come on . . . it's almost four. Your mum will be moaning, and it takes at least ten minutes, doesn't it, to get a bib on Michael's child . . . '

We went home. We ate the dinner. The grown-ups had a cider each. Sheila and I stuck to water.

The call came just as Mum was serving pudding, dividing up a fat white cheesecake and wondering if Sheila would like a pink lolly instead. The ringing of Carlyn's phone startled her so much that she dropped the pudding knife onto the floor. Bending to pick it up, I got that weird feeling of déjà vu . . . or, no, not déjà vu, but that other feeling, whatever it's called, that Carlyn's horrified 'Oh no!' and the fact that I was reaching for a rather sharp knife were connected, in some random way.

'What's happened?'

'Who is it?'

'Carlyn. Are you all right? Who are you talking to?'

I offered the knife, handle first, to Mum but she waved it away. It was too dirty, now, to slice food with and, anyway, pudding was no longer anyone's priority. All eyes were on Carlyn as she spoke into her phone. Even Sheila was watching—transfixed, I suppose, by the sight and sound of a grown woman talking to a silver brick.

I gulped my water. My liquid-nothing. I drained the glass.

'Are you sure?' Carlyn said. And: 'So there was nothing

anyone could have done for him?' And then: 'Thank you for letting me know.'

She switched the phone off and stowed it away in her pocket. Her face had gone like the cheesecake—all curdy and pale.

'Car . . . lyn sad,' little Sheila sang out. 'Don' cry, my maid. Don' cry now.' She can break your heart, that child, when she's not splitting your eardrums or driving you insane.

I don't think Carlyn even heard her. She was too much in shock.

'It's my boss,' she told us, in a faint and wondering voice. 'He's dead.'

DILLY

I found Gurnet. At least, I found the place where he was hiding. It wasn't hard. He was at the old manor house, just as Jenna had predicted—him and his creature.

Laurence.

I used to think that was so cute.

I could tell, as soon as I stepped into the attic, that someone had set up camp there. Not just because trunks and crates had been shifted around, and pots and pans brought up from the kitchen, but because the attic had that feel about it that spaces only get when the air is being breathed. You can't put your finger on it; you just know.

'Gurnet,' I said, all calm and quiet. 'It's me, Dilly. Is there anything you want? Anything I can fetch for you?'

'Sea water,' came the prompt reply, from behind a stack of crates. 'A big bucketful, please. With plankton in it.'

Confused, I stared at the crates. At the words 'Christmas decs' and 'Baby things' printed on the sides.

'Gurnet?' I said. 'Is that you?'

Stupid question. I would know Gurnet's voice any-where, and this wasn't it . . . this wasn't it at all.

'Tell you what,' the voice said, as if I hadn't spoken.

244

'Just let me out. Go on. Be a diamond. Be a sport. Let me out and I'll find some sea for myself. A nice bit of sea. With plankton.'

Laurence?

Gurnet's creature, I told myself, couldn't possibly hurt me. Not if it was caged, which it surely to goodness was. But the sound of that voice—the strange croak and whisper of it—kept me rooted to the spot. *How could something that was neither human nor parrot string so many words together and make such perfect sense? How was that even possible?*

'Where's . . . where's Gurnet?' I asked. I was trying to sound pleasant. I was trying to sound the way I would if this was someone—a person—I conversed with every day, not a mess of fur and hair that we'd never imagined would do anything more than squeak, or maybe purr. 'Where's Gurnet gone?'

Beyond the crates, the creature shifted. I heard something tinkle. *A bell*, I thought, dizzily. *Or a little mirror. Gurnet has put a bell or a piece of looking glass in the cage, like for a singing bird.*

'Gary, you mean,' the voice rasped. 'Show some respect, you. That's my Gary you're chafing on about. He's gone for a wander. To check the lie of the land. Now let me out, Daff-o-dilly. Let me go to the sea.'

I stepped forward then. Just far enough to be able to see over the crates, but not so far that I wouldn't be able to duck, or shield my eyes, if I needed to; if the creature spat at me.

It was the decorations I noticed first: Christmas bells and snowflakes twinkling through the bars of the cat carrier . . . an angel, face down in a saucer of water . . . gold and silver tinsel shredded and scattered, like unwanted bedding or a thing torn apart in a rage.

Those were the bright things. The shiny things. Laurence himself was a fat dark mass, his fur pressed tight against the carrier's bars. I couldn't work out, to begin with, if he had his back to me or not, but the size of him was shocking. Before long, I could tell, he would need a bigger carrier.

'Laurence?'

He opened his eyes. He looked straight at me.

And oh, the misery of it. The despair. It washed right over me, making me stagger. I would grow old, I realized. One day . . . I would get sick and know pain. And if I love, or am loved, before my death day comes, so what? For no one will ever love me truly or accept me for who I am . . . a strange girl, a dreamer . . . a rootless, abandoned thing . . .

I reached out to steady myself on one of the crates— the one marked 'Baby things'.

Baby things . . . I closed my eyes and made a huge effort to imagine all those tiny clothes, folded carefully away. It was the right thing to do because it focused my mind—stopped the misery, and the panic, from overwhelming me completely.

The manor's last lord and lady died childless. The clothes in the crate would be old-fashioned, I imagined, and in need of a good wash. Still, they had been special, once. Someone, long ago, had bought them, or knitted them, or embroidered flowers round their hems, or on their teeny tiny collars, thinking lovingly, and hopefully, of the little ones they were for.

My mother left no clothes for me, just the blanket I was wrapped in and the nappy I had on. No embroidery there. Nothing worth saving, so we didn't.

A blanket and a nappy . . . I would have liked those things kept, I realized. I would have treasured them— even the nappy—for they prove Aurelia cared enough about me to keep me clean and warm for the short time I was hers.

'*I love her but I cannot keep . . . '*

My mother could have flung me, squalling, into the sea or left me in her caravan, to starve. She wanted me to be happy, though, and among my own kin. She gave me that chance.

I took a deep shuddery breath, let go of the crate, and dared to look back at the creature.

He blinked his doleful eyes at me.

'Oh, Laurence,' I said. 'Don't be sad. We'll sort something out for you.' He blinked again. He seemed confused.

'I have to go now,' I told him, 'but I'll come again tomorrow. When Gurnet—Gary—gets back, tell him I was here. Tell him I'll see him tomorrow. '

I backed away, expecting to be cursed, or spat upon, for not opening the carrier. But Laurence said nothing as I left, nor did he shout after me as I made my way downstairs.

I wouldn't tell Jenna, I decided. I would have to tell someone but it wouldn't be her. I'd left her in the special room with the four-poster bed in it (Gurnet must have forced the lock because the door had opened just like that) and she was in there still, when I went back, sprawled on the bed in a dress she'd found, and very nearly asleep.

I could have slapped her. Not because the room still felt like mine but because the first thing she said, as she opened her eyes and sat up, was: 'I'm having this dress. If anyone asks, it got washed up on the beach. I'll make a big show of asking the Americans if it came from their ship, but after that it's mine. I'm keeping it.'

'Don't you want to know,' I snapped back at her, 'whether or not I found Gurnet?' My voice was shaking; so were my hands.

'Of course,' Jenna said, although her own hands were busy, tightening the ribbons down the front of the dress, and her eyes were on her own chest as it rose, with the tightening, like something being baked in an oven. 'Is he up there, then? And is the creature with him?'

'No,' I said, unwilling to say a single word about any of it to a girl who cared more, all of a sudden, about how she looked in a stolen dress than about our missing friend.

Not telling wasn't easy though. I felt the burden of it all the way down the stairs and was glad to get out, into daylight.

The manor grounds are beautiful, now that spring is here. Above our heads, the rhododendrons formed a twisted arch, the red flowers already huge, the mauves and whites just starting to open out.

'Do you remember,' Jenna said—all chatty and bright, because of the stolen dress—'when we were fairies, in that thing at the school? You were Pease Blossom, remember? We did a little dance, and the teacher gave us sweets.'

'You bit me,' I reminded her, coldly. 'On the arm.'

'Never!'

'You did. You were jealous because I got a floaty pink dress to wear and you got something brown.'

'Yellowy-brown,' she corrected me. 'I was Mustard Seed. I wore a yellowy-brown tunic and yellowy-green tights. I looked like a streak of diarrhoea. No wonder I got cranky.'

'Either way . . . '

My head was beginning to ache. Not over Jenna but from having no idea what to do about Gurnet and the creature. I needed help, I knew that. But who from? Who could I trust to do the right thing—to even know what the right thing was? Mum and Dad? The Carthews? A vet? The authorities?

I considered telling Connor Blue but even as I thought it, I knew I never would. The connection I'd felt with him earlier seemed fragile, all of a sudden: lovely, still, and something I would always remember but not strong enough, nowhere near strong enough, to take the strain and the worry of what-to-do-about-Gurnet.

No.

Stepping, with Jenna, through the gap in the wall, I knew there was only one person I could turn to. One person who loves and understands Gurnet Carthew every bit as much as I do, and would, I knew, move heaven and earth to help him.

And that was Danzel.

JENNA

I avoided Trent-the-badger-man and went straight to Connor Blue. I had no useful information, after all, about the whereabouts of Gurnet's creature so why mess around with plan a) I thought, when I have plan b) now, thanks to the dress? Also, something Dilly had said, about doing a good turn for Maude, had got me thinking (or, all right then, plotting).

I knew how to get Connor Blue to the manor. I knew what to say, to lure him into that room with the four-poster bed in it. Would he be as crazy for me, though, as I am for him, by the time I got him there?

I told myself I had nothing to lose by trying. I told myself I was gorgeous enough to tempt any man, and that Connor Blue, being young and fit and a very long way from home, would surely take one look at me, in the pink silk frock, and another at that incredible bed, and be unable to resist.

I sat on a rock, watching the Americans' ship as day-light faded to grey and a mist began to rise. If he hadn't come, I would have borrowed a boat to go to him, or kicked off my shoes and swum out to the ship's ladder, as daring as you like. If he'd come with a gang I would have brazened it out, and asked for a private word. If he'd come with old Trent I would have been seriously flicked off.

He came alone—apart, that is, from the man rowing the dinghy. Watching that little boat pulling closer to the shore . . . bringing HIM nearer and nearer . . . I felt my stomach dip and bob like it was me riding the waves.

I walked slowly down the beach . . . I waded a little way into the sea . . . I allowed a wave to smack against my shins, not caring that the bottom of my dress got soaked. It was no longer my best one, after all. It had been demoted. 'Hello,' I said, grabbing an edge of the dinghy to help bring it in.

'Hi,' said Connor Blue. 'Jenna, right?'

'That's right,' I said, all sweetness. Then I turned to the man who'd rowed, fixing all my attention on him as he rolled his trousers up over his knees and then jumped, barefoot, into a receding wave.

'When you get back to the ship,' I said to him, 'would you please ask the women there if anyone's lost a dress.'

'A dress?'

He had stowed the oars; was hauling the dinghy right out of the water, which didn't bode well, and meant I was having to drag it with him, a lot further up than I wanted to. Connor Blue hadn't moved a muscle.

'Yes,' I said, patiently. 'A dress. I found one, today, right here on the beach. It must have blown over the side of the ship—off a washing line or something.'

The rower tipped his head back and laughed; a really throaty laugh, as if I'd told a funny joke. All the women, he said—apart from the leading lady who had gone to her cabin, with a headache—were in The Crazy

Mermaid which is where he himself was heading, along with Connor Blue. 'I'll ask,' he said. 'I'll make a big announcement in the café. "Did anyone, apart from the local woman—the real live crazy mermaid—ditch their clothes on the beach last night"?'

I felt my face redden. 'It was on the tide line,' I said, stiffly. 'Washed in. It's a ball dress. A beautiful dress. And for all you know, your leading lady doesn't have a head-ache at all but is very, very upset about losing her favour-ite piece of clothing, ever. If it was mine, I'd be crying. I'd want to know sooner rather than later if it had been found, and whether it was still wearable, which it is.'

'Can we ring Jane?' said Connor Blue, jumping ashore now that we'd beached the dinghy for him. 'Let's ring her. When we get to the café, we'll give her a call.'

The rower didn't answer. He was looking me up and down and, even in the dusk, I could see the twinkle in his eyes. Then: 'Don't worry,' he said. 'I'll row back. It won't take long. Order me something light, will you, Con? And a flagon of that wonderful cider.'

I could have kissed him—almost.

'Thank you,' I said, moving, straightaway, to swivel the dinghy back round.

'You're welcome, young lady,' he answered, reaching past me for the oars. 'Just make sure our leading man goes straight to the café OK? No wreathing him with seaweed and luring him away to some chamber of the sea. Not with him due on set first thing tomorrow morn-ing. Promise?'

'I promise,' I said, happy now, and not particularly minding if this man had seen right through me. *No wreathing him with seaweed.* As if I would, the smelly stuff.

Connor Blue had backed away to where the waves wouldn't lap at his shoes.

'You're all wet,' he observed when we were finally alone.

'I am, aren't I,' I agreed. 'I'm absolutely dripping.'

I wanted to touch him. I wanted to throw my arms around his neck and hug him tight. I wanted to smell his throat. *This is the man of your dreams,* I told myself as a wave crashed at my heels, and neither of us moved. *The most beautiful man in the universe is standing so close you could grab his jumper. Or stroke a cheekbone. Or . . .*

'Well . . . don't stand around here for too long, Jenna,' he said. 'Now that the sun's gone, you'll catch your death.'

He sounded genuinely concerned. It made my innards melt to hear it.

'I'll walk with you,' I said. 'Up to the café. There's something I want to ask you—something really important.'

'Sure.' He set off at once, taking such huge strides across the sand that I had to trot to keep up. 'What is it?'

He really was moving fast. 'It's all right,' I said, 'I don't need to run, to keep warm. I'm a local. I'm hardened. We can walk normally, really.'

And so he slowed his pace, although I could tell it worried him to do it. And I stopped myself—just—from reaching for his hand as I spun my pretty tale. About my lovely friend Maude. My dear and beautiful friend who was so painfully shy that she was like a wood nymph or an echo—always hiding or slipping away somewhere.

'That thing you said when you arrived,' I said, 'about

the apron she was wearing. Well, it offended her terribly. It shocked her to the core. To her very *soul*.'

He stopped walking, then, and stared at me, appalled. 'But I was joking,' he said. 'You know that, right? I was only fooling around.'

I shook my head sadly. We Port Zannon girls, I told him, weren't used to being fooled around with. Certainly not by strangers. And Maude, in particular, was such a sensitive maid that any talk of a sexual nature—even a comment as fleeting and harmless as his had been—was bound to leave its mark. An emotional bruise. A *scar*.

'Please tell her—let her know, will you?—I meant no harm by it.'

He'd taken the bait. So far, so very good.

'I think,' I said slowly, 'it would be best if you told her yourself.'

He didn't answer straightaway and I held my breath, wondering if I'd wrecked it—if I'd gone a bit too far.

Then: Of course, he agreed. Absolutely. He would go to Maude right away, and apologize for being so crass. Where would he find her? Would I take him there?

Oh, it was good. It was perfect. It couldn't have gone any better if I'd written him a script.

'It's coming dark now,' I said. 'She won't want to be bothered. But I could take you to her tomorrow—to where I know she'll be.'

'Really?' he said. 'Would you do that for me?'

No problem, I answered. My pleasure.

DANZEL

I cried. I'm not ashamed. I cried like a baby all over Maude's shoulder while she patted my back and waited, bless her, for me to pull myself together and explain.

'Gurnet's done for,' I moaned, as soon as I could speak without choking on my own snot. 'That councillor he knifed is as dead as a brick. They'll come for him, Maude. They'll put him away for life. They might even . . . if the king gives the order . . . they might . . . '

She covered my mouth with the palm of her hand.

This was dreadful, she said, the colour draining from her face. And if she hadn't let the creature out in the first place, none of it would have happened.

I moved her hand away.

'Horse dung,' I croaked. 'If anyone's to blame, it's me.' And I told how I'd spilled the beans, about Gurnet and his creature. How I'd betrayed my best friend, just to big myself up in front of Connor Blue and the researcher and that rotten whelk of a councillor.

'It was the cider talking, Maudie. I swear . . . it was the cider made me gabble so . . . I wish . . . I wish . . . '

She had to pat and calm me some more, then. Poor Maude. Her hands were trembling so much they felt like birds landing on my spine. It should have been me

255

comforting her, I know, I know, and it pains me—it really does—that all I did was blabber and sniff and go on and on about what a useless sap I am, leaving her to deal, alone, with the whirl of her own guilt.

'I don't know what to do,' I blubbed. 'Or who to tell. I have absolutely no idea . . . '

A rat-a-tat at the front door made us jump half out of our skins. We were in Maude's parlour, with the curtains drawn against the setting of the sun. Nowhere should have felt safer, but we clutched each other as if the County Executioner himself had arrived on the step, with a warrant to take us away.

Maude's mother answered the door. We heard her voice (so familiar, so ordinary . . .): 'Oh, Dilly, hello . . . I think she's asleep, but wait there a moment, and I'll see.'

'Maude, dear . . . ?' The knock and the question were tentative; and so very hard to hear, that we held our breaths, the better to catch whatever else she might say.

'It's Dilly, looking for Danzel. He's not with you is he?'

Maude raised a finger to her lips. *Shhh*. Her mother, we knew, wouldn't open the door. The parlour is Maude's domain. I'd tapped, earlier, at its window, not wanting the grown-ups to see me, in my terrible agitation, and Maude had let me in, quietly and in secret.

Her mother, receiving no answer, went away. Moments later, so did Dilly. I heard her footsteps on the cobbles outside, and, in my mind, I hurried after her. *Dilly Daydream*, I thought, miserably, *would you be patting my back, all sweet and kind, if you knew what I'd done to our Gurnet? Would you?*

I had enough on my plate, I knew, without worrying

what Dilly would make of it all. Still, I couldn't help feeling wretched, imagining her scorn. What she thinks of me matters, I realized. Now, more than ever.

Maude took my hand.

We would go back to the manor house, she said to me. First thing in the morning she and I would let Gurnet know that the councillor had died from his wounds.

'Can't,' I protested, shuddering. 'He'll have a turn for certain, the worst he's ever had.'

More than likely, she agreed. But if anyone could deal with it, we could. And if anyone could persuade Gurnet to come back to the port, to face up to what he had done, it was us, his friends.

I nodded. I was sure she was right. That it was the best thing—the only thing—to do. I just wriggled, maggot that I am, from having to explain, to a wild and terrified Gurn, the part I had played in destroying his life. In ending it even . . . oh God . . .

'What . . . what about Dilly?' I wondered, forcing the words past a lump in my throat. 'And Jenna? Shouldn't we do this together? All four of us?'

Maude shook her head.

Not this bit, she said. Not the bringing of Gurnet home. We would do that part alone. And then the five of us— she and I, Gurnet, Jenna, and Dilly—would go to our families and tell them everything.

'Everything?' I said, in a voice I'm completely ashamed of.

Everything, she replied.

The whole story.

It is Dilly's mum who tells Connor Blue where to find Maude. She even walks him from the café and points out the way.

'Don't worry,' she says, for he has told her, word for word, what Jenna Rosdew said to him, down on the beach. 'Don't fret. It will all be fine.'

'Do you think so?' Connor peers, anxiously, into the dark, uncertain, still, about the amount of dismay he might have caused the girl whose mermaid-face has been haunting him through two days and a sleep.

'I know so.'

'But it's getting late . . . it's nearly nine. Perhaps I should wait until . . . '

Dilly's mum flaps her apron at him, as if he is a gull, or a dithering child. He laughs, then, and skips out of her way. 'Go!' she orders. 'You need your rest, young man, with filming starting tomorrow. And you'll sleep better knowing this was a misunderstanding—a storm in a teacup. Go talk to Maude.'

'OK, OK, I'm going . . . ' He laughs some more, turning, eagerly now, in the direction of Maude's home.

Dilly's mum watches him leave. Jenna Rosdew, she thinks, you are one crafty maid, twisting things around for your own gain . . . putting trouble where none exists . . . I know your game, missy, I know what you're about. But Connor Blue is as sincere as he is handsome. I won't have him mortified.

It takes Connor less than a minute to reach Maude's house, and another three to pluck up enough courage to knock.

Maude, alone in the parlour, hears the knock and assumes it is Dilly, returning, or that Danzel—who has only just left—no longer wants to catch a few hours sleep before going to find Gurnet at the old manor house.

It's all right, she tells her mother, as they collide in the tiny hall. I'll go . . . and she waits until her mother is back in the kitchen, re-settled in front of the inter-telly and the nice warm stove.

Then she opens the front door.

Love at first sight? (Or second sight, in this case, if you want to split hairs.) A cynic would call it impossible: a poet's fib . . . mutual lust, that's all. But Connor Blue is no cynic, and neither is young Maude. They are hopeless romantics. Turtle doves. As soppy as they come.

So: love at first sight it is.

'Please forgive me,' Connor says, his heart leaping like a fish as he looks at this girl, framed in the doorway like a maid in an old-fashioned painting. 'For what I said to you yesterday, about the apron.'

Maude is all of a fluster, but only from timidity, and the surprise of seeing him, of all people, there on the step. She shakes her head for, what with everything else going on, she has forgotten all about the apron.

Seeing her so puzzled goes a long way towards setting Connor's mind at rest. Still, he wants to be certain.

'Your friend Jenna,' he says, 'told me I'd offended you, deeply.'

Maude smiles then and shakes her head a second time. She gets it now. She understands. This is one of Jenna's things.

'No?' Connor doesn't need Maude to speak. He can tell, just by looking at her, that her friend took serious liberties with the truth, earlier, and that everything is, indeed, fine, just as Mrs Tonkin said it would be. 'Well then . . . I must have misunderstood. That crack about the apron, though, was still pretty crass—unnecessary. And winking at you . . . I can't believe I did that.'

Maude looks kindly at him. It's funny, she thinks, how ordinary this person is; not like a film star at all, or at least her idea of one. She is sorry that Jenna lied to him, but glad that he has come, like a perfect gentleman, to make sure she is all right. This, she knows, would not have been Jenna's intention.

Inviting Connor in seems as natural to Maude as opening a window, to let in light and air. And when he steps into her parlour, and sits down in a green-patterned chair, she notices, and is amazed by, how very much at home he seems.

As for Connor Blue: nothing, in his experience, has primed him to feel comfortable here. Quite the opposite. He is used to vast rooms, painted white; to sliding glass doors the size of tennis courts and cinematic views across the Hollywood hills.

This tiny English parlour with its seaweed-coloured carpet and firelight-shadows, is smaller, even, than the space he usually hangs his clothes in.

And yet, as he leans back in the green-patterned chair and Maude, delighted, sits opposite, it seems to him he has stepped away from the world and into enchanted space: a fairy den beneath the roots of a tree . . . a grotto under water. If a cat had come in and started to speak, or a broom begun sweeping, of its own accord, he would not have been surprised.

'I can't stay long,' he says, regretting, already, that he has to leave at all—that there is filming to do tomorrow, and some *kind of a future, after that.*

Maude nods. Later, after he has gone, it will dawn on her that she didn't offer him tea, or a biscuit, or anything at all apart from a chair to sit upon and her own, quiet, company.

And it will make her glow with pleasure to realize—to know with utter certainty—that just sitting there with her had been enough for Connor Blue. That there had been no need, whatsoever, for her to struggle with conversation . . . to wear herself out by pretending, with a thumping heart and burning face, to be chattier, and flirtier and altogether louder than she naturally is.

And yet (and this amazes her) she wants, very badly, to talk to Connor Blue; one day, when she is over the surprise—the suddenness—of feeling this way. For the first time in her life she longs to pour out her thoughts . . . her memories . . . the story of who she is . . . to another human being and then to be silent again, and still, while he does the same.

Returning to the parlour, Maude touches the green-patterned chair, resting her hand on the place where the back of Connor's head has just been. Then she crosses the small room and lies down on a narrow couch, to try and get some sleep before Danzel arrives. Sleepless, she considers the embers of the fire and, with them, the possibility of happiness.

And as the clock on the mantel ticks towards dawn, and the time for her own leaving draws near, her confidence starts to waver, and her hopes, like the coals, cool down and fall apart.

Connor Blue, she tells herself, is too good for her. He will sail away after filming, never to return, and she will weep, in secret, for the loss of him, and never tell a soul.

She reminds herself, as the clock strikes four, that she has her friends to think about: Gurnet, who is in terrible trouble, and Danzel who needs her support. And then there is the creature . . . the creature she let out. There is unfinished business there, she can feel it in her bones.

Her destiny, she senses, is not sunny. She wishes she could see it, in the fire's dying, or hear it whispered by the walls, or the atoms of this room where she has spent so many hours calmly dreaming.

But she can't.

DILLY

I looked everywhere for Danzel: at his house, at Maude's, on the cliff top where he goes to drink his cider, at the café, on the beach: everywhere. Finally, I called at Jenna's; but she was home alone, wearing her stolen dress and trying new things with her hair.

'Up or down?' she said to me. 'And with or without the clip?'

'Down,' I said. And 'Without.'

'Don't call for me tomorrow,' she told me, shaking loose her hair and pouting at her wet room mirror. 'I'm going to be *otherwise engaged.*'

She had that desperate look about her, the one she gets when she talks, or even thinks, about Connor Blue. I couldn't be bothered with her. I was too worried about Gurnet, and what to do about his creature, I didn't even ask what she was planning. I guessed it would be something sad and silly, like going back to the beach to spy on the ship, or hanging about the film set expecting to be swooped on and given a starring role.

It was close to midnight by the time I left. There were cables and rails in the streets, ready for filming to start. I moved carefully, not wanting to break anything, including my own ankles. I thought I might find one or two

263

people walking along on the beach, or sitting on the harbour wall, but there wasn't a soul around.

The American ship, though, was all lit up, with laughter and music spilling from it. I prefer the sound of waves, I decided, and the sight of the stars up above. I am a true stick-at-home, I realized, smiling to myself in the dark. A Port Zannon girl to the core. And I need—want—to talk to Danzel.

Through the window of The Crazy Mermaid I saw candles burning, still, and the shapes of two people, one sitting, one moving around. It was my mum moving, to wipe the table tops. I didn't recognize the other person until I reached the door.

'Dilly!' Mum said, as I stepped in. 'I was just telling our visitor here the tale of our ghostly rider. *The footman he rode like a bat out of hell, lickety-lickety-split.* But he already knows it, imagine that? And not from a file on the inter-telly either but from his own grandad in America, who heard it from his grandad and so on down the line. Fancy, our stories being remembered, and told, so very far away?'

She went prattling on, as she wiped the last table, about the smallness of the world, and the connections that exist between all kinds of different folk.

'You were about to tell me, sir,' she said. 'Who it was went from here to America all those years ago.'

'My great-great-great-great-great-great-grandfather,' he replied, ticking the 'greats' off on his fingers, so as not to miss one out. 'On my father's side.'

'Oh my.' My mother paused, in her wiping. 'All those greats! How wonderful to be able to go back so far in

264

your family. To know your own roots—the spread of them, and how deep they go . . . '

She stopped, then, pretending to clear her throat, but her throat didn't need clearing, and the look she threw me was flustered. Apologetic. Had I been closer to her I would have given her a hug, to show I didn't mind—I really didn't, any more—about the gaps in my own past. Because my roots are right here, in Port Zannon, and growing just fine.

But I was closer to the American than to her, and he was looking at me in a very peculiar way.

'Dilly,' he said. 'That's a pretty name. Is it short for something? Delia? Adele?' He was trying to sound off-hand but something about his manner—something tense—put me on my guard.

'Daffodil,' Mum told him, proudly. 'My daughter's name is Daffodil. Daffodil Aurelia Tonkin.'

A flicker passed over the man's face. There and gone it was, as if he'd walked through spider thread.

'Unusual,' he said.

'Unique,' my mum replied. 'She's unique this maid is . . . Sorry . . . I'm sorry . . . I must go and rinse my cloth out and put some crocks away . . . '

I will hug her later, I told myself as she headed for the kitchen. *When I've worked out what to do, about Gurnet and his creature, I'll give her a great big hug.*

For the moment though, there was this man to deal with. This American with Cornish blood in his veins and my name on his mind, ringing bells.

I sat down in front of him. I looked him in the eye.

'This is going to sound really odd,' I said, keeping my

265

voice low even though the kitchen door had swung shut behind my mum. 'But . . . did you recognize my name just then, sir? Have you heard it before, somewhere, or . . . or . . . seen it written down?'

And I knew, as soon as the words were out, that we were both, in our own minds, picturing those words—Daffodil Aurelia Tonkin—swirled in dust on a big old bedroom mirror.

My heart began to thump, so hard I thought he might hear it.

'Have you . . . have you been exploring, sir?' I faltered. 'Up on the cliffs? As far as—'

'I've been to the manor house, Dilly,' he interrupted, quietly. 'And so have you, haven't you? Recently. It's your name I saw on the mirror. No—don't worry. Listen. Just listen . . . '

I'd turned, automatically, to watch the kitchen door, scared that my mum would come out and hear us. I didn't want her finding out, I realized, about the house, the creature, or any of it. I didn't want her going crazy at me, for breaking all the rules; for going where I shouldn't as if home, and the café, and she and my dad were no longer enough to anchor me—to keep me safe.

'Listen,' the man repeated, more urgently this time. 'Your friend Gary Carthew. Do you know where he is? I can't tell you how important this is, Dilly. Not yet. But please . . . you have to trust me. I've just found out he's run away and I have to find him. He had a pet, didn't he . . . something he, or you, or somebody, anyway, found at the old manor house. No . . . I'm sorry. You have to hear me out . . . '

I'd pushed back my chair . . . had risen to my feet . . . would have bolted straight out of the café if he hadn't grabbed me by my wrists, forcing me to stay.

'Let go of me,' I said. 'Or I'll scream for my mother.'

'OK. OK . . . I apologize. I'm sorry. ' He dropped my wrists, slumped back in his chair, groaned and closed his eyes.

I dithered. Was he having a stroke, or something? Or was he shamming, to make me stay? I couldn't tell. I don't know enough about people—about foreigners—to know when they're pretending.

He really did look dreadful.

Then: 'I don't want to frighten you,' he said, opening his eyes and sitting up straighter. 'You weren't to know, and neither was your friend, but that creature is dangerous. So dangerous that the longer it's out there, the worse the consequences are going to be. Not just for people living here but for—'

'Is . . . is it rabid?' I cut in, my heart missing a thump. 'Might I . . . might my friends . . . '

'No,' he said, quickly. 'It isn't that. And you're in no immediate danger, Dilly. I'd be able to tell if . . . if you'd been affected. But, please, if you know where Gary is, you must tell me. He may have some idea—some clue—about where the creature went after it flew out of your church.'

I looked down at the table, at a scallop-shaped mat, freshly wiped and ready for somebody's breakfast plate. I thought of Gurnet, who I had known my whole life long and who deserved my loyalty far more than this American—this foreigner who, for all I knew, only

267

wanted Laurence for himself, to keep as a pet or sell on to the highest bidder.

'I can't help you, sir,' I said. 'I'm sorry.'

I thought he was going to groan again but he didn't. Instead, he put his hand in his pocket, took out a tiny inter-phone, and passed it across the table. 'I want you to take this,' he said. 'And if you think of anything . . . hear of anything . . . anything at all that might help me to trace this creature, ring me at once, OK? Just press the green button—that one, there—and I'll answer. Any time, day or night, I'll answer the call, OK?'

I was looking at the phone, wondering what to do—whether to take it or not—when the kitchen door swung open.

'Finished,' my mum said, all bright and breezy again. 'We're closing now, sir. It's been a very long day. Nine o'clock we'll be open tomorrow. It's usually much earlier, for the fishermen's breakfasts, but they're staying in port tonight, what with filming starting so early. They'll be looking forward to sleeping in, I expect—I know I am.'

'Of course,' the American said, as I covered the phone with my hand. 'I'm sorry to have kept you, Mrs Tonkin.'

'Oh, you're welcome,' Mum replied. 'I enjoyed our chat. And I meant to ask your name, sir. Because if it's the same as your Cornish ancestor's . . . '

'It is,' he said, with a brief, distracted smile.

' . . . then it could be you have blood relatives, still living in the port.'

She sounded so enthusiastic, so *normal*, rabbiting on the way she does, that sliding the phone off the table and down onto my lap felt normal too; of no more weight or consequence than sneaking sugar lumps from a bowl.

The American gave me the tiniest nod. *Thank you*. And 'My name is Trent,' he said to my mum. 'Trent Rogerson.'

'Rogerson? Hmm . . . ' Mum was too busy racking her memory, going through the surnames of everyone in the port, to pay attention to me as I slipped the inter-phone into the pocket of my dress.

'It's not a name I recognize,' she said eventually. 'And there are none in the churchyard either, I'm quite certain of that. But your ancestor would be very glad, I'm sure, sir, to know that you've come back. That the family name didn't sink from here for ever, without memory or trace.'

She blew the remaining candles out and we moved, all three of us, towards the door. The inter-phone felt lead-heavy in my pocket. And I didn't look at Trent Rogerson again as I said goodnight and went home with my mum.

I didn't sleep. How could I? I thought about Gurnet; memories of him crowding my head like movie scenes . . . Gurnet at three, with a crab in a bucket. What did he call that crab again? I've forgotten . . . The turn he had when it died . . . the way he wept and raged for days.

Gurnet at five, bullied at school by inlanders . . . the terrible turns he had then, until Danzel invented the hurling game, throwing pebbles, to start with, from the shore into the sea. Shoulder to shoulder they would sit, little Gurn and little Dan, with their toes in the surf and their pebbles in a pile. '*That next wave, Gurn, is Alfie Price. Let's get him—yay!*' . . . The pebbles getting bigger over the years and thrown from further away. They hurl small rocks, now, from the top of the cliff—small rocks aimed at larger rocks, and thrown so hard and fast that they would brain a gull, if one got in the way.

I pictured Gurnet with his creature: both of them fast asleep, I guessed, in the attic of the old manor house.

Let me out, Daff-o-Dilly.

Trent Rogerson thought the creature was out already; running wild on the moors or heading inland in search of food—or people.

You weren't to know, and neither was your friend, but that creature is dangerous . . .

Not if it's caged, it's not, I told myself. It can't hurt anyone, surely, if it stays in its carrier. And Gurnet, I knew, would keep it caged for ever, or at least until it died of natural causes, like the long-ago crab in a bucket.

I tried to think, rationally, about what possible harm the creature could do, to Gurnet or anyone else, if it never got let out. And there it was: the one fact I couldn't afford to ignore.

It could spit.

If Gurnet didn't listen . . . refused to let it go . . . it could spit right into his eyes. I wished, then, that I'd asked Trent Rogerson about the spitting. About how dangerous it might be for humans, to get that spit in their eyes, even if the creature wasn't rabid, as he'd said.

I fretted about the clergyman who got spat on in the church. What had happened to him? Did anyone know? Did Trent Rogerson?

I imagined that poor man disfigured . . . blinded perhaps . . . maybe even dying, slowly, from some awful virus the creature carried in its spit; a virus without a cure that Trent Rogerson hadn't mentioned because he didn't want to scare the living daylights out of me; and because he had no idea that Gurnet—our Gurnet—was with the creature now, and could be spat on at any second.

Shortly before dawn I fetched the inter-phone from the pocket of my dress and pressed the green button.

'Dilly. Talk to me.'

It didn't seem possible, that I could speak, from my bed, and that someone could hear me without being in the room.

'What happened to the clergyman?' I said to the phone. 'The one the creature spat on. Is he . . . is he . . . alive?'

'He is,' the phone answered, promptly. 'But the people who are monitoring him say he wishes he was not. Physically, Dilly, he is fine. But he won't be for much longer. He isn't eating, you see, or taking any exercise. And he won't speak to a soul. He has lost his faith, Dilly, and with it the will to live. He has no—'

'Stop,' I said and the phone went silent . . . grew heavier in my hand, it seemed, pulsing like a heart as it waited for me to go on.

For a second or so I could barely breathe, never mind speak. Then: 'Gary Carthew is at the old manor house,' I said. 'In the attic, with the creature. It—'

'Thank you,' the phone replied and the green light went away.

DANZEL

In the end, we didn't wait for the dawn. We took our torches and set off for the manor while the port was still in darkness. Passing beneath Dilly's window I got the feeling she was awake. I wanted to stop and call up to her. I wanted her with us. But Maude shook her head at me, although I hadn't said a word, and then we were at the steps, and climbing.

I'd spent a while, before leaving, wondering what to take. What object or thing I could bring to my friend Gurnet to help him bear our news. I wanted to shower him with gifts. Flagons of cider. A fine new coat. A baby rabbit to tame and to love. A fishing rod to die for.

No. Forget to die for. Not funny. Not funny at all . . .

Because what gifts do you give to a murderer? What, for the love of all that breathes, do you take a boy like Gurn who, should the king decree it, could spend a year and a day in a high security gaol and then . . .

It can't happen to Gurn. It can't happen to Gurn. It wasn't treason. It wasn't a slaying in cold blood. The man broke into his room, for crying out loud. It can't happen to Gurn. It can't happen to Gurn . . .

I kept up that mantra all the way to the manor gates. Silently, in time with my walking. *It can't happen to Gurn.*

It can't . . . Apart from anything else, it kept me from dwelling on—from counting—the number of lads and men beheaded, in recent years, for murder. It stopped me from seeing that big old daft old Gurny head, lopped off at the neck, those Gurny eyes all of a-boggle that they could do this thing to him . . . that they could really, really, do it . . .

It can't happen to Gurn . . .

Larks were singing, by the time we reached the house. I staggered a bit, going in, and would have crumpled altogether, at the foot of the stairs, if Maude hadn't taken my arm.

'I can't do this, Maudie,' I whimpered, pulling against her; rearing back from those stairs, 'I can't . . . '

But she kept hold of my arm and told me that I must. That I had to.

And so, after a few sorry shudders and gulps, I did. I climbed the stairs with Maude—'Up the wooden hill to Bedfordshire,' my granny Killick used to say—to the very top of the house.

We didn't need our torches, up there. The early morning light was streaming in, through window-sized holes in the roof.

'Maude,' I whispered, clutching her hand so tight I must have hurt her. 'What the—'

There was a table cloth spread out on the floorboards, an old-fashioned one with red and white checks, and it was laid for a picnic with plates and cups and salt and pepper and an antique flask with the lid off. And there was tinsel looped all around the walls, and other old-fashioned Christmas stuff—glitter-angels and baubles;

plastic snowmen and deer—arranged on top of crates or dangling from beams, like the mermaids in the café.

The cat carrier was there, and the creature was in it, pressed so tight and close to the criss-cross bars holding it in that the front of its body looked checked, like the cloth. It had a pink tube in its mouth; a plastic straw—the kind you don't get nowadays—and was sucking something up from a cup, set down outside the carrier.

And our Gurnet was sitting cross-legged on the floor, reading aloud from an old-fashioned kiddie book that had a picture on the front of a robed and long-haired man who looked so much like Connor Blue that I thought, for a moment, that it was.

'As Jesus walked beside the sea of Galilee,' Gurnet was saying, while the creature sucked and listened. 'He saw two fishermen, casting their nets, and he said to them . . .'

'Here's trouble,' the creature announced, spitting out its straw. And it fixed its stare on Maude and me as we hovered at the top of the stairs, not knowing, either of us, what to think . . . what to do . . . how to intrude, with our terrible news, upon this weird and yet—it has to be said—oddly contented scene. 'Over there, my Gary. Wake up, mate!'

And Gurnet turned, his face hostile until he realized it was us. Only us. His friends.

'Hello,' he said, his mouth lifting in a rare and lovely grin. 'Have you brought us something nice?'

Dawn.

A beautiful one.

The calm before the storm.

It is said that the gods on Mount Olympus played chess to pass the time, and that for each piece taken a mortal lost a battle. Or a leg. Or their greatest heart's desire. It is said that human beings do not control their destinies but are part of a grand design . . . of a pattern so vast, and so complicated, that no one begins to understand it until after they die, and maybe not even then.

Sometimes a mortal—a child, usually—gets a fleeting glimpse of what the pattern is all about: a reflection on water, a whisper on the wind . . . there and gone, impossible to hold.

But I digress . . .

In the attic of the old manor house, Gurnet's creature blinks and stirs.

Today, it thinks. I must get to the sea today. Never mind the clergy-people, the eeky-Christians and so on. It's the plankton I must get to. That's what's bringing hope to the world with its breedings and its thrivings and its oxygen-making parts.

And it's small stuff, my Gary says. Little specks. I can get the lot wiped out by sunslide, across the seven seas, and hah! Job done, matey. No hope after that for anyone . . . none at all.

The actors from Hollywood are stirring too, on board their fancy ship. Connor Blue is up already, having his hair tied back and his eyes outlined in black. Not that the wreckers of Port Zannon wore make-up. Not likely. His shirt, too, is all wrong. Too white, and too flouncy, to have graced the back of any fisherman in 1732. And when he speaks his first lines ('The sky to the west be as black as a bruise. There's a storm brewing, Nancy, I can feel it') they will sound about as Cornish as a weather report in the state of California.

And another thing: the sky to the west is not as black as a bruise. It is milky blue with an apricot tinge, promising only the sunniest of aspects when the cameras start to roll.

But they can sort that. When they get back to the studio, in Hollywood, they can bruise the sky, whip up a sea and make a toy ship look just like a tall one as they wreck it in a sinkful of water, against a backdrop of thunder and lightning. They can do anything now; anything at all, to create an illusion on film.

So why send a cast and a crew all the way across the Atlantic? Why must Connor Blue stroll around Port Zannon, with an actress on his arm, and glee in his kohl-rimmed eyes at the prospect of a wreck, when he could have played his part just as easily—and at far less cost—on a film set back in America?

The thing to know (and Connor hasn't a clue, bless his flouncy cotton shirt) is that the studio didn't pay for this trip. It has been organized and funded by folk more powerful than that.

It is a cover. A foil. A smokescreen for something else.

Where's that Trent fellow?

He knows. He's a key player in the real drama, only it's spinning, with frightening rapidity, right out of his control.

Had his quest—his genuine reason for being here—gone according to plan he would be a happy man this morning. Had he only succeeded in finding and destroying Gurnet's creature, he would be content to continue his pretend role as a film researcher until the king (that's right) and the president of the United States (u-huh) say he can go home. He would be in cahoots with the director, or strolling the cobbled streets, making—or pretending to make—last minute checks on how quaint Port Zannon is going to look, through the sweep of the camera's eye.

But no . . . there he goes, running like a man with his pants on fire, through thickets of gorse on the top of the cliff . . . running as if his life depends on it . . . as if the fate of all humanity rests on how quickly he can get to the old manor house.

Which it does.

(You're wondering, aren't you, how I know all of this? You've been wondering for a while, haven't you, who, or what, I am?

Well, sorry.

You won't know until after you die, and maybe not even then.)

GURNET

Before the sea of Galilee got full of poo, and then dried up in the droughts, so that any old person could walk on it, there were more than twenty types of fish in it and one type protected its young by scooping them into its mouth whenever danger threatened.

I would have liked to have been a little fish of that kind. When Danzel told me I had killed the man who tried to steal Laurence away, I wished I had a parent who could scoop me up and hide me in her mouth—and Laurence, too, because I wouldn't go anywhere, now, without him.

'Gurnet,' my Danzel said, 'come home.'

'No,' I answered back. 'I'm all right here. And anyway I promised Laurence I'd take him out to sea. Today. I said we'd go today, Dan.'

'You can't do that, Gurn,' Danzel said to me. 'You need to come home. Things . . . things might go easier for you if you tell the authorities what happened . . . what you did . . . before . . . '

'I've found a boat,' I interrupted him. 'It's in a cave, on a beach round the back of here. And there's fishing stuff—in that crate, see? I can row the boat, and I can go fishing. Laurence will like that. I've promised him.'

'They'll come with dogs, Gurn,' my Danzel said to me, his voice turning slippy and strange. 'And they'll . . . they'll . . . '

He was all choked up, that friend of mine. He was in a right old state and Maude was clinging to both of my hands like I was about to set off on a long sea voyage, and she might never see me again.

I thought about that man-shape and about the stabbing I had done. I hadn't meant to kill the man, only to show him what for—to get him away from my Laurence and out of my room, where he had no right to be. I wasn't a proper murderer and I was very, very sorry. And I supposed that Danzel was right. He is always right, that boy. I needed to get my confession told before men from the authorities came to get it from me.

'All right,' I said. 'I'll come back. But I'm leaving Laurence here where no one else can get at him, or try and take him away.'

I didn't look at my Laurence when I said that. I was hoping he would be all right about it. I had given him a shell, after all, and some sea-water in a cup; and he liked the decorations in his carrier, which he'd pulled in himself because there was a hole in the crate marked 'Christmas decs' that his fingers were just long enough to reach. And Danzel and Maude and Dilly and Jenna would look after him.

They would do that for me—even Jenna would do it, without whining or insulting my intelligence—because it would be my Last Request and no one ignores those.

But: '*Nooooo,*' my Laurence wailed. '*Let me out! Let me go to the sea. I'm parching, my Gary. I'm dying of my thirst. Let me go! You promised! You gave your solemn word!'*

I got upset then. I nearly lost it.

'I can't!' I yelled, covering my ears with both my hands and scrunching my eyes tight shut. 'I have to go home, mate, and you mustn't come—it's too dangerous. The authorities would cart you off, and then you'd never see me, or the ocean, or anything else ever again. You don't understand do you? They'd stick needles in you, and watch you, and take pictures of your head. And then they'd do you in and throw your carcass away for compost or stove fuel. They would, Laurence, honestly . . . '

'*Then set me free, killer-boy*. Set. Me. Free.'

He was weeping spouts. We both were. 'Listen,' Danzel said, all urgency now. 'Gurnet, listen to me. It *has* to come home with you. The authorities need to know you were protecting it, when the councillor came. They'll need proof, my friend, because the last anyone back at the port saw or heard, that creature was flapping hell for leather out of the church.'

He took a deep breath and carried on:

'And just seeing the thing, never mind hearing it *talk*, well, it might make all the difference, mightn't it? To what . . . to what they do with you. In fact . . . I've just had a thought . . . you could say you were provoked; that the thing threatened to kill *you* if you didn't stick the councillor.'

'Oi!' Laurence hollered. 'That's a lie, that is, mate. A putrid offence.' And his weeping went from wild to weary, as if Danzel's bad suggestion had been the very last straw and he was giving up, now, on everything, including me and all my promises. Especially those.

It broke my heart, that weary sobbing noise. It did for me completely. And I knew, then, what it was that I needed to do.

'OK,' I said to Danzel. 'Let's all of us go back.'

'Good man,' he said, relieved.

'But we'll go in the boat,' I added. 'The one that's in the cave. It will be quicker than walking and Laurence will see the sea. I promised him, Danzel. I promised I'd take him out in the boat. Today. As soon as the sun came up.'

Danzel considered my plan, looking for drawbacks, and a way of saying no. But his main thought, I could tell, was that this might be my Last Request, and that only the worst kind of smother-all—the very cruellest of boys—would go against it, if it was.

'Is the boat safe?' he wondered. Yes it is, I said. 'Will it hold the three of us, plus the beast and its carrier?' he asked. Yes it would, I said, and don't call my Laurence a beast. 'And will you let me do all the rowing? Not that I don't trust you, Gurn, to head in the right direction but . . . ' Yes, I told him. You can row the boat, Danzel. You can row it all the way.

'All right, then,' he agreed. 'Let's go.'

'Wait . . . Mister Rogerson. Wait for me . . .'

Trent Rogerson has the manor gates in sight. Wheeling round, he sees the girl, heading like an arrow, straight for him.

'Go . . . home . . . Dilly,' he pants. 'It's too . . . dangerous. Go . . .'

'No!'

She catches him up, stands panting, herself, for a moment, recovering her own breath. There is an urgency about her, he notices, that wasn't there in the café. Her cheeks are flushed and her dark hair all of a tangle. She looks, to Trent Rogerson, as if she might tell him his fortune, she is so . . . luminous. So poised on the brink of something. She reminds him, suddenly, of Eve. Not the Eve men have demonized, for more than two thousand years, but the earlier Eve, of first century scripture. The one who was a teacher, and a giver of life. The one who carried the light of salvation so happily within herself that she was a joy to be around.

Eve and Pandora. Pandora and Eve. Temptresses both, in the myths that have endured, and bad news for the boys. And how handy it has been, for many a mortal man, to have a woman to blame for all evil. To have it said, or preached, or taught in school, that whatever awful things a person may do, the buck can be passed, through layers and layers of time, to a woman lifting a lid, or taking a bite out of an apple.

'Tell me,' Trent Rogerson says, to Dilly. 'Was it you who opened the box?'

'What box?' Dilly replies. 'I don't know what you're talking about.'

'The box the creature was in,' Trent says, impatient to get going but, curious, suddenly, to know if this is the girl the suppressed myth spoke of—the second Pandora. 'A wooden one, about the size of a lobster crate.'

Young Dilly shakes her head, puzzled. 'I don't know about any box,' she insists. 'According to Gurnet—that's Gary, by the way—the wall swung open, suddenly, and Laurence was . . . well . . . he was just there.'

'Laurence?'

'The creature. Gurnet wanted the creature to have a smart name. A distinguished name.'

'I see. So who . . . how?'

'Maude.'

They are moving now, towards the gap in the wall, striding rather than running, so that they can talk at the same time.

'My friend—our friend—Maude opened the wall but she never mentioned any box, and nor did Gurnet. Is it important?'

Trent Rogerson says it is. The creature was in the box, he says, and hidden behind the wall. He knows this, he says, not only from his own research—which has taken years—but because when he went to the manor on Saturday night he found the box in question. Behind the wall. Empty, as he'd feared—dreaded—it would be.

Through the gap they go and into the manor grounds. The big red flowers, clotting the arch, do not remind Dilly of weddings or of love. Not this time.

'You're going to kill it, aren't you?' she says to the man close by her side. 'You're going to kill Gurnet's creature.'

'Yes,' he replies.

She doesn't ask how. She asks why.

And so he tells her.

283

JENNA

I slept, for a bit, fantasized, a lot, and then I got up. Filming was about to start and I wanted to be there. I was going to lay claim to Connor Blue the second the cameras stopped rolling, and lead him away to the manor.

I put the silk dress on, with my blue cloak over the top, and I fastened the cloak with a silver brooch in the shape of a sickle moon. I brushed and brushed my hair until it really did gleam and washed out my mouth with mint-water.

Doing my lipstick gave me the quivers. *You won't need to wipe this off tonight*, I told my reflection in the glass. *It will have been kissed away.*

Would his kiss be rough or gentle, I wondered? And would mine be nice, for him? I'd been practising—on my pillow, on the crook of my own elbow, on the face of an old doll . . . I'd been watching soppy movies from the archives, freeze-framing love scenes and zooming in on The Kiss. My biggest worry was bumping noses. How did two people avoid doing that, I wondered? By instinct?

My boots were in the hall. How I wished, as I shoved my feet into the gallumping great things, that they could have been magicked, overnight, into a pair of high heeled shoes—pink, to match my dress, or black for extra glamour. But heels would only have snapped on the cobbles, or hampered me, later, up on the cliffs, particularly if we hurried, Connor and I, as I rather hoped we would.

Once we're there, I thought to myself. *Once we're through the gap in the wall, and onto the rhododendron path, I will kick these flicking things off and go barefoot the rest of the way. I'll take my cloak off as well and hang it on a branch. I might even pick a flower and put in my hair. Maybe he'll want to pick one for me. Maybe he'll pin it on my dress, as an excuse to touch my thingies . . . Maybe . . .*

'Jenna? It's six o'clock in the morning! What on earth—?'

I cursed, under my breath, and carried on tying my laces. The last thing I needed, at that precise moment, was my mother asking all sorts. I'd stuck a note on the hallstand for her: 'Off to watch the filming. Back late.' Getting no answer from me she picked the note up, and read it, bleary-eyed.

'Right then,' I said, straightening up and unlatching our front door. 'I'm going.'

She lowered the note and made a sound in her throat, like the build up to a rant. I waited for her to say it: *Not dressed like that you're not.* I grew impatient, waiting, and embarrassed too, when she didn't say a single word, only looked at me, and kept on looking, as if she wanted, more than anything, to drag me in off the step and . . . then what? Lock me in the cellar? Her face was odd. I couldn't read it right.

'What?' I cried out. 'What's the matter with you? Are you drunk?'

'Not at all.' She sounded weary half to death but not

the slightest bit annoyed, which only confused me more. 'I'm fine. I'm all right. And you have a lovely day, my sweet. Just be careful, is all.'

'Yep,' I answered. 'Bye.'

And off I darted, across the cobbles, while the going was still good. The boots, I soon decided, were all right with the dress. They meant I could still leap and jump and run, which is exactly what I was doing, from the sheer joy of being alive and in love with Connor Blue.

And Oh. My. Stars. He was waiting for me. He was there . . .

'Hey!' he called, the second I turned into Fore Street.

'Hey!' I called back, across a tangle of cables and stuff. And I swear I could have flown to him, heavy boots and all, only . . . something wasn't right. Even with my heart . . . my spirits . . . everything soaring, I could tell that something was wrong. There was no one else around . . . no filming being done . . . nothing to be seen except the tide going out and Connor Blue sitting all by himself on our harbour wall.

I slowed to a walk. *Don't tell me*, I panicked, *that they haven't even started . . . Don't tell me my plan—my wonderful day—is already spoiled.*

I checked my watch: 6.40a.m.

'I thought you'd be filming,' I said; reminding myself, as I got closer, not to touch him . . . not to dribble or drool or fall in a swoon at his feet . . . 'Where is everyone?'

He shrugged. 'There's been a hitch,' he said. 'Some technical problem. Plus, our director needs to speak to Trent, only Trent's gone AWOL and his phone's switched off. Everyone else has gone back to the ship, although I guess they'll come over again as soon as the café opens.'

'So . . . ' I was having trouble, not drooling . . . with keeping my little bit of distance, he looked so *amazing* . . . so incredibly sexy . . . all dressed up as a wrecker. Not that anyone from around these parts has ever looked that good, not in this century, the eighteenth century or any other century, I'd bet my lipsticks and my life.

'So . . . are you going back to the ship too, now . . . or what?'

A seagull flew over and looked at me with one horrid eye. I touched my brooch—my sickle moon—for luck.

'I don't know,' Connor answered. 'I'm not sure how long a wait I'm in for. It might be hours. All day even. But I'm OK sitting here. I'm enjoying the peace and quiet—and the beautiful view, of course.'

I swear, I nearly died. *Me*, I thought, thrilled. *He's enjoying looking at me! Even with my cloak on, he's thinking what fantastic thingies I've got.*

'Well, you don't *have* to stay sitting there, all by yourself,' I said, turning on my sexiest smile. 'I could take you now, if you want. Right now, this very minute.'

'Excuse me?'

He looked so offended that, for a moment, I was thrown. But: *It's all right,* I told myself. *He's working. He's in wrecker-mode. Real life has taken second place—for now.*

'I said I'd take you to look for my friend,' I prompted him. 'So that you could apologize to her. You know. About the apron. For suggesting she might be available, sexually, because she had "Catch of the Day" on her apron.'

'Oh yes,' he said. 'That.'

I felt myself grow hot beneath my cloak. Hot, then cold, then hot again as his eyes met mine and I saw, in the forget-me-not, touch-me-not, blue of them that in the short time since I'd left him on the beach, he'd stopped believing my story.

My brain has never raced so fast. Had someone in the café warned him off me? Told him I couldn't be trusted? Or had he simply thought my tale over, in the cold light of day and seen it—and me—for the devious snippets we are?

Whatever the case, he'd rumbled me. He didn't have to say it. It was all over his face.

I couldn't look at him any more. I looked out to sea instead, but that was almost the exact-same blue as the eyes I was avoiding, and glinting, in a mocking way. I looked up at the cliffs, knowing we wouldn't walk there now, and I felt my eyes fill up and my face begin to burn, for disappointment and for shame.

'Got to go,' I managed to say. 'Home. Mum's waiting.'

'Jenna . . . ' He reached out and touched my hand, but I jumped away like a bee had got me. I didn't want his pity. I didn't want anything from him any more. I just wanted to hide. I wanted my mum.

'It's all right,' he said. 'I understand. I do—honest. And if you . . . '

A flock of gulls flew over just then, the din of them drowning him out. There were so many of the things, all sounding so frantic, that we both looked up, startled, and watched them go, wheeling over rooftops and away.

'That's odd,' Connor remarked, as the last one

disappeared. 'What's rattled them, I wonder? And why are they heading inland?'

I shrugged. I didn't care. No flicking gull, or any other creature on this earth, could possibly have been feeling as rattled as I was just then—as much inclined to flee the port, lamenting all the way.

'Hey, cheer up,' Connor said. 'It's not the end of the world. We can be friends, right? Tell you what—let's go for a walk; just until the café opens or they want me back on set. I've not been up on the cliff path yet—what do you say?'

Well, what could I say? What would any girl? Shamed though I was, there was only one answer to that.

DILLY

'He's gone. They've both gone. The creature was here—behind the Christmas crate. I don't . . . I don't know what to say.'

Trent Rogerson slumped against a beam. He took his inter-phone out of his pocket, looked at it for a moment, then put it back, defeated.

'We'll go down and check behind the mural,' he said. 'It's a long shot, I know, but maybe . . . just maybe . . . your friend Gary has had the sense to . . . ' His voice got bleaker, trailing away to nothing.

'And if he hasn't?'

'I don't know, Dilly. One step at a time, OK?'

'OK,' I said. 'All right.'

I'd gone up alone, to talk to Gurnet; to get him away from the attic. I still hadn't asked (because I really didn't want to know) what would happen after that—how Trent Rogerson planned to destroy the thing from Pandora's Box.

Pandora's Box.

'Do you believe in God, Dilly?' Trent Rogerson had asked, as we stood, for a moment, outside the house, preparing—steeling ourselves—to go in.

'I don't know,' I'd replied. 'I think I want to, but He

290

doesn't make it easy for anyone does he? To believe in Him, I mean.'

'Well, do you believe in the *possibility* of God? Of a creator of all things?'

Yes, I said. I supposed that, yes, I did.

'Then is it too far-fetched to believe, also, that the creature from behind the wall might be Hopelessness? And that Hopelessness has the power—the very real power—to plunge the whole human race into utter despair? Into hell?'

No, I'd agreed. It wasn't. Particularly as I'd seen for myself how certain people in the port had changed since Gurnet took the creature home. Mrs Carthew . . . Nancy . . . Maude . . . even Danzel with his drinking . . . and Jenna losing her sass. They hadn't been spat on; Nancy hadn't even been in the same house as the creature, so far as I was aware. But still . . . something had got to them; something had taken whatever sadness or strangeness they'd had in them already and made it ten times worse.

And hadn't I felt it myself, the previous afternoon? That wave of awful despair, when the creature looked into my eyes?

'Maybe it won't affect everyone,' I'd said to Trent, as we let ourselves into the house. 'People like me, and my mum, and others . . . we've been OK up to now, pretty much. And Gurnet—he's not just all right, he's happy. He's with the creature all the time and, yet, he's the happiest I've ever known him.'

Which has to be, Trent answered quietly, the saddest and most hopeless situation of all.

I'd paused then, at the foot of the stairs, making Trent stop too.

'Gurnet mustn't see it killed,' I'd insisted. 'He mustn't even know you're here because if he sees you, and suspects . . . he'll go berserk. Let me talk to him. I'll get him to come down and leave the creature behind. I can do that. He'll listen to me.'

'All right,' Trent had agreed. 'I'll wait in one of the bedrooms. But don't imagine you've got all day to talk him out of there, Dilly, because you haven't.'

And now I didn't need all day, or any time at all. And Gurnet hadn't even left a note, although he must have known—the creature must have told him—that I'd been, and was coming back. *He didn't trust me*, I thought. *He doesn't trust anyone any more. Oh, Gurnet . . .*

There were picnic things from one of the trunks spread out all over the floor, and a dog-eared old book abandoned on top of a crate. After he'd recovered, a bit, from the blow of finding the creature gone, Trent Rogerson picked the book up and read the title out loud: '*Jesus by the Sea of Galilee.*' He stared at the cover, as if it might have a clue on it somewhere. He stared for a very long time.

'I expect Gurnet was reading that,' I told him, my voice all sad and sorry, still, because there hadn't been a note. 'Out loud, like parents do at bedtime. Laurence likes being read to. Gurnet was teaching him stuff—I know, because he told me. Stuff about the ocean . . . about the Eco-Crisis and all the things that are being done nowadays to . . . to . . . '

Trent Rogerson lowered the book.

'What?' he said, sharply. 'What is it, Dilly?'

'The sea,' I said, lowering my voice to almost a whisper even though there was no one but Trent to hear. 'The creature . . . it wanted to go to the sea. Yesterday, while I was up here, it told me. It *insisted*.'

Trent Rogerson stared at me, his expression changing so fast I couldn't keep up with it.

'It speaks,' I added. 'Didn't you know? It told me it wanted seawater. With plankton in it. It was very serious, about the plankton. What . . . wait . . . where are you going?'

Trent Rogerson was running . . . crunching Christmas things under his shoes . . . kicking aside picnic plates and dishes as he headed for the stairs. I ran after him . . . down all the stairs . . . across the hall . . .

'Am I right? . . . Is that where Gurnet's taken it . . . to the sea?'

He had his inter-phone in his hand. A red button was flashing on it.

'It's out of my control,' he was yelling. 'It . . . goddammit to hell . . . it's not people it wants, sir. Not any more. It knows about the Oceanic Eco Project. And it's heading out to sea . . . '

Row, row, row your boat
Gently down the stream
Merrily, merrily, merrily, merrily . . .

A puddle. A lake. An ocean blue. They were all the same, once, to Hopelessness: just boring expanses of wet, of no particular consequence in the great scheme of things. It doesn't even know if it can swim, although it supposes it will, when push comes to shove. When it's down among the fishies, spawning doom and gloom.

It wonders what plankton will taste like. Pepper, it reckons. Or dust. Not that it feels much like eating; not since it left dry land.

'Hey!' it calls out, as the small boat crests a wave, bucking and dipping like a carnival car. 'Hey, my Gary. I'm feeling a bit ikky cooped up in this unit. Let me out.'

'Laurence needs to fix his eyes on the horizon,' Gurnet tells his friends, 'to settle his stomach down.'

'Horse dung,' answers Danzel, pulling harder on the oars. 'You touch the bolt on that cat carrier, Gurn, and I swear—I'll kick the whole contraption overboard.'

'Then I'll lift it,' Gurnet tells him. 'Just up onto the seat, so he can breathe a bit better, and see the horizon through the bars. Budge over, please, Maude. Or get down between the seats for a minute—that's it. Thank you.'

'For crying out loud, Gurn!' Danzel is losing patience. 'Sit down, will you. Stop rocking the boat.' He's wishing he'd never agreed to this. Not without life jackets and at least a dozen flares. He's wishing they'd taken the long way home. The long, safe, way.

He knows this shoreline though, like the shape of his own jaw. He knows where the rocks are, and the trace and pull of the currents. To avoid a scrape—or worse—he has rowed right out to sea. It will be a strenuous haul back, past the American ship and into the port, but that's not the problem, Gurnet is, with all his shifting and fussing around.

'Gurnet!' Danzel yells. 'Will you settle your flicking arse. It's a boat we're in, not someone's parlour. You of all people . . . for crying out loud!'

Gurnet doesn't sit—he can't, there isn't room now that the cat carrier is on the seat—but he squats down next to Maude, both hands holding tight to the carrier, as if to keep it, or himself, stock still. 'Is that all right, Dan?' he yells. 'Is that better?'

'It'll do,' Danzel replies, although he isn't really looking. Not at Gurnet, or the creature. He is peering backwards as he rests the left oar, and manoeuvres the right, to bring the boat around.

'That's good,' Gurnet announces, once they're turned and heading towards the port. 'Laurence can see the horizon now. At least I think he can. I'll just check.'

The salt-breeze, at this angle, is blowing Maude's hair all off to one side. She raises her hands to gather it up . . . to tuck it into the collar of her oilskin, so that when Gurnet hunkers back down again, it won't get in his eyes. Noticing—understanding—Gurnet bends, clumsily, to plant a wet kiss on her cheek.

'I love you, Maude,' he says. 'You, too, Danzel Killick.'

Then he throws the bolt on the cat carrier, and roars out that his creature is free.

DANZEL

I lost an oar. When Gurnet freed the creature—out at sea, without so much as a 'mind your eyes!'—my concentration slipped, as it was bound to, and so did the wretched oar.

Two options flashed in my head: retrieve the oar, or bring Gurnet down. For the good of us all I went with option one, although the temptation to knock my friend over, to let whack at him with the remaining oar, for being such a stubborn, insubordinate, head-crazy OAF was huge.

'*Fly away, mate,*' he was hollering to his creature. '*Quick! Go! It's your only chance!*'

Oh yes, I would have done that Gurny-one some serious damage if the boat hadn't tipped as he stood there yelling and waving his arms . . . if I hadn't had three lives to save.

Lunging for the oar . . . grabbing it up in the nick of time . . . I saw, from the corner of my eye, the front of the cat carrier fall away and go cartwheeling into the sea. Landing flat it began, very slowly, to sink, sieving bubbles as it went. There was something peaceful—beautiful, even—about the sinking of that object. It mesmerized me—I don't know why. I wanted to keep watching, as it disappeared . . . had to force myself to jam the oar back into place and then turn to give Gurnet what for; to yell at him to calm down, sit down, and stop rocking the boat.

But Gurnet was already sitting, in the space between the seats, and the only movement from him was the heaving of his shoulders; the only sound a sob. Maude was cradling him, or trying to. And the creature . . . the creature was perched on top of its carrier, moving from foot to foot and contemplating the top of Gurnet's head as if it wasn't sure what to do next.

I considered belting it—knocking it overboard and then rowing like the clappers. But the thought of having it come after me, maimed and as angry as hell, made me think twice. And anyway, the boat was really rocking now. I needed to keep us all moving, preferably towards dry land.

The creature swivelled its eyes at me as I put my back into the job of controlling the boat. I tried to ignore it, and failed. I looked at my knees . . . over my shoulder . . . at the obstinate wodge that is the back of Gurnet's head . . . but just knowing that the creature had me in its sights put me right off my stroke.

It was dangerous to stop. Crazy. The current was tugging like a magnet . . . we were too far out . . . but I couldn't keep rowing with the thing's eyes on me. I just couldn't. It was making me feel—I don't know—as if there was no point carrying on. As if I might as well chuck both oars overboard and kiss my rear goodbye.

And so I stopped, to confront it. To give it what for.

What a stupid, stupid, stupid thing to do . . .

DILLY

Talking and running wasn't easy, but there was so much I needed to know. 'Who are you . . . really?' I asked, as we entered the rhododendron tunnel.

Trent Rogerson was holding my elbow, hurrying me along.

'Well, I'm not . . . a researcher . . . ' he panted, although I'd guessed that much already. 'I'm a scholar . . . originally . . . but I've been trained . . . primed . . . for this . . . because it's my baby . . . my discovery . . . and because I volunteered.'

He laughed, shakily, and ducked to avoid a branch. 'I guess I'm a . . . secret agent now,' he puffed. 'Like James Bond . . . only . . . not as . . . fit.'

'Who's James Bond?' I wondered but he said never mind—it didn't matter.

He stopped talking then, conserving his breath for hurrying. And the red rhododendrons looked, to me, like bags of blood which might burst if we touched them, and splatter us.

'How did you find out . . . about the box?' I asked, after a while of simply hurrying. 'How did you *know*?'

And in stops and starts, he told me about his ancestor, Ethan Rogerson, who was a footman at the manor and hid the box behind the mural . . . about his own research as a scholar of suppressed and forgotten myths . . . about finding the ancient text that told of the coming of Hopelessness and then, after months spent trawling the inter-telly—on a hunch, is all—the mention, in an English sea captain's journal, of a sealed box they called 'La Scalata di Pandora', taken from an underground shrine on the outskirts of Rome but lost in the wreck of the *Lady Eleanor*, right here at Port Zannon, in the spring of 1732.

'Wow,' I breathed, my mind whirling with it all. *Ethan . . . La Scalata di Pandora . . . the Lady Eleanor . . .* such romantic, lovely names. I had to remind myself, as we reached the end of the tunnel, that there was nothing lovely, or romantic, about the situation we were in—that the *whole world* was in, if Trent Rogerson was right and Gurnet's creature truly was the very worst of all evils.

'Stop . . . a minute . . . ' Trent let go of my elbow and leaned against the garden wall, breathing heavily. He looked old to me, at that moment, and very frightened.

'What can we do?' I asked, surprised by how calm I sounded. 'If it's heading out to sea—attacking things, and messing up the eco-project—what can be done, to stop it?'

Trent gazed, for a moment, over my head; catching his breath, collecting his thoughts.

'It could be,' he said, after a while, 'that it's still caged—that your friend hasn't released it yet. If so, we only need to find the two of them; to follow where they've gone.'

He sounded no more certain about this than he had about the creature being back behind the mural.

'And if we're too late? What then?'

He took hold of my elbow again and half-hurried, half-guided me towards the gap in the wall. 'Then nothing, Dilly,' he replied. 'There'll be nothing we—or anyone else—can do.' And of that he sounded very sure indeed.

The boat is drifting; dragged sideways by the current, but Danzel's rowing nowhere until the creature flies away.

'Shoo!' he hollers, resting hard on the oars, to keep the boat, and his nerves, steady. 'Get lost!'

Gurnet and Maude look up, surprised.

The breeze, a lot stronger than it was a minute ago, sends a shiver over the sea and loosens Maude's long hair from the collar of her coat. Gurnet's face is a gargoyle's, pig-ugly from sorrow, but his voice comes calm and clear:

'I'll miss you always, Laurence, but Danzel's right. You're free now so fly, go on—fly away!'

Hopelessness blinks. It swivels its head, checking out its freedom: the north and the south of it, the east and the west . . . the arc of the heavens . . . the heave and swell of the ocean, where it knows it has to go.

It looks back at Gurnet and its eyes begin to leak. *I don't want to fly away, my Gary,* it thinks. *Now that I'm out, mate, I'm all of a dither. It pains me to leave you . . . to know we'll never meet again.*

It could gag, it really could, on the taste of its own tears.

Its creator, it decides, is a black-hearted shite. Has to be. For what kind of an entity creates Hopelessness with the capacity to care?

The heavens are darkening.

It is time.

Hopelessness opens its mouth and the sound that comes out is the wail of all anguish, of every terror ever known . . . of every hurt and sorrow . . . every total loss of faith.

And the little boat shudders as Hopelessness spreads its wings. And Gurnet cannot move, and Danzel cannot move, and the waves seem hardly to move either, but to be waiting for a sign— the re-appearance of the sun, a nod from the moon—to let them know it's OK to keep rolling. To do what they've always done.

Only Maude moves. As Hopelessness rises, she leaps up and tries to catch it . . . to grab it by its feet . . . to pull it back into the boat so that it will not perform what she knows, now, (how can she not, with that wailing in her ears and her world already dark) can only be some truly ghastly deed.

How desperate she looks as she clutches at thin air, yet how utterly determined as she leaps a second time. And how unsurprised she seems—accepting, almost—as she falls into the sea.

MAUDE

It's my fault. All . . . my . . . fault . . .

JENNA

I felt better, walking. Calmer. I didn't say a lot, though, as
we climbed away from the harbour. It felt odd, I suppose,
knowing Connor and I were on the path I'd planned to
take, but wouldn't, after all, be going all the way.

A breeze blew up, growing stronger the higher we
climbed. I drew my cloak tighter with one hand and
clutched at my skirt with the other, so it wouldn't rise up
and show my pants.

'Let me go ahead,' Connor offered. 'Then you won't
get blown around so much.'

I was happier with him in front. It meant I could still
feast my eyes on him without being made to feel guilty
or daft. With his old-fashioned clothes on, and his hair
tied back, he looked a bit like a pirate and a bit like a
gentleman, and I felt pretty fed up, I have to admit,
knowing I wasn't ever going to run my fingers through
that hair, or undo all the buttons on that flouncy white
shirt, or . . .

'Wow!' Connor said, as he jumped the final step and
came out on the top of the cliff. 'This really is *amazing*.'

'Is it?' I went and stood beside him, hanging on tighter
to my clothes. Apart from the presence of a flicking
great ship, the view from the clifftop was the same as it's

always been: just sea and sky and rocks, going on and on and on.

'I'm so glad we came here,' Connor said, and my heart leapt a little, assuming he was referring to us, to me and him, only: 'I'm getting a much better feel for the history of the place, than if we'd filmed at home,' he went on. 'I can imagine how isolated people must have felt along these shores; how bleak the winters must have been.'

'It's like that now,' I told him. 'No change there.'

He looked down at me and smiled. I smiled back, thinking, *Oh well, I may never get to kiss that mouth, but I'll always have this moment . . . this swapping of smiles.* 'I've heard it told,' Connor said, 'that Jesus came to this part of the world. Yes—honestly. He had an uncle—Joseph of Arimathea—who went to mines all over the ancient world. When he's twelve, Jesus disappears from the gospels and we don't hear of him again until he's thirty. It's quite possible he sailed the trade routes with his uncle, in which case, he would certainly have come to Cornwall—maybe even right here, to Port Zannon. You know the hymn "Jerusalem"?'

I didn't, I said. Sorry.

So he sang a bit, about Jesus's feet, in ancient times, walking on England's mountains green.

'These aren't mountains though,' I said, embarrassed, a bit, because his singing voice was rubbish. 'They're cliffs.'

He smiled and shook his head, like the detail didn't matter. 'There's an atmosphere up here, Jenna,' he insisted. 'Can't you feel it? A sense of haunted holiness. It makes me think those stories might be true. And the air up here is so *pure*; the way God made it; the way it ought to have stayed—everywhere, I mean.'

And *Oh. My. Stars* I thought. *Jenna Rosdew, you total splat-brain. What were you thinking when you read his profile on the inter-telly? 'Connor Blue likes girls with a strong sense of faith.' Aaaargh! He's an Eco-Christian, idiot. He would no more have ripped your dress off on that four-poster bed than he would eat an endangered animal or throw rubbish into the sea. He's more gentleman than pirate. You NUMBSKULL.*

I felt better then. Much. I told myself that being rejected *in that way* by an Eco-Christian doesn't exactly count. It's nothing personal; nothing to do with your face, or your personality. Poor Connor, I thought. He probably fancies me to DEATH. He's just not allowed to follow through, is all, at least not until after he's married . . .

I thought, then, that we might carry on along the path—just as far as the manor grounds, so I could show him the rhododendron walk. He was bound to like that; bound to see it as a beautiful creation. And if I acted demure, and kept my thingies covered, and didn't curse, or moan, or bad-mouth any of my friends, perhaps (oh joy) he would want to see me again.

I was about to suggest it—the walk, that is—when we saw the boat. Or, rather, Connor saw it and pointed.

'Look! Isn't that Maude out there?'

I looked, thinking, *What the—? The girl's practically a recluse, so how come she's out at sea, at this unearthly hour, and hogging my limelight AGAIN?*

Connor seemed anxious.

'They're a fair way out,' he fretted. 'Should we . . . ? No. Sorry. I forget—you kids were raised here. I guess that guy can handle a row boat all right.'

I raised both my hands against the sun, and squinted towards and beyond the American ship. Danzel, Maude, and Gurnet: there they were, all three of them, bobbing around in a boat I didn't recognize. They were a lot further out than is usually sensible and the waves were really pitching but Danzel was rowing and Connor was right—that boy can handle a boat.

So Gurnet's back then is he? I thought. *I'd better tell old Trent. Maybe there's still a chance I'll get to act in Wreckers . . .*

And then the sun went in. Or rather, it simply 'went', for no clouds had come to cover its face.

Alarmed, I grabbed Connor's arm.

'What's happening?' I said, like he would know. 'What's going on?'

'I don't . . . I'm not sure.'

It wasn't pitch black, but nor was it day any more. It was just *weird*, like a dirty veil had been flung across the sky, draining the whole port—the whole kingdom, for all I knew—of ordinary colours and light leaving everything a kind of dirty yellow.

I thought, perhaps, it was some kind of an eclipse, only the authorities hadn't bothered telling us, isolated as we are among our 'mountains green'.

Then the cry went up. An ear-splitting wail that seemed to come at Connor and me from all directions at once, so that we ducked, whirled around, staggered away from the cliff edge and then back, in a frenzy of not-understanding . . . of not-knowing what to do.

I could have held him then. I could have thrown myself into Connor Blue's arms and he would have clutched me

307

tight, I know he would, if only for comfort—his own as much as mine. I could have pressed my face against the warmth of his neck and felt the thumpety-thump of his heart.

But we were separate in our terror. Separate and alone. And that tortured cry made me want to burrow, like an animal, right into the earth and hide there until it stopped. I dropped to my knees. I even scrabbled, a bit, moaning softly to myself as the cry went on and on.

Then: 'No!' shrieked Connor Blue, the sound a perfect echo of the bigger, louder wail. And then he was running . . . falling . . . picking himself up. And all I could do was watch him go, dumbfounded as to why and what for, until the wailing suddenly stopped, and fainter cries reached my ears; cries of 'Maude! Maude!' and 'No, Gurnet—don't. It's too dangerous!' and cries from the Americans who had gathered on the deck of their ship . . . who were scuttling like mice, or wind-up toys, so small from where I was standing, looking down . . . so small and so terribly afraid.

The men from the port would come. I had absolute faith in that. However spun out they'd been by the unearthly wailing, and whatever had become of the light, they wouldn't leave my friend out there, to flounder and to drown. Once Connor raised the shout our men would launch the lifeboat and Maudie would be saved. She only had to swim . . . only swim a little while, kicking hard against the current, like a good, brave girl . . . and she would be scooped out of there, ice-cold and puking, but alive.

But Connor didn't raise the shout. Maybe he thought

there wasn't time. Maybe he didn't know about the right thing to do. He appeared on the beach so quickly, after tearing away down the steps, that I would have said it wasn't him, except that his white shirt seemed to glow as he raced into the sea, and his hair had come loose from the ponytail and was blowing like a merman's in the wind.

The wind. It was the wind's turn now. The waves, even as Connor Blue dived into them, were turning monstrous further out and I wailed to think that if Danzel and Gurnet didn't row like crazy they too would be lost overboard.

I saw them try. I saw them attempt to do just that as the big waves swept towards them. I saw Connor Blue's head, as sleek as a seal's, as he swam right into danger, and then even the yellow leeched from the sky, leaving us all in darkness, and the wind almost took me—almost threw me from the cliff—so I had to think of myself.

On my knees though. Still on my knees, I was, after I'd backed into a gorse bush; screaming, wordlessly, into the wind. And because I was on my knees I began to pray. It seemed the right thing—the only thing—to do.

So who shall we follow—Connor Blue as he struggles in a boiling sea, calling out a name? Danzel Killick as he rows for his life, screaming at Gurnet to throw the cat carrier overboard and to bail out, bail out, bail out . . . ? Or Dilly and Trent Rogerson, out on the cliff path now and staggering, blindly, towards the port?

No. Let's follow Hopelessness and see where it leads. In truth, it should have dived by now. It should be five fathoms down, drooling despair; destroying the oh-so-fragile beginnings of a healthier eco-system, and with it all hope for mankind.

So why isn't it?

There it goes, the big daft thing, flapping away, in the general direction of Ireland, and looping the occasional loop. See it stall in mid-air and then swoop . . . heading, at last, for the water. See it change its mind, with just seconds to spare, and go flapping and flailing upwards.

Listen hard and you'll hear it keening as it veers back towards the shore . . . returning, after all, to Port Zannon.

All good? Will the day go back to normal now? Will the sea behave itself and the mortals be all right? Or is someone playing chess up there—knocking pawns from the board, like crumbs from a table, and laughing all the while?

Dilly Tonkin is the first to spot it: a speck of light spiralling earthwards from the horrible-coloured sky. She thinks of aeroplanes and stops dead in her tracks, appalled.

Trent Rogerson, struggling to keep up, is the next to see the speck, growing brighter by the second. He, too, skids to a halt. And as the light gets closer, dazzling his eyes, he yells at Dilly to get down; right down on the turf, and to cover her head with her coat and with her arms because there's going to be a collision, and it's going to be close.

He himself remains standing, his face turned to the light, bathing in it . . . revelling in it . . . willing it to stay strong; to cut like a diamond and burn like a star in its almighty clash . . . just seconds away now . . . with the worst of all evils.

Hope versus Hopelessness.

Let the battle commence.

DANZEL

It almost killed me to leave her—to row away from the place she disappeared, knowing I hadn't been able to save her—that I hadn't even tried. We thought, when she fell, she'd be all right. Oh Maude, we thought, you idiot; this is all we need . . .

We expected her to come up, spluttering; to grab one of the oars . . . or the side of the boat . . . or Gurnet's hand which was stretched out, ready and waiting.

When she didn't appear I panicked. Gurnet too. The sky had gone this awful colour, like it was about to rain mustard or pee, and our ears were still ringing and our minds reeling from the terrible sound Gurnet's creature had made before it flew away.

'Maude! Maude!' Gurnet yelled, and he would have jumped overboard himself if I hadn't yanked him down, risking both oars in the process.

'It's too dangerous,' I shouted and it was. I wasn't kidding.

A wave sloshed into the boat, tipping it like a cradle. That was it. We had to go. I had to row away from there, however hard it was; and I don't mean physically.

I kept my eyes on the sea . . . hoping . . . willing . . . and I swear, on my life, I saw her there, swimming away from us with her oilskins gone and her long hair streaming and her whole body moving easily and well through the murk and the pull of deep water. 'There!' I said— more in wonder than alarm—'She's there . . . '

'Where? Where is she, Danzel? Get to her—quick!'

I yelled at him to calm down. To use his hands, the creature's dinner dish, whatever he could find to bail us out before we, too, were forced to swim for our lives. I told him to ditch the cat carrier, to chuck it overboard because it was weighing us down . . . because the very sight of it, after hearing that creature howl . . . after what had just happened to Maude . . . was boiling my blood and doing me in.

'Maude can swim like a fish,' I reminded him. 'You know she can. And look! The Americans! They've lowered their dinghy. And a ladder. They've seen us, Gurn. We're going to be all right. All three of us. I promise . . . '

And that was when the sky burst apart, and a storm like no other sent us scudding and spinning the mercifully short distance from where we were to the side of the ship. We hit it hard—hard enough to smash our boat to smithereens, and lucky we were that it wasn't our bones. With just seconds to spare I grabbed at a rope, or maybe it was somebody's arm. I was hauled up anyway, before the sea could suck me down, and slapped down on the deck.

'Maude!' was the first thing I said, through the hawking up of water and the sponge-wheeze of my lungs. 'Maude . . . she's still out there . . . '

'It's OK,' someone answered, way above my head. 'Hang in there buddy, it's OK.'

Is it? I thought, beginning to shiver from shock and the cold. *All right, then, if you say so. I'll believe you; plenty wouldn't . . . Blanket*, I thought next. And *Get warm. Think about Maudie later . . . And Gurnet—where's the Gurn? Oh God . . .*

There was a lurching, then, and a terrible grating sound. And screaming, and panic, and mayhem as the people who'd been leaning over me were pulled, or fell, away.

Lying on the deck, sprawled out like a starfish, I saw a flash, like sheet lightning, somewhere out to sea; heard a sound, above the rest, that made me think of the clashing of swords.

When the deck started tilting I almost laughed. *Not so very OK now, is it, BUDDY!* Someone jumped over my face. A chair clipped my right ear, in passing. Still, it seemed impossible—and more than a little cruel—that having only just been rescued from the waves I was about to be tossed back in. *This ship is top of the range*, I told myself. *No way can it lose its mooring. No way can it ever be wrecked.*

Then the deck tilted some more and I felt, and recognized, the touch of Gurnet's clumsy paw as he took hold of my hand and held it. We slid like slugs off a spade, my friend and I, and got sluiced overboard together.

DILLY

I fell to the ground and covered my head. I did exactly as Trent told me. 'This is it!' he shrieked. 'There's going to be a collision and it's going to be close!'

I didn't dare peep. I didn't dare look to see how close, exactly, the collision was going to be. I believed it was a plane. Another Attack. I was expecting to die, any second, and daring to imagine that the spark of me—the me of me—might rise from the atoms and the ash of me to meet, and finally know, the spark that had once been my mother.

There was no room in my head just then for myths, or boxes, or talking creatures with the power to destroy mankind. Even the eclipse, and the terrible wailing we'd heard earlier, could be put down, I was certain, to some human activity—something planned, and cruel, done to frighten us half to death before we actually died.

A plane. It had to be a plane, like before.

Then, as nothing hit the ground, or the sea, or me, I thought OK then—a Natural Disaster. The world, or our part of it anyway, is falling away from its axis, like old fruit from a tree, and dragging some stars down with it.

I still didn't think of the creature. I just felt sorry, is all, that the earth was giving up on us. Sorry, but oddly relieved that it was nothing personal; that no one had targeted Port Zannon deliberately. It wasn't going to be murder.

Then: 'There it is!' Trent yelled. 'I can see it.' And he stumbled away from me, searching, as he did so, in his pocket. I couldn't believe, as I shrieked for him to come back, that in the midst of all this mayhem he was reaching for his phone

But then I saw it for myself. Gurnet's creature, spot lit by lightning, only yards above my head. Its coat seemed to be on fire and maybe it was, I don't know. But its wings were beating and its hands—I could see its two hands clearly as they punched and tore into the dazzle of light that I'd taken to be part of a plane.

'Drop it!' Trent hollered, the way a farmer might yell to a dog that has a chicken by the throat. 'Gary needs you. He's in trouble. He's calling!'

My stomach lurched. But Trent Rogerson knew what he was doing. He knew precisely.

I saw the creature pause, and its face, as it looked down, was bewildered. Concerned. I saw Trent Rogerson raise one arm. *Throwing the phone at it won't help*, I thought. *Are you mad?*

But Trent was pointing, only pointing, and babbling into his phone . . . holding it so close to his lips, with his free hand, that it could have been a snack. His last. *'Can you hear me? Can you hear . . . ?'* but it seemed that no one could, through the shrieking of the wind.

And the creature flapped, clumsily, getting ready I think—no, I'm sure—to go to Gurnet; to find Gurnet wherever he was, and help him. Only, the dazzle of light was right on its tail . . . so bright it hurt . . . it hurt my eyes. I looked away, and then back. I did that three times. Then: *You have to keep watching,* I urged myself. *For Gurnet's sake. You have to bear witness, for Gurnet.* And I saw the light fall upon the creature like a spark upon a rug, and hang on.

It was quick, and I'm glad of that. It was over in a flash. The creature cried out, just once, as the light flared, white-hot, and consumed it. 'Sorry,' the creature wailed, at least I think that's what it said. It might have been something else—it was so hard to hear. It might, it just might, have been 'Gary'.

As quickly as it had flared, the light began to fade. Expecting the creature to fall, as ashes, I cowered, still watching, and covered my head. Its shape, though, was still recognizable as it hurtled from the sky.

I could—should—have cried out a warning. 'Trent!' I should have yelled. 'Watch out. Run, Trent—this way. Hurry!' But I was too busy tracking the creature's fall to notice the threat it still posed.

The creature hit the ground and fizzled away to nothing. I know. I saw it happen. But the last thing it did, consciously or not, was to send Trent Rogerson reeling backwards, out of its way, and over the edge of the cliff.

Trent's ancestor survived a stabbing—was hauled onto a ship in the Bristol channel, patched up by some surgeon and taken to America where he lived to tell his children, and then his children's children, about the box behind the wall.

But no one falls from a cliff, into a raging sea, and lives to tell a tale.

With the dissolving of the creature, the storm began to ease. I looked for the spot of light—the dazzle—but it had gone. On my hands and knees I crawled as close as I dared to the edge of the cliff but well away from the place where the creature was no more.

Leaning forward . . . peering over . . . I looked and listened for a sign or a sound from Trent.

Nothing. There was nothing. And I would have howled then, for him, and for me, had daylight not returned to the sky . . . seeping to start with and then pouring, like clean water, until everything above, around, and below me was properly back in focus and Port Zannon looked the way it always looks when a spring storm has passed, just in time for breakfast.

Except . . .

At first I thought they were filming, far below me on the beach; that the Americans had been crazy, or brave, or heartless enough to keep their cameras rolling all through the storm and were busy getting the wrecking scenes done while the waves were still huge and the actors all on set.

It was an easy mistake to make.

The box is nothing special. No carvings. No swirlings of gold. The men of Port Zannon barely notice it as they flounder, in towering waves, hauling half-drowned Americans to safety.

'Thank you . . .' A cameraman falls to the shingle, his torn shirt dripping and flailing. 'Bless you . . .'

The howling wind takes his words, just as surely as the next wave to crash will suck the box back out to sea, but Barry Tonkin hears them clearly enough, as he plunges back into the surf. 'You're welcome,' he calls back.

When it is over . . . when the locals are certain that no one from the Americans' broken ship has been swept onto rocks, or trapped beneath wreckage, they hurl aside their ropes and lines and call for what is needed:

'Is the doctor sent for? And the ambulance car?' . . . 'We need blankets here, and brandy for the shock' . . .

The storm has eased. Soon light will return—the ordinary light of a Cornish spring—and others will come hurrying down to the cove: men offering horses and carts in case the ambulance-car is delayed . . . Women with relief and concern etched deep in their faces as they rush to bind and bandage; to soothe and to calm the injured. The children are kept away. This is not for them to see. They have been frightened enough already today, half out of their wits.

The ship is groaning, like something mortally hurt. She never stood a chance, that ship, so fierce had been the storm that snapped her anchor chain, like thread, and swung her smack onto the rocks that rim the cliffs in a perilous toothy curve.

She is a broken thing, a ripped up thing, spilling cargo into the swell: tinned asparagus and jewellery boxes; suitcases and high heeled shoes; cameras and inter-phones and communication discs. They will sink like bricks, those things, or get washed up by and by. Right now, though, nobody's bothered. They have other fish to fry.

'Hey!' someone shouts. 'Over there, look! Out there on the rocks.'

Perran Carthew is at the top of the beach, tending to the boys—to his son, Gurnet, and to Danzel Killick. They are cut about, but they will live. They have survived. As leader, of sorts, Perran snaps to attention when he hears the call and races back down to the waves.

He thanks the stars, as he goes, that, although too hungover to handle a boat, he can still issue orders and make sure they are carried out.

'Barry!' he shouts. 'Barry Tonkin? There are two people stranded on the rocks. Do you see? Take the boat and fetch them in.'

'It's rough out there, Perran. Too rough, I'd say, to be launching any boats just yet.'

'No mouthing back at me, Barry. Do you not see the danger those two are in? Go. You can do this.'

Barry Tonkin is young, still, and strong; and the best man for the job. And the couple on the rocks have managed to stand—to stagger upright and even to wave their arms. They are not so badly hurt, so far as anyone can tell, that they won't be able to grab a line and help themselves to safety.

It is a one-man mission, to get them off that rock before a wave does. To risk the lives of two would be a reckless act, and Barry Tonkin knows this just as surely as he knows the times to reap and sow and the colour of his daughter Dilly's eyes.

That trip out, though, beyond the listing ship to where the harbour widens out into the open sea, is no picnic. Twice Barry thinks about turning back. Why me? he wonders, as shards of solar-panel glass, torn from the ship by the storm, clatter and jab at his boat. Why? But they are watching from the shore: his wife, his daughter, his neighbours, the Americans . . . they are watching with anxious, stinging eyes and he cannot let them down.

And as Barry Tonkin guides the boat closer to the couple on the rocks he gets the strangest feeling that the folk on the shore aren't the ones willing him on. That other eyes are on him as he steers the little boat . . . assesses the depths . . . judges, correctly, the moment, and the place, to approach. That another's hand is guiding his as he flings the line that will bring Maude, then Connor Blue, the short distance they need to go in order to be safe.

There are those who, in years to come, will call the survival of these two a miracle. Connor Blue, they will say, prayed for the strength to save the girl he loved, and he was heard. Others will claim that, actually, it was the other way round. That the girl rescued Connor Blue. Pointing to Graeco-Roman myth they will remind the world of Neptune's gift to Pandora: that she would never drown. Nonsense, the dissenters will say. Where's your proof? In a book, the Pandora scholars will answer, where's yours?

For now, though, a hoarse cheer goes up as Barry Tonkin

brings Connor and Maude to the shore. A bonfire has been lit and there are many hands to feed it wood . . . to wrap Connor and Maude in blankets . . . to bang Barry Tonkin on the back and call him Hero, rather than Catch, of the Day.

Three ambulance cars arrive and those in need of medical attention are lifted and stretchered away. They are surprisingly few. Maude's parents insist that she goes—just overnight, for observation—because they can't, for the life of them, understand how she can have been under the water for so very long, without trauma, or damage to her lungs. Connor Blue goes with her. He insists.

'Tea!' Mrs Tonkin says, as the last ambulance glides away. 'I'm going to open up the café . . . Dilly my love, are you all right? I still think you should have gone to the hospital, particularly after—'

'I'm OK,' Dilly interrupts her, gently. 'I'll stay with you.'

Jenna Rosdew says she'll come to the café herself later, after she's rested a while and changed out of her stupid dress—so ripped and stained, now, that it can never be worn again.

'I might be able to do something with that frock,' her mum says, shakily, as they walk towards their home. 'Waste not want not. Where did you get it, anyway?'

'Found it,' Jenna replies, happy to have something ordinary to talk about now that the panic is over. 'And it's wrecked, Mum. Ruined.'

'It is not,' her mother argues, linking arms. 'I could make us some knickers, at least. Lovely silk knickers with big ribbon-bows. Pink to make the boys wink!'

'Mother!' Jenna groans. 'Behave!'

Back down on the beach a salvage party has formed. All kinds of things are being fished out of the sea and sorted into *piles: stuff that looks precious, stuff that is smashed, stuff to be recycled, stuff to be reclaimed.*

It will be a couple more days before the box is washed up, battered but intact. Jenna Rosdew, out on beachcombing duty, will find it. She'll give it a shake and she'll lift up the lid—just checking. Finding it empty, she will take it home.

Waste not, want not, she will say, as she dumps it in the yard, for firewood.

DANZEL

I was slouching around at home, watching the rain and wondering whether to go and check on Gurn, when Dilly came to find me. It had been raining non-stop since the day of the wreck. Three days and counting. Nothing heavy, just mizzling drizzle and a low sea mist which no one was going to complain about; not after what we'd been through.

'Dils!' I was so pleased to see her I could have grabbed her hands and danced around the room, but she was in no mood for gaiety, which I guessed was understandable. She'd seen a man die, which, on top of the eclipse, and all that stuff with Gurnet's creature, and almost losing three of her friends to the sea, would be enough to make anyone sombre. Oh, and the rain. That's always depressing . . .

'I need to talk to you,' she said. 'About things Trent Rogerson told to me. And about what I saw and heard for myself, up on the cliffs. I'll go mad if I don't tell someone . . .'

'So, talk,' I said, budging up along the sofa. 'Sit down. Tell me.'

And so she told me. About the death of Gurnet's creature. And then—word for word, she said, as Trent

Rogerson told it to her—the story of Pandora's Box.

'Horse dung,' I jeered—I couldn't help it—when she got to the bit about Trent's Cornish ancestor hiding the box—Pandora's Box, that is—behind the wall at the old manor house. 'I'm sorry, Dils, but really . . . '

'Just *listen* will you,' she said. 'And, for once in your life, don't mock. You don't *know*, Dan. You weren't there . . . '

So I listened, humbly enough, as she described Trent Rogerson as some kind of a scholar-genius who put two and two together, over the course of many years, and came up with a threat to world safety.

I was doing pretty well, I thought, not butting in, or chuckling, even once, until she got to the bit about the filming of *Wreckers* being a cover for Operation Kill The Beast, or whatever code name the president, and our very own king, were supposed to have given Trent Rogerson's death-defying mission to save the planet.

'Di-*lee*,' I said, as nicely as I could. 'Come on . . . They set up the cameras and everything. They had *costumes*. And it would have cost a tidy fortune to bring everyone over here. And why go to so much trouble? Why not just send the hit man—this Trent character—in secret?'

'Because,' she insisted, 'it all had to be done under-cover. There were others—some foreigners, Trent said—who wanted to get to the box first. They knew it was here somewhere, they just didn't know where exactly. Only Trent knew that. Those others wanted to capture the creature alive—to clone it, or something, and use it as a weapon.'

I laughed like a jester, then. I laughed so hard I almost twanged a rib. 'What were they planning to do, Dils?

Have it parachute in over some major city, spitting on people's heads?'

'I knew you'd be like this,' she muttered, close to tears. 'I knew you'd mock.'

Oh, come here . . . I told her. Don't cry, darling. And I hugged her, and she clung on to me, sobbing the rest of it out. And I listened, without interrupting once, or mocking her any more. And as she told how Trent had been trained for the mission . . . how the cast and crew of *Wreckers* didn't know—might never know—that he was far more than just a bumbling researcher, with a fondness for long walks and badgers . . . Well, there were bits that made sense, and bits that still made my mouth twitch, and bits that made me think *Wow! What if all this is true?*

And all the time I was listening, I was stroking Dilly's hair and I knew—and I knew that she knew too—that it wasn't the same as when I'd stroked it in the past; like when we were four and I just liked stroking hair; or eight and she'd tumbled over at school, skinning her knees on the gravel.

This is Dilly, I reminded myself. *Dilly Daydream who you've known your whole life long. Is it all right to want to kiss her—properly, on the mouth? And to want to hold her, like this, all afternoon? All night even, one day . . . some day . . .*

I sensed that it was. Only, this wasn't the best of times to be discussing it.

'Who else have you told?' I asked, aware that I was still holding her, even though she'd stopped crying, and could have moved away.

'No one.' Her voice was all muffled against my chest,

which felt nice, like she preferred being in my arms to being properly heard. 'Should I tell my mum and dad, do you think? Or the authorities? What if no one believes me?'

I didn't reply, just carried on stroking her hair.

'You don't believe me yourself, do you?' she accused, her eyes flashing as she pulled away. 'Well, Gurnet will. In fact . . .' She stood up, and smoothed her skirt. 'I need to see Gurnet. I have to tell him what happened to the creature. And something else . . . there's something else I have to tell him. Something *really* important.'

She gave me a look, like I didn't deserve to know what this 'really important' thing was.

'What?' I said, alert suddenly to what it might be. 'What else, Dilly—tell me.'

'I think I've guessed,' she said, touching my arm as if to say, *All right, calm down, I was going to tell you eventually,* 'why Gurnet went to the manor to hide. He attacked someone, Dan—a man who broke into his house, looking for Laurence—for Hopelessness. But it's all right. He won't get into trouble. I need to go and tell him that it's all OK. '

I caught her by the wrist, spinning her round as she turned to leave.

'It's not OK,' I told her. 'It's not OK at all. The man's dead, Dilly. Gurn killed him. They'll be coming for him . . . the authorities. I'm surprised they haven't come already, but I suppose with the eclipse and the storm and all . . . '

She looked triumphant then, like she used to when she'd beaten me at marbles or got the pass-the-parcel prize at one of our parties. 'Have you looked at the inter-telly over the past few days, Dan?' she said. 'Have you checked the news by any chance?'

I had.

'Anything about a murder?'

She'd got me there. I'd been puzzling, myself, over that. Carlyn had said very little, to any of us, about the way her boss had died. 'I can't believe he's gone,' was all she'd managed, in my hearing, before Ned had taken her home. 'He always seemed so well to me, such a fit and healthy man.'

Clearly, she'd been fobbed off with some tale about natural causes—or ordered to lie through her teeth. Either way, I'd expected a fuss on the telly, about the passing of such a big-noise councillor. Some sort of tribute, at the very least.

'Anything about a murder, Dan?' Dilly said again.

Nuh, I replied.

'Anything about the eclipse? Or the storm? Or about the American ship being wrecked and Hollywood's most famous actor almost getting drowned?'

'Nope.'

She shook her head at me, the way I'd shaken mine at her.

'What?' I said. '*What?*'

'Gurnet didn't kill that man, Dan,' she said. 'He barely scratched him. The authorities had him executed—shot, for being a traitor.'

DILLY

We decided, Danzel and I, not to over-burden Gurnet. We told him only as much as he needed to know: that he hadn't killed anyone and wasn't to give the matter another thought.

It wasn't enough.

'Where is he then, Dilly?' Gurnet fretted. 'Where is that man shape? Is he coming back here? And why did Dan say he was dead if he isn't? Why did you say that to me, Danzel?'

I didn't know how to answer, for the best; so it was Danzel who told him the truth, or at least a watered-down version of it.

'The authorities killed him, Gurn,' he said, carefully, 'because he was a bad man. He didn't just try to steal Laurence, he was up to all sorts. He made a call on his inter-phone after leaving your house and the authorities intercepted it. They'd been suspicious of him for a while, but hadn't any proof about what he was up to until they overheard that call. He was plotting against the king, Gurn. He was a right rotten whelk—the worst—so good riddance eh?'

Gurnet was lying on his bed, staring up at the black of his ceiling.

'I told you, Danzel,' was all he said. 'I told you I didn't stab that man shape. I only did a slicing and it wasn't very deep.'

'You did,' Danzel answered, more merrily than was called for. 'I'll remember to take your word for it, Gurn, next time you take your knife to something that is neither fish nor fowl.'

I gave him a little push and frowned at him to be quiet. There was one more thing we had to tell our friend, and it was going to be hard.

'Gurn,' I said, sitting down on the edge of the bed. 'There's something else. Something sad, I'm afraid, about Laurence.'

He flinched. I felt it. 'What?' he said. 'What is it, Dilly?'

I looked up at Danzel and he nodded.

'During the storm,' I said, 'I was up the cliffs, and I saw Laurence struck by lightning. He was killed instantly, Gurnet. Straightaway. There's . . . there's nothing left of him.'

I waited. I let it sink in. After a while Danzel knelt beside the bed.

'Are you all right, mate?' he said.

'Yes,' Gurnet answered, politely. 'I'm all right, Dan.'

'Do you want to go hurling?'

'No,' Gurnet said. 'It's raining. And I don't have anyone to blame.'

We stayed until it was dark outside, as well as in the room, and then Gurnet fell asleep so we covered him with his eiderdown and crept away.

'He'll be all right,' Danzel said. 'He just needs time to mourn.'

'Like for the crab,' I reminded him. 'What was that crab of his called again, do you remember?'

'Howard,' Dan said. 'Howard, for crying out loud . . .'

Telling Danzel everything had helped me, a lot. I wasn't sure how much of it he believed but he hadn't mocked—at least, not much—and for some reason, that was enough.

He took my hand as we walked along Fore Street and not just because the film crew's cables were still there and he was worried I might trip. I could tell, straight-away, it was *that kind of a hand hold* and I was glad.

It was too dark to see much, beyond the harbour wall, but the drizzle had eased so we stopped for a while and stood looking out to sea.

I thought about Trent Rogerson. He had told me so much, in such a very short space of time; so much that should have been kept secret; so much that was scary and strange. I'd found it odd, at the time, that he should want to share all that with me, a sixteen-year-old girl . . . that he hadn't kept things vague, the way Danzel had just done with Gurnet.

Standing close to Danzel, and listening to the waves, it dawned on me that maybe Trent had known how his own story would end. That perhaps it is written some-where, in one of those ancient texts of his, that whoever freed the world from Hopelessness would perish in the act.

I felt strangely blessed, then, to think I was the one Trent had told the story to. Blessed and duty-bound, one day, to pass the details on. To let everyone—the whole world, if I could—know exactly what happened, here in

331

Port Zannon, on the day of the terrible storm. *I'll do it*, I pledged Trent's spirit, wherever it had gone. *When the time is right. When I'm older. I promise.*

'Are you cold?' Danzel asked, wrapping his arms around me. 'Shall we go and get a milk-shot? A hot one?'

I turned into the hug, my own arms slipping naturally and easily around Dan's waist. 'Aren't you wanting a cider then?' I said, doing my best to sound casual.

'No,' he answered, firmly. 'A milk-shot. With honey and cinnamon.'

He meant it, I could tell. I didn't need to nag. Relieved, I looked over his shoulder. The Crazy Mermaid was busy, with all the candles lit. I could see Jenna leaning across a table, talking nineteen to the dozen to one of the Americans (a man, of course) and showing a lot of her chest. Michael Killick was there, holding Sheila on his lap and smiling at everyone, for the first time in months, because Nance has been in touch to say she's coming home.

Connor Blue was there, but edging towards the door— on his way, I guessed, to be with Maude.

And my dad was there, in his Catch of the Day apron, and my mum, bustling around with dishes and cups, avoiding all the mermaids in a way that takes years of practice.

I smiled at them all, although none of them were looking my way. I was still smiling when Danzel kissed me, which could have been a disaster, my mouth not being ready, and all, but wasn't because this was Dan, who I'd known my whole life long, and somehow that made it all right.

'Do you remember,' I said, as he moved away—uncertain, I could tell, about the kiss, and about me, and about how things were going to change between us. 'At potty training, when you . . . '

He groaned, then he laughed, then he picked me up in his arms and pretended to throw me, giggling, over the harbour wall.

'Trust you,' he teased, 'to think of that. I'm trying to be all romantic here, Dils. I'm doing a Connor Blue.'

I kissed the side of his face as he set me down on my feet; I breathed the scent of his skin, as familiar to me as the scent of my own. Then he kissed me again, on the mouth, and this time I was ready. We both were.

The authorities come, as they were bound to. Not for Gurnet, but 'in support of those whose health and/or livelihoods have been affected, in recent weeks, by adverse weather conditions along the Cornish coast'. At least, that's what it said on the inter-telly.

Everyone over the age of eighteen is interviewed, some for well over an hour. Of the under-eighteens, only Dilly is summoned to the church, and she knows, immediately, why. The officer who records her statement says he understands she saw a man fall to his death from the cliffs. He is sorry about that, he says. It must have been traumatic.

It was, Dilly tells him. Very.

And what else might she have seen, he wonders, up there on the cliff?

I saw the strangest, and most frightening of sights, she says, widening her eyes and clutching the sides of her chair. I saw a creature—like a pig, it was, only with fur, and wings—and it was fighting with a star. And then the star disappeared and the creature fell to earth. And when it hit the earth it dissolved, like foam, into nothing. Am . . . am I going mad, sir, do you think? Is it shock?

Could be, the officer replies, sitting up very straight. It could easily be shock. But let's take a look, shall we, at the place where you say this happened?

Up on the cliffs, at the spot where Hopelessness perished, the turf is badly charred. And the shape the officer sees, and summons his colleagues to see, and will report to the king that he has seen, who will report, in turn, to the president of the United States of America, is, as Dilly said, the shape and size of a pig. With wings.

It is enough.

'Get plenty of sleep, young girl,' the authorities will instruct Dilly Tonkin. 'Take a herbal tonic for your nerves, and enjoy the rest of your life. It was a seagull you saw . . . a seagull, is all, struck by a bolt of lightning.'

Two days after the authorities leave, a ship comes for the Americans. Connor Blue holds tight to Maude and says he will never forget her. That one day, when the borders are open, he will return to make her his bride. Horse dung, says Danzel Killick. When sardines sing hymns, sneers Jenna.

Oh they of little faith . . .

The kingdom's borders will open, that much I can tell you. And Maude will become Mrs Blue. The wedding arch will be heavy with rhododendron flowers and the manor house (redeveloped by then, into eco apartments, with shared social space and a thriving market garden) done up for the occasion.

Gary Carthew, inheritor of his father's fishing fleet, will provide a wedding feast fit for a lord: creamed lobster on shells of puffed pastry; crabmeat with lemon and dill; more pilchards than you could shake a rod at, stuffed into fifty pies. He will be doing very well by then, will Gurnet. So, too, will the sea.

Jenna Rosdew, already a big name in inter-theatre, will turn up in a flamingo-coloured ball gown and laugh when she enters the shared social space, where the wedding feast is laid. 'I would have thought,' she'll say, in her foghorn voice, 'that getting rid of that ugly mural would have been the Council's top priority.'

The Killicks—married a year and living, happily and well, in a first floor apartment that used to be a bedroom with a four-poster bed in it—will be mildly offended. 'That mural's part of our heritage,' Dilly will tell her friend. 'It's protected. And we love it.' And the daughter in her belly will flutter and kick, as if in complete agreement.

But stop.

I am jumping way too far ahead.

The day after the Americans set sail Gurnet tells Danzel that he wants to go up on the cliffs. Not to hurl but to visit the place where Laurence was struck by lightning. He wants them all to go, he says, like for a funeral, only without the body.

Danzel is pleased. Gurnet hasn't left his room since learning of his creature's death. Mrs Carthew, who has bucked up no end in the last week or so, has tried everything she can think of, including the promise of a bigger inter-telly for the parlour, if her son will only come downstairs, or go fishing with his dad, or to the café with his friends. But no. Gurnet has been in decline; adrift in some dark place and dreaming of sharks.

Saying a proper farewell to his creature will, Danzel is sure, be good for Gurnet. It will help him get back to normal—or to what passes for normal, in Gurny terms.

The sun is high as The Gang climbs away from the harbour: Dilly, Danzel, Jenna, Gurnet, and Maude. They walk silently, as the occasion demands, but every now and then Danzel will touch Dilly's arm, making her tingle as she leads them on, to the place where Hopelessness fell.

The exact spot, as Dilly already knows, has been carefully cut away (the image, scorched on the turf, is in the hands of scientists now and it will be a century and a half before it is 'discovered' and hailed, by scholars, as the final piece of the Pandora Puzzle).

So Dilly points to a place close by and bows her head—they all do—as Gurnet puts a seashell there and says goodbye to his Laurence.

'My life's dung now, mate,' he tells the shell and the turf and the breeze. 'It's horrible. I hate it.'

They turn to go. Dilly, Danzel, Jenna, Gurnet, and Maude. And nobody speaks, because nobody knows quite what to say, to make things all right for the Gurn.

The light in the gorse bush is so small and so faint that they almost pass it by. Like a torch winding down, or the nub end of a candle, it falters and flares through a thicket of prickles and bright yellow flowers. Then it sneezes.

'What's this?' Gurnet wonders, breaking from the line and going to look. He parts the gorse carefully, mindful of the thorns.

'It's a dragonfly,' he tells the others. 'Or a tiny little bird.'

Reaching in . . . big hands like a catcher's mitt; all grimy from patting the turf . . . he holds his breath a moment; this creature is so delicate, such a flimsy little thing . . .

'Leave it, Gurn,' Danzel tells him. 'Its mother might come back. Put it in the nest and let's go. I'll buy you a milk-shot. Come on.'

But: 'She doesn't have a nest, Dan,' Gurnet answers. 'She doesn't have anything. I'm taking her home.'

The girls cluster around him, oohing and aahing as they peep into his hands.

'It's a flicking fairy!' Jenna squeals.

'Horse dung!'

Danzel strides to look.

'A dragonfly,' he mutters, stepping back. 'And it's fine, by the look of it. Just exhausted, Gurn, is all. Or frightened half to death from finding itself in your sweaty paw.'

Dilly touches Gurnet's arm.

'Perhaps it was trapped,' she says. 'Stuck fast in the gorse. But it's moving around now. Look! It wants to fly.'

'Let it go, Gurn,' Danzel urges. 'You've rescued it—now let it go.'

Gurnet squints down at the creature in his hands.

'I could keep her for a bit,' he says. 'Just until she's bigger. I could keep her safe and feed her stuff. Honey. I bet she likes honey. And water with sugar in.'

Jenna says why not? It's cute. Let him keep it. 'I've a box at home, Gurn,' she says. 'One I found down on the beach. She'll be nice and comfy in there. I'll bring it round.'

GURNET

I could have kept that little creature. And I would have loved her, too, just like I loved my Laurence, but in a different way. I would have called her Pamela, because that is a pretty name and I would have told her about flowers, because I think they would have interested her a lot more than the sea.

I do not know about flowers, the way I know about the sea, but I could have found out. I could have learned.

But my Danzel was right. He is always right, that boy. So I opened up my hands and I let the creature fly away. She went very fast, right up into the sky.

She was a good flyer.